Tokens and Omens

First Edition
Second Printing, 2016

Jolly Fish Press, an imprint of North Star Editions, Inc.

Jolly Fish Press
North Star Editions, Inc.
2297 Waters Drive
Mendota Heights, MN 55120
www.jollyfishpress.com

Printed in the United States of America

THIS TITLE IS ALSO AVAILABLE AS AN EBOOK.

Library of Congress Cataloging-in-Publication Data

Names: Baird, Jeri, author.
  Title: Tokens and omens / Jeri Baird.
Description: First Paperback Edition. | Provo, Utah : Jolly Fish Press,
  2016. | Summary: "Zander, Adanna, and the other fourteen-year-old
  children of their village must prepare for their quest, a dangerous rite of
  passage, by earning tokens through good deeds to combat the deadly omens
  incurred for wrongdoings"-- Provided by publisher.
Identifiers: LCCN 2016007927 | ISBN 9781631630828 (paperback)
Subjects: | CYAC: Magic--Fiction. | Adventure and adventurers--Fiction.
  | Rites and ceremonies--Fiction. | Fantasy. | BISAC: JUVENILE
  FICTION / Fantasy & Magic. | JUVENILE FICTION / Science Fiction.
Classification: LCC PZ7.1.B33 To 2016 | DDC [Fic]--dc23
LC record available at https://lccn.loc.gov/2016007927

For my niece, Emily, who shares my love of fantasy, reading, and animals.

TOKENS and OMENS

Jeri Baird

JOLLY
FISH
PRESS

Mendota Heights, Minnesota

PROLOGUE

Moira

I am called by many names: Destiny, Fate, Fortune; however, I prefer Moira, for it sounds as if I have a heart.

I do not.

I oversee human destinies, and all things happen exactly as I intend. Some try to deceive me, but I am Moira. I will not be cheated.

CHAPTER ONE

Outskirts of Puck's Gulch, North Province

Zander

On the eve of the New Year, Zander hiked beneath a crescent moon. Tomorrow his life would change, but today he hunted.

The crunch of his leather boots against fresh snow quieted the evening call of the birds until silence surrounded him. He stopped to inhale the crisp air and check the snow for tracks. Rabbit prints led him to a pile of twisted fur and blood. Perfect. The leftover carcass, likely from a hawk kill, would draw the prey he sought. He leaned against the rough bark of a Scots pine, his hemp pants and leather tunic blending with the dried winter thicket, making him nearly invisible—just as he liked it.

A single white feather hung down the side of the ebony hair Zander tucked behind his ear. He closed his eyes to listen for sounds of Elder Terrec, upon whose land he poached. He tamped down the anger that rose. The elders had no right to control the land when so many in the village hungered.

He willed his energy into the earth, connecting himself to the quiet of the forest. An owl hooted behind him. Although the feathers would fetch a nice price in the market, tonight the owl would live. Father wanted a pelt.

The comfort of the woods tugged him into his center, where his thoughts split between the hunt and the time of magic that would begin the next day. Along with the other sixteen-year-olds in his village, he'd have six months to gain tokens before the five-day quest; six months to win the favor of Moira; six long months to avoid earning omens.

A crunch in the snow caught his attention. He lifted his bow, pulled back the arrow, aimed, and released. His arrow flew true. A coyote twitched and lay still, dead before it could yelp. Father would be pleased if he wasn't drunk when Zander returned. He strode to the carcass and tied the legs. As he worked, a yip from the dense brush startled him.

"Stars!" He wouldn't have shot if he'd known she had a pup. It was the wrong season for pups. A tiny amber body trembled in the bush. Zander knelt in the snow and dug in his pocket to offer a sliver of deer jerky. "Come here, boy," he whispered.

A tiny, black nose appeared and sniffed at Zander's hand. The pup inched closer and grabbed the meat before pulling it back in the brush. It would be a mercy to kill it. A pup that young wouldn't survive on its own.

Zander rubbed the back of its neck. It was his fault the pup was motherless. And Zander knew how that felt. He had to care for it or it would die. He could train the coyote to hunt, and Zander could use a friend. Even if it was a scraggly, four-legged one that didn't talk. Maybe better it didn't talk.

The pup popped his head out, and his ears twitched forward. His alert blue eyes matched Zander's. It didn't make sense unless it was an early patron from Moira.

Zander tensed. He felt a tremor before he heard the three-beat drumming of horses as they cantered across the frozen forest floor—lots of horses. Trying hard to keep from panicking, Zander scooped the pup into his pack, grabbed the dead mother by her legs, and ran. As he fled the land only the elders and Protectors legally hunted, he glanced back.

Elder Terrec.

Zander sped up, the panic rising in earnest. Terrec was the one elder who wouldn't hesitate to chop off Zander's hand for poaching.

He smirked. Good thing he could run where a horse could not. He zigzagged through a maze of dried, tangled weeds and disappeared over the edge of the gulch. His feet scrabbled against the rocks as he slid down the steep slopes. After leaping over a fallen log, Zander skidded across a patch of ice and dropped the dead coyote. He scrambled to grab the tied feet and sprinted for the largest oak in the gulch. He followed a small stream, mostly covered in a thin crust of ice, that wound past the tree's gnarled roots. Once he knew he wasn't followed, Zander slackened his pace and caught his breath. As he walked eastward down the gulch, Zander heard his name floating from the treetops and winding along the stream.

"Zander," it whispered.

"Leave me alone, Puck," Zander hissed. It was a hazard of hiking in the gulch. The founder's ghost liked to tease him.

"Unite the tribes and save the village," the tortured voice murmured.

"Tell it to someone else," Zander muttered. "It's not my job."

At an old elm tree, he turned and hiked up the steep wall of the gulch. He grunted as he reached the top edge and bent over to catch his breath. No matter how many times he climbed the steep sides, it winded him, but he was safe. No one could prove he'd hunted the coyote on private land. As if a coyote was dumb enough to venture to the fringes where every boy with a bow stomped around. No matter. Elder Terrec hadn't seen him.

Another successful hunt. Another escape. Another day to keep his hand.

Whistling as he hiked along a worn path, Zander soon came in sight of his home. His cheerful mood evaporated as he watched his father stumble through the door. The jug of mead he carried warned Zander to keep his new pet a secret. He darted to the back of the mud-covered, twig-and-straw hut. Another chunk of clay had fallen off the side, and Father hadn't seemed inclined to fix it. Zander was the one who slept on the other side of the wall, shivering when the wind blew through.

The stink of lye drifted from the tanning pit and burnt his nostrils. How Father stood it day after day was a mystery. He cleared out a corner in the pelting shed and moved the skins to a higher shelf, where the coyote wouldn't be tempted to chew them. That would be a sure way for Father to turn the pup into a pelt to match its mother.

He knelt and opened his pack. The pup whimpered as Zander lifted him out. He held out another piece of dried venison. The coyote snatched it and scampered to a corner with the strip hanging out his mouth. A pang of guilt ran through Zander. He'd made the pup an orphan.

"Don't worry, boy. I'll come for you after Father passes out." It never took long. Zander set a bowl of water in the corner and latched the door. He'd be back soon enough.

Zander stepped into the single-room and blinked to adjust to the dark, wondering what mood Father'd be in. He shared his father's Kharok tribal traits of straight black hair and brown skin, but not his black eyes. After two-hundred years in Puck's Gulch, most of the tribes had intermingled. It showed in Zander's blue eyes.

Father slumped over a cup of mead. A loaf of raisin bread and a carrot cake sat on the lone table. Even as the sweet aroma made his mouth water, anger burned in his gut. Father shouldn't be wasting what little coin they had on treats meant for the rich.

He breathed in and held it, pushing down the fire. Showing

emotion had no place in his life. Father had taught him that. Zander felt a perverse satisfaction that he hadn't cried since he was five. Controlling his anger was taking longer.

"Good hunt?" Father slurred.

"Coyote. I hung it from the post to bleed. I'll skin it tomorrow."

Bloodshot eyes glared at Zander. "Only one?"

Zander crossed his arms over his chest. Seconds ticked by as he sifted through a dozen replies. He settled for the one least likely to bring his father's contempt. It also happened to be the one that was true. "I was lucky to shoot one. Elder Terrec rode through and made enough commotion to scare the prey for miles."

"The stupidity of the elders knows no end," Father grumbled. "Were the useless Protectors with him?"

"I'm not sure. I ran."

Most of the elders were arrogant, but the Protectors were different. Zander had a gift with the bow. He dreamed of training with the men who protected their village, rather than apprentice as a furrier with his father.

"Fancy dandies, all they are." Father stumbled to his feet and punched his fist in the air. "Parading around protecting us from what? Our own people aren't allowed out at night or to hunt the forests that should belong to all of us. The elders are idiots if they think anyone would invade a piss hole like this."

Father cared about others? Zander turned to hide his grin. But his ranting about the elders meant Father wasn't yelling at Zander.

Glassy-eyed, Father teetered in the sparse light of a single lantern. "This came for you today." He held out a package wrapped in purple cloth and tied with a gold cord. "New year, new group of questers," he muttered. "Moira loves her drama."

Zander accepted the parcel. He unfolded the cloth, and rubbed his hand across the white journal. The scent of lavender drifted from the pages. He stilled himself by breathing slowly as he'd learned from hunting. He wouldn't give away his excitement to Father.

He'd first learned of the time of magic as a ten-year-old. His dream of becoming a Protector had risen the day he'd heard the fortune-teller talk of Moira choosing your destiny.

"Moira's a foul mistress." Father rubbed at his eyes. "We raise our kids for sixteen years, and Fate decides who lives and who dies."

We? The villagers? What did Father mean? Zander had vague memories of a mother rocking him, but Father wouldn't speak of her. Zander wanted to ask, but he wouldn't interrupt now. This was more talking than Father had done for a long while.

"You're prepared for the quest in the gulch. You'll survive." Father scratched his forehead. "And then maybe our lives will be good again."

Zander nodded, but couldn't remember a time he'd called his life good. After the quest, life would be good if he could move away from Father's drinking and lying.

Father said, "Tomorrow, you'll join the other questers in the dedication ceremony. Tonight we'll roast outside, and let the scent go as it pleases."

Living so far outside the village had its advantages. Zander snorted. Many times they'd broken the law requiring abstinence of meat before a holiday.

With the quest in his future, three things stood between Zander and his dream. First, he had to prove himself to Moira. His shoulders relaxed. He could do it.

He ran his tongue over a chipped front tooth, a constant reminder of the second. He also had to overcome his terror of riding a horse.

And of course, he had to survive the quest itself.

CHAPTER TWO

The Market at Puck's Gulch

Alexa

The yeasty fragrance of baking bread pervaded Alexa's bedroom from the kitchen below. She threw open the window, knowing it would make no difference. The smell suffocated her. She scowled at the slice of moon floating above the forest as if it were to blame. Leaning over the sill, she inhaled the sharp sting of winter. The cold burned her lungs, but did nothing to replace the stink.

Living above the kitchen meant the odor permeated her clothes and her hair. One sniff and strangers could identify her as the baker's daughter. With the Festival of the New Year starting the next day, Alexa had spent the past week helping her mother bake the special treats in demand for the private celebrations. It paid well, but Mother was exhausted.

Alexa's time of magic would begin with the festival and end in six months with the quest. Then she could leave the bakery and its smells behind. A jolt of guilt shot through her gut. She ran her fingers over the bloodstone beads threaded throughout her golden hair. What would Mother do without her help?

No matter. She couldn't explain it, but Alexa knew she would not be a baker.

Periwinkle yarn sprawled across the yellow coverlet on her narrow bed. She wound it into a ball and added it to the other colors in a willow basket on her nightstand. As Alexa threw the covers to the side, an errant needle jabbed her thumb. "Stars!" She pressed against the spot of blood with a finger. It wasn't the first time she'd pricked herself.

Her door opened, pulling Alexa from her thoughts.

"Alexa?" Flour smudged Mother's face, and her hair glistened from working in the hot kitchen. Dark circles under blue eyes reminded Alexa of the late nights Mother worked.

"You've worked hard these last days." Mother held out a warm bowl of rabbit and carrot stew thickened with mushroom gravy.

This scent tickled Alexa's nose, and her mouth watered. She smiled. Mother risked the ire of the church for eating meat the day before the holiday, but then, her mother never was one for following the priest's rules. "Thank you."

Like most descendants of the Chahda tribe, Alexa and her mother had light hair and skin, but Alexa's eyes were dark while Mother's were the blue of the sky. A familiar sense of loss overwhelmed her. She'd never known her father.

Mother smoothed her apron. "It seems like yesterday I cradled you in my arms, and now you're a young woman of sixteen and beautiful." Searching Alexa's face, she sighed. "After the quest, maybe our lives can be perfect again."

What was Mother thinking? When had her life been perfect?

"There's much you can't understand until you've completed the quest. Moira will choose the bakery as your apprenticeship, I'm sure of it." Mother shuddered as a breeze fluttered in from the open window.

Alexa flipped her hair. "Mother! Are you worried I won't return from the quest?" Her mother paled. "How could you think I would fail? Really, Mother, do you think so little of me?" Her heart thudded. Not everyone returned from the quest, but surely Moira would find her deserving.

"No, no, of course I don't doubt your return." Mother twisted her hands. "But you need to be careful not to tempt Fate."

"Moira? Why would I tempt her?" Alexa's stomach tightened.

As her mother picked at the dough under her nails, Alexa suspected she was hiding something. But then, Alexa had her own secrets, and apprenticing anywhere except the bakery was one of them. She took a deep breath and scooped a bite of stew. "It's wonderful, Mother. Thank you."

Smiling, her mother caressed Alexa's hair. As she turned to leave, she glanced back. "Soon now, Alexa. I promise everything will be better."

"Yes, Mother. It will be better."

Alexa had her own plan she shared with no one. Not her favored teacher, not her mother, who would be shocked to know her daughter capable of such an idea, and not her best friend, Merindah. With a small favor from the fortune-teller, Alexa felt confident she would not be a baker, whatever Mother might think.

CHAPTER THREE

First Day of Magic

Zander

Zander woke as the sun struggled to light the room through dust-covered windows. Father stood over him. Too late, Zander pulled the ragged quilt over the pup nestled under his arm.

"What's this?" Father whistled. "Moira gave you a coyote?" He grabbed the pup by his scruff and shook him. "You better watch yourself, Son, if Moira thinks you need a predator for your patron." He dropped the whimpering pup to the straw sleeping mat.

Panic twisted through Zander's chest at the thought of losing the pup in the quest. "I won't need him to protect me. I want to train him to hunt."

Father leaned down, the stink of the night's mead on his breath. "There's no room in this world for a soft heart. You learned that long ago." He stood. "Train him and use him when you need him." Father stomped across the room. "Get up."

After cutting thick slices of the carrot cake, Father slathered butter across the soft surface, where it stuck in large clumps. He handed a slice to Zander, and said in his way of blessing, "Eat and be grateful."

"Eat and be grateful," Zander murmured back. It was about as much church as Father allowed, which was fine with Zander.

As much as he hated what Father must have spent for the cake, Zander loved baked sweets. But today the aroma of cinnamon and sugar triggered a memory of his mother's embrace. His happiness vanished like the flame of a snuffed-out candle. He struggled to finish and held the last bite out to the pup, which he'd named Shadow. The coyote sniffed, licked the butter, and gulped the cake. Shadow didn't seem to miss his mother, so why did Zander?

Sitting at the hewn table, Zander swallowed hard and cleared his throat. Father was sober. This was his chance. "Tell me of your quest. Did anyone die?"

Father bowed his head into his hands. "One. He was my best friend."

So that was why Father never talked about his quest. "What happened?"

"What happened? Moira deemed him unworthy to live. That's what happened."

"But why? Was he bad?"

"He was reckless. He turned sixteen the day before the New Year. Byron was the youngest quester, and he never took it seriously. He spent five months not caring and earning every omen he could." Father let out a jagged laugh. "And he misplaced every token he earned."

He stabbed his finger at Zander, and Zander jerked back. He never knew when Father would connect that finger to his chest. That time, he kept talking.

"Keep track of your tokens. If you lose them, you can't fight your omens. But if you lose your omens? They'll come. You can't escape them."

Zander nodded. He had an old brown leather pouch to keep them in.

"Byron got scared in the sixth month. He fasted, he cared for the old, he did good deeds for the priest, but it was too late."

"Why didn't you help him? Give him some of your tokens or find him in the forest and fight together?"

"No!" Father slammed his fist on the table. "You go it alone. You can't cheat Fate. Remember that, Zander. Moira cannot be cheated." Peering at Zander, his father grimaced. "Everyone gets omens, but try to limit them. The omens come when you do a bad deed or your thoughts are dark. These are your challenges during the quest, and some cannot be overcome."

Zander's heart thudded. How could he control his thoughts?

"And remember to stay on the good side of the priest and the fortune-teller. They hand out tokens and omens as they see fit." Father sucked in a deep breath. "There's one other thing. Moira hands out favors after the quest. Whatever she gives you will benefit your calling, but she's tricky. Sometimes she bestows the favors during your time of magic. If she gives it early, you know you're in trouble, 'cause you'll need it. You never know what Moira plans for you. She's a fickle one, Fate is." His father stood. "I'm done talking. The priest and fortune-teller will tell you what you need to know. Go. You have time to hunt before the Welcoming Ceremony."

With his father's instructions rolling through his head, Zander grabbed his bow. He'd wanted to ask about Father's patron, but he didn't dare. He knew enough to understand Father had needed it in the quest—that's why he didn't have one now. Zander raced toward the calm of the forest, but he'd be careful. On the first morning of the holiday, the elders hunted too.

After shooting three rabbits and a pheasant, Zander returned as Father opened a jug of mead. Zander laughed as he laid the game on the table. "We'll feast tonight, Father."

He stared into his father's dark eyes. For a few seconds, a vision played out in front of him. Father hugged a woman. Zander couldn't see her face, but it was evident Father loved her. Zander could feel it. Who was she? Who was this woman and why did Father hide her? Why was he seeing Father's secrets?

Confused, Zander mumbled, "I left my pack in the forest." He grabbed Shadow, bolted from the house, and ran until his legs collapsed. He dropped, face to the ground, inhaling the musty leaves under the snow. Anger coursed through him, and he beat at the cold earth. Father kept too many secrets. He shivered while the wind whipped at his hair and drove snow down his tunic.

Then, he rose as if compelled.

A young woman stood before him. Silver hair flowed to her waist. "Zander," she said.

Her emerald eyes enthralled him. "Who are you?"

"I am called by many names. Destiny, Fate, Fortune; however I prefer Moira." She held out a green stone. "Your first omen. Learn to control your anger."

Zander breathed deeply, trying to regain his composure, before he reached to claim the stone.

"Do you enjoy seeing secrets? I chose your favor after much consideration."

Zander gaped at Moira. "My favor? Why now?"

"You'll find it useful, Zander. But it's best to hide it. Others will avoid you if they know you see their hard-held secrets. And what fun would it be to have your favor and not be able to use it?"

She lifted Shadow and breathed into his mouth. "He came early, but he's delightful. Shadow will be your patron." She glanced at the sky. "Run, Zander. You'll be late for the ceremony." And, as fog evanesces in the sun, she vanished.

Rolling the stone in his hand as he raced home, Zander vowed to control his emotions. He wouldn't reveal the vision or his visit from Moira to Father.

When he burst into the house, his father held a mug. From the look of him, it wasn't his first.

Father slurred, "Th'noon bells've rung."

On his first day of magic, Moira had given Zander an early favor of seeing secrets, the green stone omen, and a predator patron. And now he'd be late to the Welcoming Ceremony. It wasn't a good start. After a backward glance at his father, Zander sprinted to the Quinary.

CHAPTER FOUR

Six Months until the Quest

Alexa

Alexa felt a pinch on her cheek. "I'll get up, Mother," she murmured. She yawned and opened her eyes. A long, black and brown, furry animal danced on the bed. Its white face with a brown mask stared at Alexa.

"A ferret?" Alexa squealed. "Moira gave me a ferret for my patron?"

The ferret leaped off the bed and hid under a pile of clothes. Alexa slid off the bed and knelt next to the clothes. "Come here, girl. I won't hurt you."

A tiny nose poked out and sniffed Alexa's outstretched fingers. The patron crawled out and sidled toward Alexa, who scooped the weasel into her arms. The ferret rubbed her nose against Alexa's cheek.

"You're beautiful!" Alexa whispered. "I thought I'd get a canary like Mother's. You're much better than a bird." She studied the little furball curled in her arms. "What's your name?"

The ferret's black eyes peered back.

"Fiona? I think that fits you."

Alexa smiled as she recorded the ferret's name in the black journal that had appeared on her doorstep the night before. It came wrapped in a purple cloth, tied with a golden cord, smelling of lavender. She ran downstairs for a bowl of water and scraps of uncooked rabbit. After Fiona ate, she curled up on Alexa's pillow and fell asleep.

Time to get ready for the ceremony. Alexa separated three long strands of hair and braided, adding turquoise and clear quartz beads onto the golden curls. The Twelve Day Feast began that day, and she wanted to look her best. She dressed in the clothes Fiona had hidden in. All questers dressed alike during their time of magic. She pulled the wheat-yellow undershirt over her head, marveling at the softness. Hemp pants dyed green from the roots of sorrel came next, and she cinched the waist with a braided hemp tie. Alexa had helped gather and boil the acorns that colored the brown tunic she slipped on.

As she pushed the buttons fashioned from deer antlers through the slits, pride warred with fear. How long she'd dreamed of this day! To be a quester and on the cusp of adulthood. But wearing the clothes and having her patron animal made it all too real. Last, she slipped the strap of a leather pouch over her head and settled the pouch at her hip. As she collected tokens and omens, she'd store them safely in the bag.

A sudden memory jarred her. Last year, Saul had earned plenty of tokens, but he'd died from a snake bite in the quest.

Pushing away the fear, Alexa tied her curls in a loose ponytail, leaving the braid to hang free. She'd do her best to earn tokens and avoid the deeds that brought omens. She picked up Fiona and gently placed her in a loose woven pouch and slipped it over her shoulder. She skipped down the stairs and out to the market. The noon bell would signal the start of the Welcoming Ceremony. She had time to find Merindah.

Light snow fell as she searched for her best friend's black curls. Merindah's dark skin identified her as a descendant of the Dakta

Tribe, the creative ones. Most of the artists and musicians were Dakta. They were the dreamers, but not Merindah. She saw everything as black and white. Alexa spied her friend and ran to meet her at the five-sided Quinary. Five massive oaks formed the living cornerstones for the oldest structure in Puck's Village. Each represented one of the five tribes.

A sparrow perched on Merindah's shoulder. A headband woven of horsehair and seed beads crossed Merindah's forehead and tied in the back. When she reached Alexa, Merindah asked, "Where's your patron?"

Alexa opened her bag and a sleepy ferret poked out her head. "This is Fiona."

Merindah laughed. "You *would* get a ferret."

Alexa reached up to stroke the sparrow's head. "What's her name?" When her friend blushed, Alexa hid her annoyance. This was going to be good.

"I'm calling her Angel. She's a messenger from God."

"She's not from God, she's from Moira." Alexa shook her head. Merindah tied everything to God.

"Well, I don't care what you think. I believe she's from God."

"It doesn't matter. She's perfect for you." Alexa could give Merindah that. She grabbed her friend's hand. "Let's get drinks."

The scent of meat roasting over open fire pits drew them to the festivities scattered throughout the market. Laughing men labored to turn the spits laden with boar and deer. The first day of the New Year was one of two yearly celebrations where no coin was needed for food. The elders supplied the meat, and each family shared what they could. Alexa's mother had baked through the night to provide sweet apricot and hickory nut bread. Alexa rushed past a table of roasted red potatoes and honey-glazed purple turnips. A group of ragged-looking children stood at the tables and stared at the food with big eyes. Alexa took a quick breath. It would be a day when the shack house kids would go to bed with full bellies.

She and Merindah headed for cider. The year's abundant fall apple harvest had left plenty to store over winter and press for the sweet drink.

Alexa grabbed two mugs of hot spiced cider. As she handed one to Merindah, Alexa giggled. "Let's check out the boys."

"You mean let the boys check *you* out?" Merindah rolled her eyes. "You want to prance about in your fancy new clothes?"

"At least there aren't any girls from the elders' families questing this year."

Merindah frowned. "Rank doesn't matter during the quest. We're all equals."

"It matters." Alexa blushed. "We just pretend it doesn't."

"Alexa? Don't hope for an elder's son as a boyfriend. You know it won't happen."

And that was why Alexa wouldn't share her plan with Merindah. It *could* happen. Sometimes a boy chose a girl from beneath his class instead of riding to another village to find a wife. If she was honest with herself, she had to admit it hardly ever happened, but Alexa had a plan. And this was a day for hope. A new year, a new beginning. She pushed away her fear that Moira could doom her to the bakery and a life of drudgery.

As she stood at the two-hundred-year-old Quinary, Alexa searched for the other questers. Across the market, Dharien, the second son of Elder Warrin, stood tall and aloof. His black hair swept across his forehead. Brown eyes glared with contempt at the other teens. No one would doubt his Kharok background.

First born and heir to Elder Rowan's estate, Paal's dark blond curls and soft physique made him look feminine. She giggled. He could pass for her brother. He spotted her staring and grinned.

Dimples formed in both cheeks. Cute. He stooped to pick up a brown and white retriever pup that barked at a feral cat.

The peasant cousins, Odo and Kaiya, stood under the far tree of the open Quinary. They lived in the alley set apart for the Yapi tribe. Odo clutched a yellow kitten. Kaiya's patron, a black crow, perched on her shoulder. Unless Moira found them exceptional, Odo could expect to work in the fields or stables, and Kaiya would likely be a kitchen maid. Alexa laughed to think of how a crow would be any help in a kitchen. But then, maybe Moira had other plans for Kaiya after all.

Cobie, whose scrawniness gave him away as the youngest quester, was always smiling and ready with a joke. Like Merindah, Cobie descended from the Dakta tribe, and his father was a coppersmith. Already gaining a reputation as a talented ornamentalist, Cobie's flowered utensils were sought after by the elders. Moira was sure to allow him to apprentice with his father. Cobie held a small cage of wood slats. Alexa peered to see what was inside. A lizard changed its colors as she stared. Not a lizard, a chameleon—a suitable patron for an artist, she thought.

The other questers huddled together. Alexa ticked them off in her head. Tarni, daughter of the candle maker, hardly ever spoke and held a canary in her palm. All the questers had been required to help Bindi's mother, the clothier, prepare the cloth for the questing clothes. Bindi nervously stroked a calico cat. Yarra's father worked leather. She held a wiggling piglet that would never be a pair of shoes.

Jarl, large like his bricklayer father, scowled at everyone. If anyone might not survive the quest, it would be Jarl. A large black and white shepherd pup sat at his side. Waku carded yarn for his father's weaving business. He'd lost his mother two years ago in the fever that had ravaged their village. He'd taken her place at the spinning wheel. A red cardinal sat on his shoulder, shifting from leg to leg.

Dharien caught her eye again. She didn't see his patron. He

scratched at his long sleeves and scowled at the brown tunic hanging to his knees. He twisted the hemp rope cinched at his waist and flipped it against his pants. He didn't seem to enjoy giving up the fancy clothes of the elders. Alexa blushed. She couldn't help it. Dharien's good looks made her shiver.

One boy was missing. Where was Zander? She'd seldom seen the furrier's son, but she was sure he was sixteen. He should be there for the ceremony.

After Alexa finished the cider and shared a small meat pie with Merindah, the noon bells rang. Alexa grabbed Merindah's hand. "It's time."

Together they joined the others and lined across the pavilion. She held Fiona, as was the custom. Alexa glanced down the line. Each teen stood tall with their patron animal next to them, on their shoulder, or in their arms. Who would die this year? Whose family would mourn at the end of the quest? When Saul didn't return from the quest last year, his family had searched the forest and carried his lifeless body home.

Father Chanse and the fortune-teller, Melina Odella, stepped to the front. They shared duties in the yearly ritual. Wearing the traditional black robe and white cap over the red hair found predominantly in the Odwa tribe, the priest began. "I represent God, the Church, and tradition."

Melina Odella stood next to him. Her patron animal, a silver wolf, sat at her side, her black eyes intent on the questers. A long, red, embossed tunic flowed over the fortune-teller's purple skirt, tied by a gold cord at her hips. A triangle of black velvet covered the unruly, dark Kharok hair cascading down her back. As her violet eyes gazed across the crowd, the villagers grew silent. Thick black charcoal lined the top and bottom of her eyelids and lifted at the corner of her eyes.

Alexa wished Mother would let her line her eyes. Maybe once

the quest ended and she was acknowledged as an adult, she could do as she pleased.

The fortune-teller began the speech she repeated every year. "I embody Moira, our Fate, and things hidden. On this day, Father Chance and I remind you of the balance between the faith and mystery upon which our village was founded."

Alexa had heard the story many times, but now she paid attention as the priest's voice rose. "Two-hundred years ago, our God protected Hedron Puck as he gathered those weary of war from the Five Tribes. He dreamed of creating a perfect society by the shores of the Merope Sea. But Moira decreed they should remain here when they camped in our gulch during a lightning storm."

Melina Odella picked up the thread of the story. "While they climbed the steep sides of the gulch, every wagon broke a wheel. Only Moira works in this way. Our ancestors built the village on the upper rim of the gulch. The first building Puck constructed was this Quinary, to represent the five tribes living in harmony. He dedicated it to both the God who led them to safety and to Moira who kept them here. Unfortunately, Hedron Puck died in a hunting accident in the gulch before he could establish his dream of equality for all, regardless of tribe or lineage. Without a leader, five elders stepped forward and created the order we live in today." She stared out at the elders. "Puck's vision of each tribe having an equal voice died with him."

Clearing his throat, the priest said, "At the first New Year celebration, Moira came in a vision to the priest and the fortune-teller and told them of the quest she ordained for our young people. Moira would reward or punish the sixteen-year-olds with tokens and omens for their actions. She gave the priest and fortune-teller the duty of teaching the questers how to use them in the five-day quest. Only the teens worthy of joining our society as adults would survive. Each year since, it has been our tradition."

Alexa caught her mother's tear-filled eyes and took a quick breath. Mother worried too much.

"Today we celebrate our past and look to our future," Melina Odella said. "These young people, standing before you with their appointed patrons, represent our hopes for a productive society."

"Let us pray." Father Chanse raised his arms, fingers pointing to the sky. His green eyes drifted across the crowd as his voice boomed. "We bless these questers and ask our God to keep them safe. May their good actions and pure thoughts bring the tokens needed to survive their quest. Purify their sinful nature that they may take their productive places among us. And if they refuse to bend to thy will, we release them to the fate of the quest."

The priest strolled across the stage, sprinkling holy water on each bent, submissive head, blessing them. When he reached Alexa, he said, "Blessings, my child, in your time of magic."

A young acolyte followed, swinging a metal censer. Alexa swallowed a cough as the burning sage wafted over her.

As Father Chanse reached Merindah, who stood last in line, Zander dashed in to stand next to her. A coyote pup pressed into his legs.

The crowd murmured and cast worried looks at each other. Alexa's heart quickened. There would be thirteen questers. She hadn't realized until that moment. Unlucky thirteen.

CHAPTER FIVE

Zander

With his sides heaving from his run, Zander joined the group as the priest blessed the last in line. Having never been to church, he looked at the priest, hoping for guidance. Instead, Zander glimpsed the priest's secret and staggered as the unhappiness hung like a noose around the priest's heart. Zander glanced at the fortune-teller, the source of the priest's pain. Anger colored Father Chanse's face, and Zander remembered his father's warning to stay in the priest's good graces.

The priest sprinkled Zander with water and stepped to the side. When the fortune-teller took his place, Zander shuddered. The woman frightened and fascinated him at the same time. Tradition gave the priest and fortune-teller equal power in the village affairs, but when the elders controlled the land and the people who worked for them, it gave the elders an unspoken power.

Zander hated the elders and their first-born who inherited their power. A hornet buzzed by his head, turned to stone, and dropped by magic into his pocket. He sucked in a sharp breath. Another omen.

Turning to the questers, the fortune-teller seemed to float down the line. One by one she gazed into their eyes. She gave each a single word to symbolize his or her journey through the quest. "Rain, oak, pheasant, rock, rose." Melina Odella's hesitated in front of Alexa, the girl with golden curls. The fortune-teller touched Alexa's cheek and paused as if listening. "Night," Melina Odella whispered. On she drifted, her garments swishing. "Pearl, silver, owl, lily, wind." To Merindah she said, "Anchor."

When the fortune-teller faced Zander, he trembled. He viewed so many secrets in her eyes, he couldn't sort them. Melina Odella held his chin and her face softened. When a smile tugged at her mouth, Zander longed for the mother he couldn't remember.

She whispered, "Day."

He didn't understand, and he thought he should.

CHAPTER SIX
Five and a Half Months until the Quest

Alexa

The Twelve Day Feast ended with a storm that blanketed the village in fluffy, white snow. On the thirteenth day of the New Year, quester lessons began twice each week. Alexa already missed Fiona as she trudged through the snow to the church. The priest had been adamant about leaving their patrons at home during their lessons. She'd had twelve days to bond with Fiona and hated leaving her.

Alexa trailed Dharien and Paal to the white stone church. Round windows curtained in purple silk flanked each side of the thick oak door. An X imbedded with dark and light pebbles graced the top of the door, representing God and Fate working together.

Merindah fidgeted inside the door. "I got my first token—a dove! I can't wait to learn what it means." Her eyes sparkled as she pulled the inch-long, ivory-colored bird from her pocket. "I stopped to help an old woman who spilled her wagon of parsnips on the way to market. As I turned to go, her eyes shone like emeralds and she pressed it into my palm."

Alexa and Merindah wound through the dark halls of the church until they found the lecture hall. Thirteen oak chairs formed a circle in the room. Alexa hesitated at the door. The other questers fiddled with their journals and glanced nervously at the priest and fortune-teller standing on opposite sides of the room.

"Find a seat," Father Chanse grumbled.

"Yes, Father." Alexa pulled Merindah across the room and sat next to Paal.

Dharien called out, "Paal, sit with me."

Paal shrugged and moved next to Dharien as Zander burst into the room. The priest pointed to the empty chair next to Alexa.

Zander slouched in the seat, staring at his hands clutched around the pouch on his lap. He turned to Alexa with wide eyes. "You . . . you smell of bread!"

Eyes flashing, she hissed, "I live at a bakery!"

Zander paled and then turned red. His eyes bore into hers before he dropped his gaze. What was wrong with him? She hated smelling like bread, and she didn't need him reminding her of it.

The priest rapped his knuckles against a side table. Alexa ignored Zander, but she couldn't forget those blue eyes.

"We're here to help you understand the use and importance of tokens and the dangers of omens," the fortune-teller said. "It's important you hold safe your tokens, for if lost or misplaced, they cannot help you during the quest." Her face darkened. "However, the omens will appear during the quest whether you carry them or not. Over the next several months, we'll play games of strategy to help you learn to use your tokens to defeat your omens. This is theory. The quest will play out as it will, and is always full of surprises, testing your limits. But those of you who survive the quest will be prepared to join a guild as an apprentice and become a productive adult in society."

Gazing around the circle, Alexa assumed most of them shared the same questions as they stared at each other. Who would return? Who would not?

Melina Odella encouraged good deeds and wholesome thoughts. "Earning tokens assures Moira of your worthiness."

Father Chanse tapped his foot as he spoke. "The easiest way to receive omens is by committing the five deadly sins." He sauntered around the circle. "I'll begin with the sin of pride. When you think of yourself as better than another, or that your gifts come from yourself and not as given by God, you are prideful. The omen for pride is a peacock."

Melina Odella stepped in front of the priest. "Humility cures pride. Practice allowing others to come before yourself. The token given for humility is a sparrow. It may seem foolish now, but when you're tired and alone in the forest, a muster of peacocks can overwhelm you with their pecking. Tossing out one sparrow token will vanquish one peacock. If you've earned more peacocks than sparrows, then you'll have to find another way to fight them."

The priest continued, "The second sin is envy, longing to possess something belonging to another. The omen is a scorpion."

"And the cure is kindness," the fortune-teller added. "The token being a dove. When a scorpion appears during the quest, if you throw out a dove token, the bird will eat the scorpion."

Merindah's face lit. "It's a good one," she whispered to Alexa.

"The hornet represents anger and is the third sin," the priest said. "Too many stings in the quest can be fatal."

Melina Odella smiled. "Patience cures wrath. The token is a turtle. The lowly turtle loves to snap up hornets. You may receive other tokens and omens. Moira is creative and delights in surprises."

Alexa raised her hand. "What about our patrons? Does the kind we get mean anything?"

"Your patrons are given by Moira as an extra encouragement to do good deeds." The priest smiled. "One of your tasks is to discover how your patron might help in the quest. They are a token you can use if needed."

"However," Melina Odella added, "if you use them in the quest, they disappear. By the time of the quest you will have bonded with your animal and you may wish to keep them. You need to earn enough tokens to avoid the heartache of losing yours." She walked around the room and handed each teen a wooden token representing their patron. "Guard these well."

Alexa marveled at the small carved ferret. She already loved Fiona. She wouldn't risk her life. Besides, how could a ferret help in the quest?

"Keeping your patron through the quest strengthens your favor." Melina Odella smiled at the silver wolf sleeping in the corner. "I can't imagine life without Sheba. She's been my constant companion. And because of Moira's magic, your patron will live as long as you do, so it will be your life-long friend."

The priest cleared his throat. "Sometimes using your patron is the only way to survive the quest." His cheeks were tinged pink. "You'll notice I don't have a patron. I had a hard decision to make, and I regret that I had to use mine, but he saved my life."

Next to her, Zander gasped and then stared at his bag. What was his problem?

CHAPTER SEVEN

Zander

He hadn't meant to offend Alexa. The smell of bread had caught him by surprise. It was when he scanned her black eyes that Zander had been shocked. He didn't want to know her secrets, and Alexa's stunned him. Without understanding why, he vowed to do everything he could to prevent *that* secret from becoming truth.

He glanced across the circle at the peasant cousins, Odo and Kaiya. He knew them from the festivals. For his size, Odo was a decent wrestler, and Kaiya was always at the competitions, cheering for him. They shared the Yapi traits of straight brown hair and open hazel eyes. Both were big-boned, but too thin. When they returned his stare, their hunger punched his gut. He ate well every night and flushed at the unfairness. A Protector would help, and Zander resolved to find a way to ease their pain.

Although Father had taught him his numbers and how to read instead of sending him to the church school, Zander knew the other questers from the festivals. The elders' sons, Paal and Dharien, benefitted from regular training with the Protectors and always did well in the tournaments. Zander had chummed around with Cobie when they didn't have to work at their fathers' booths.

Zander glanced at Father Chanse as he talked of the omens. Father hated the priest as much as he hated the elders, so they didn't attend church. If the priest was as boring in services as he was in class, then Zander was happy he'd spent his Sundays in the forest. The elders attended church, so it was the perfect day to poach.

When Father Chanse admitted using his patron in the quest, Zander lost any respect he might have had for the priest. What kind of person would do that? He couldn't help the gasp that escaped him. He'd never put Shadow in danger.

With the promise of the other two sins to be discussed in the next class, the priest dismissed them at the noon bell. Most of the questers rushed out the door. They had chores or needed to work in the family business. Zander lagged behind, hoping to speak privately with Melina Odella.

As he stood, Merindah brushed against his pack.

Her eyes widened. "What's in there?"

He pulled the flap open, and the coyote poked his nose out. Merindah jumped, and Zander laughed. He whispered, "This is Shadow."

Merindah scratched the pup's head. "Why did you bring him?" She glanced at the priest. "Father Chanse said to leave them at home."

"I don't trust my father not to toss him in the gulch." Zander closed the flap and put his finger to his lips. "Our secret?"

Merindah hesitated and then nodded.

When Zander turned, the priest loomed in front of him. Father Chanse held out a thorn. "You were late today. This omen will trouble you in the quest. Take care to earn no more."

Zander rubbed the wooden thorn between his fingers before he met the priest's eyes. Once again he witnessed the priest's unhappiness. He blushed and stared at the floor.

"The correct response is 'Thank you Father, for helping me become a better person,'" the priest spat.

Zander clenched his jaw and said tersely, "Thank you . . . Father." He jerked back when a hornet omen fell from the ceiling and dropped at his feet. It rattled against the stone floor as if to mock his lack of self-control. Already he needed to earn two turtles.

The priest smirked before turning to march out, his heavy footsteps echoing down the hall.

Alone with the fortune-teller, Zander considered his words. "Melina Odella?" Her fragrance calmed him and reminded him of the scent from his journal.

She searched his face. "You have a favor from Moira you don't understand." It wasn't a question.

Moira had warned him to keep his favor a secret. Could he trust his teacher? He took a deep breath. He needed to know what to do. "When I look in someone's eyes, I see things I shouldn't know."

"Ah," she said, "and you wonder what to do with those secrets."

He nodded.

"Zander, do you know the meaning of your name?"

He rubbed the back of his neck. "I didn't know my name had a meaning."

Melina Odella opened a green velvet pouch tied at her waist and held out a small red heart carved from wood. "Follow your heart, Zander, and you will understand."

"Ma'am? The priest…"

"The priest's secrets are best kept, Zander."

"Yes, Ma'am."

"And Zander?"

"Yes?"

"Don't let the priest know you bring your patron to class."

Zander blushed. Did the fortune-teller know everything?

After leaving the church, Zander hesitated outside the door. He lifted Shadow from his bag and set him on the ground where the pup promptly squatted to pee. Zander slung his bag over one shoulder before he trailed after the cousins. He kept his distance so they wouldn't notice him. Invisible. He rubbed the red heart before stuffing it in his leather pouch. They didn't have to be hungry. He would help. He would do as Melina Odella advised and follow his heart.

CHAPTER EIGHT

Alexa

After the lesson, Alexa and Merindah threaded through the streets avoiding the carts, horse-drawn wagons, and the swarm of shoppers with overflowing baskets of vegetables and baked goods. Clamorous vendors hanging over wooden stalls hawked bright bolts of cloth and leather goods. The harsh clang of metal against metal reverberated from the copper workers pounding out bowls.

Alexa held her sleeve against her nose to filter the metallic tang. "I hate that boy, Zander."

"I think he's cute," Merindah replied. "Even with his chipped tooth. And those blue eyes. Aya! I think he likes you. He kept sneaking glances at you during class."

They rounded the corner to the west side of the market. Alexa's mouth watered when the aroma of smoky grilled pork and spiced nuts drifted from their stands. She stepped around a band of ragged dogs sniffing for dropped food.

"He thinks I smell like bread." Alexa wrinkled her nose.

"You do smell like bread. There's worse. Your mother could be the butcher, and you'd stink of dead pigs."

Alexa muttered, "I still hate him. And what about the bag he carried? He clung to it like it was gold."

Merindah smiled and shook her head. "It must be important to him."

As they parted, a hornet buzzed Alexa and fell to the ground as a stone. She tossed her hair and grabbed the omen for anger.

When she reached the bakery, Alexa ran upstairs to check on Fiona. The sleeping ferret opened one eye and yawned before stretching. Alexa rubbed her belly and kissed her nose.

"I have to help Mother. I'll be back later."

Alexa skipped down the steps and took her place at the counter. Her grumbling stomach would have to wait for the buyers to thin out. She spent the next three hours selling bread. She handed oat bread to the peasants, rye and sweet breads to the merchants, and fancy cakes to the elders who clamored for Mother's secret recipes. Mother's favor from Moira was understanding how to mix herbs for flavor. Lavender was one of many herbs Mother used to make her cakes unique.

Business slowed in late afternoon, and after a quick meal of oat bread and cold rabbit, Alexa pulled her embroidery from behind the counter. She retrieved a needle from the hem of her tunic.

From across the kitchen, Mother frowned. "Alexa! How many times have I warned you not to store a needle in your clothing? If you fall, you'll stab yourself."

"Mother, I'm sixteen." Alexa laughed. "I don't stumble around like a two-year-old." She threaded pink silk into the eye and pushed the needle in and out as she completed the cross-stitched border. She'd started the scene during the Twelve Day Feast, and it was almost done. As she held it to the light, pride surged through her. This was some of her best work. A small copper peacock materialized next to her. With a sigh, she stuffed it in her pouch and examined the stitching.

A black and white dappled horse stood beneath a towering oak. Grasses in six shades of green were speckled with yellow flowers. With a thin gold thread, she stitched her name above the bottom border. As she tied the last knot, Alexa gasped. To her astonishment, the scene came alive. The yellow flowers swayed in an imaginary breeze. Two doves fluttered around the cloth while the horse bent his head as if to graze.

This must be her favor from Moira. It had to be, the way the stitched figures moved across the cloth. Now she knew for certain she would not be a baker. It was a lady's favor. Alexa pursed her lips. The women would fight like peasants to own such a treasure. And it would bring Alexa a step closer in her plan to leave the bakery.

She hid the cloth when Mother brought over fresh loaves of apple cinnamon bread.

"Can I go?" She wouldn't be able to hide her excitement for long.

After Mother dismissed her, Alexa slipped into the crowded market and wandered along the rows of stalls, lingering to admire the jeweled clasps. When the vendor waved her away to make room for a buyer with coins, Alexa stormed from the stall. Someday she'd have her own jewels. As an elder's wife, she'd have plenty of coins to spend.

She bumped into an old woman. "Oh, pardon," Alexa exclaimed.

The crone smiled, and her emerald eyes sparkled. She held out a small carved pig, the omen for greed.

Those eyes weren't natural. Was this Moira?

"Alexa," the old woman purred. "I gave you your favor early for a reason. May you use it wisely."

With that, Moira disappeared. Alexa glanced at the crowd, but no one else seemed to have seen Fate.

CHAPTER NINE

Zander

An hour before dusk, Zander hiked down the gulch and up into Elder Rowan's land. Paal's father wouldn't be hunting this time of night. Zander's hand was safe.

He inhaled deeply, smelling the heavy scent of snow on the air, and cocked his head, listening for animals that preferred to be predator over prey. Shadow slunk next to him, nose sniffing. This evening, Zander hunted for the peasant cousins. He tucked himself between the branches of a Scots pine, nocked his arrow, and waited.

A hare caught his eye. Zander lifted the bow and sighted. Rabbits were easy targets. It was if they announced, *Here I am. Shoot me.* As silent as the air around it, the arrow found its mark through the eye. It was easy enough to shoot three more.

Soon, four rabbits lay piled on the frozen ground next to him. Zander caught a flash of yellow beyond the brush. A large cat-like animal skulked from the cover and regarded Zander from golden eyes. He'd heard of mountain lions in the forest, but never believed the stories. He hardly believed now as the last light of dusk cast shadows, making the cat appear ghost-like rather than real. Shadow pressed against the back of Zander's legs.

Graceful and fearless, the cat sniffed the air as her ears twitched. The flick of the tail alerted Zander she'd scented him. Seeing the muscles tensed to spring, Zander drew his bow and hoped his shaking arms could hit his mark. But then, in the cat's gaze, he found himself linked mind to mind. As he had seen his father's secret, he observed the primal urges of hunger in the cat. The drive to feed her twin male and female cubs and the scent of blood from the rabbits at Zander's feet ruled the feline's instincts.

He lowered the bow. Without breaking eye contact, he reached to the ground and felt for two sets of long ears. So not to startle the cat, he tossed them underhanded into the clearing between them. The cat snarled, revealing long, sharp teeth as she snatched the rabbits. She disappeared, leaving Zander to wonder if he dreamed it, but no, two rabbits were missing. He let out his breath, unaware he held it. At his feet, a golden cat formed from a leaf. Zander rubbed the token and dropped it into his quiver of arrows.

Night had fully fallen before he'd replaced the rabbits. He hurried home amid the squeals of a mouse carried across the treetops by an owl. At the bottom of the gulch, the hair on Zander's neck tingled.

"Leave me alone, Puck," he said to the wind.

"Unite the tribes," came the whisper. "Save the village."

Zander rolled his eyes. "Give it a rest, Puck. I'm not your hero." Puck's ghost should've given up after two hundred years of being dead.

"Zander…" His name drifted out and stretched along the stream. It followed him up the embankment, but ended once Zander climbed over the edge. He fumbled his way home in the dark and let out a deep breath, relieved his father was absent. After lighting the lantern, Zander ate cold stew. Then he lay down, fully dressed, on his straw mattress with Shadow curled next to him.

Zander woke to the crash of a chair hitting the floor and his father swearing. He waited until Father shuffled to bed and snores replaced wheezing. Then he rose and pulled on a cloak. Three fresh loaves sat on the table, still warm from the oven. Where did Father buy bread at this hour? They still had uncut pumpkin bread and half a loaf of rye.

For several minutes Zander weighed the consequences of taking two loaves, thinking of what he'd tell his father if he noticed them missing. He ran his hands through his hair. He didn't mind lying, but found the truth easier to manage.

Listening to his father's drunken snores, Zander grabbed the pumpkin and rye. If Father asked, he'd say they were moldy. He slipped from the house, retrieved the hidden rabbits, and tied them to his waist. A quarter moon gave enough light to navigate the rutted streets as Zander and Shadow scurried toward the opposite end of the village. As he neared the deserted market area he slowed and stepped behind a booth to avoid the Protectors patrolling the village. If he was caught in the market past dark, he'd be thrown into jail, and a person could be in jail for a long time before seeing a judge.

Six men strode across the street with clubs swinging at their sides. They were Kharok like Zander, but it wouldn't keep them from knocking him in the head if they caught him skulking in the shadows. Zander waited until the men disappeared around a corner before he snuck past the stalls and darted for the alleys. A dog barked, and Shadow yipped in reply.

"Quiet, boy." Zander knelt to hold the pup from going after the dog. The stench from the garbage-filled streets gagged him as the stagnant night air held the smell close to the ground. He didn't understand how Odo and Kaiya could stand to live in the filth.

Zander closed his eyes, debating the risk. It was none of his business to provide food for two families because they had kids his age. Every Yapi family living in the alley was hungry, of that he was certain. He almost gave in to the voice in his head begging him to turn and go home, until he remembered the hunger pains he'd felt from the cousins and Melina Odella's words to follow his heart. He plunged into the dark alley, wound through the narrow streets past the trash pile, and turned left at a burnt shack.

Lingering in the dark, Zander contemplated the house he'd spied the two cousins enter earlier. They shared the house with nine others. He pressed his tongue against his chipped tooth. The imagined bravery of a Protector filled him. He shrugged and ducked under the coarse cloth that covered their doorway. Once inside, Zander laid the bread and rabbits on a table pushed against the wall to give more floor space for sleeping.

Kaiya's crow perched on the back of a chair and opened one sleepy eye to gaze at Zander. He held back a shiver. One caw and he'd be discovered. In the haze from the embers in the fireplace, a body stirred on a sleeping mat. Zander backed out and vanished into the darkness.

After slinking home with Shadow at his side, Zander fell into bed. The tension of sneaking across the village, hiding from the Protectors, and hoping the peasants wouldn't catch him made his head pound. Two tokens materialized next to him—a loaf of bread and a rabbit. He tucked them in his leather bag and sleep overcame him.

Zander woke to the morning bells. Stars, he'd be late for class again. He ran to the church and slid into a seat. The priest glared as Zander opened his journal. Father Chanse droned on, and Zander wrote the final deadly sins. The omen for overindulgence was a pig. Greed completed the list and earned a snake.

Dressed in black with a deep lavender tunic that made her eyes glow, Melina Odella said, "If you receive a pig omen, you can spend a day fasting to earn a butterfly."

Dharien laughed. "A butterfly to fight a pig?"

"Believe it," she said. "Being generous to others will earn a hawk."

"I guess I won't be earning any hawks then." Dharien smirked at the fortune-teller.

Melina Odella fixed her gaze on Dharien, and his smile faded. "Being an elder's son does not guarantee your safety in the quest." She swept the room with piercing eyes. "Do you have any questions about the tokens or omens?"

Zander glanced at the others, who seemed too timid to speak. His need for information was greater than his need to remain in the background. "What about the omens and tokens we receive that aren't from the deadly sins or virtues?"

"What others have you earned? Give me an example." Melina Odella looked curious.

Zander glanced at the cousins. He wouldn't mention the rabbit or bread he'd earned last night. "I earned a mountain lion token while hunting yesterday."

"What?" snapped the priest. "How did you deserve that?"

"I . . . I didn't shoot her. Instead, I gave her two rabbits to feed her young."

"How did you know she had young?"

He didn't want to reveal his favor, so Zander shrugged. "I guessed."

The fortune-teller smiled. "A mountain lion token will protect you from a pig during the quest." She chuckled. "Or you could disperse a whole cluster of peacocks with that one token. Well done, Zander."

Across the circle, Dharien's mouth twisted like he'd sucked on a lemon. Zander tried not to smile.

"Anything else?" the fortune-teller asked.

Zander hesitated, but he needed to know about the green stone. "On my first day of magic, Moira gave me a green stone omen. I don't know how to fight it in the quest."

The priest sputtered. "Moira gave it to you? Are you sure it was her?"

"She had long silver hair and eyes that glowed green. She disappeared while I was watching."

"Did she say anything?" He sneered. "What words of wisdom did she have for you?"

"I was late for the Welcoming Ceremony. She told me to run." He didn't add that she'd said to keep his favor a secret.

The rest of the questers laughed. Except for Dharien, who leaned forward and glared at Zander.

The priest turned red. "Does anyone else think they've had a visit from Moira?"

Merindah raised her hand and said softly, "I think I did, but I might be wrong."

"She spoke to me," Alexa said. "She told me to use my favor wisely."

Shaking his head, the priest muttered, "Preposterous. Visits from Fate and favors this early?"

Melina Odella stepped in front of the priest. "It is rare for Moira to visit questers during their time of magic, but not unheard of. Treasure the gift of her appearance."

Zander glanced at the look of awe on the other's faces.

"You'll each have a visit from Moira at the completion of the quest. She'll come to you in a dream on your final night. It is then she will reveal your calling and give you your favor." Melina Odella stared at Alexa. "We trust Fate to know what's best for you and for the village."

The noon bells rang, and Melina Odella dismissed them. "That's enough for today. Do what you can to earn tokens."

The green stone was still a mystery to Zander, but he wanted to avoid any more of the priest's ire, so he grabbed his bag and headed for the door. Before he could slide past, the priest held out a thorn.

Over the next two weeks, Zander continued to earn omens from the priest. He was either late or not paying attention. When

Father Chanse's favorite quill disappeared, he accused Zander. At the end of class, Father Chanse towered over Zander and added a snake omen for theft to the thorn. It was then Zander refused to call the priest Father. The man wasn't his father, and Zander would never think of him as one. Never.

Although Zander tried to avoid the other students' eyes, he resigned himself to the fact that sooner or later he would see their private fears. So instead, he decided he'd rather have it done with and went looking for them.

Paal's shame at his pudgy body hid behind his smiling face. Cobie hunted illegally, as Zander did, to feed his family. Tarni's mother was ill, Bindi's father beat her, and Yarra, Jarl, and Waku worried over returning from the quest.

Zander met Merindah's eyes and puzzled over her secret. She wished to enter the convent. As far as he could understand, it was a noble desire and not something she needed to hide, but she held it tight, fearful of discovery.

Dharien made Zander uncomfortable, and so he waited until the second week before he searched Dharien's eyes. What Zander discovered surprised him more than any of the others.

Dharien was a thief. Why would the son of an elder need to steal?

That was the day Zander learned secrets could be dreams held close to the heart or dark thoughts desired to be kept hidden. He didn't enjoy knowing any of them.

CHAPTER TEN

Five Months until the Quest

Alexa

Alexa slumped on her bed and wrapped the yellow coverlet around her shoulders as she mulled her plan, while Fiona played at her feet. If Paal or Dharien fell in love with her, she could leave the bakery regardless of what Fate decided. The elders' families seldom apprenticed with the guilds.

But which one? Dharien. Handsome and smart. When he smiled at her, her stomach fluttered, but he could be cruel. He hated Zander and made fun of him. Zander hadn't done anything to deserve the ill treatment, and he never retaliated. As Elder Warrin's second son, Dharien would likely train as a Protector after the quest. Most of the village girls swooned over the Protectors, but Alexa knew a girl who'd married one, and she was often alone. The Protectors spent most of their time training, hunting, and drinking with the elders. Not the life Alexa wanted.

Everyone liked Paal, and he liked everyone. He had a quick smile, even for the peasants, Odo and Kaiya. As a firstborn son, he'd train under his father and inherit their estate. She *liked* Paal. Maybe she could learn to love him.

She bit her lip. Girls had so much to consider. Which boy would make a good match? Zander? No, never Zander—not after what he said about her. Cobie was too squirrely. Odo was a definite no. The thought of kissing Jarl or Waku made her skin crawl.

Although Merindah believed she was boy crazy, Alexa wanted to wait a couple of years before becoming betrothed. Mother told her she'd married for love and wished the same for Alexa. Obviously, it hadn't worked out. Mother refused to speak of Alexa's father, no matter how hard Alexa pleaded with her. But Alexa couldn't wait. If she wanted to be certain she'd get away from the bakery, it had to be Paal or Dharien.

She closed her eyes. Paal, who looked like her brother, but was kind, was her choice.

With the decision made, she picked up her embroidery. She hoped the elaborate scene would be enough trade for what she needed from Melina Odella. She pushed the needle in and out through the fabric as she finished the purple flowers and added golden butterflies. With the final knot tied, she grinned. The fortune-teller's lavender eyes glowed from the center of the stitching as the butterflies flitted through the flowers twining around the edges.

After rolling the cloth, Alexa cuddled Fiona and slipped her into the deep pocket in her jacket. She left for Melina Odella's, hoping she could find the cottage. The day before, she'd overheard a bakery customer whispering directions to a young mother who needed a potion.

Alexa left the market and hiked north past the shack houses belonging to the field laborers. Dirty urchins stopped their play to stare. The thin children made her heart ache. Perhaps being a baker's daughter wasn't so bad. She always had food. If her plan worked, maybe she could help the poor. The wife of an elder would have influence and money. If they married, Paal would surely agree. Another reason to pick him. Dharien had made it clear he wouldn't earn any tokens for generosity.

Continuing north, Alexa searched for the wooden post carved

with moon and stars. It pointed to the left path, and she wound around until convinced she'd taken a wrong turn. She turned to leave. The dirty face of a solemn boy in too-small clothes stared from the path. He had a shock of red hair, an Odwan trait that seemed to pop up in the shack house kids more often than in the other villagers. He couldn't be more than a year younger than herself, but his bright blue eyes seemed older.

"If you want the fortune-teller, you're almost there." He waved for her to follow. "I'll show you."

How did the boy guess she wanted the fortune-teller? Alexa followed as he trotted down a narrow trail and stood in front of a low, stone cottage with a mustard-colored door marked with runes. The scent of lavender drifted from the plants surrounding the house. Alexa recognized some of the herbs from the bakery. Rosemary, thyme, and ginger crowded together with unfamiliar greenery behind a short brick wall. She shivered. The fortune-teller must use magic to grow herbs in the winter while other plants lay dormant. The stone-walled cottage showed its age. It was rumored that Melina Odella was descended from the first fortune-teller in Puck's Gulch.

She'd forgotten the boy until he leaned in and sniffed. "You smell like bread."

For the first time, Alexa wasn't offended. She reached in her bag and drew out a roll. Smiling, she beckoned. "Would you like this?"

She spotted the desire in his eyes, but his hands hung still at his side. She stepped closer, lifted his hand, and placed the roll in his palm. His fingers curled around the soft bread, and he gave her a quick smile before he turned.

"Wait," Alexa called to him. "What's your name?"

"Zephyr, but call me Zeph."

"Thanks for your help, Zeph." He skipped along the path until he disappeared around a bend.

A bread token materialized at her feet, and Alexa tucked it into her bag. Maybe Mother would allow her to bring the unsold bread to the children here. She smiled at the idea of bringing a small cake for each child, but knew Mother couldn't afford to bake cakes for the poor. It didn't matter. Day-old bread would fill their hungry tummies better than sweets.

Clouds floated across the sun and cast a chilling shade as Alexa took a deep breath and knocked on the door she hoped would lead to her destiny.

As the door opened, she recalled her mother's warning years earlier when Alexa first noticed Melina Odella in her flowing skirts in the market. *Be careful of that woman. Favors asked from the fortune-teller sometimes manifest in unwelcome ways.*

Alexa reached into her pocket and touched Fiona for courage. She hesitated only a moment before she stepped into the darkness. The pungent odor of herbs made her head swirl. They smelled of the balm her mother rubbed on her chest when she coughed, but there was more to the fortune-teller's magic than healing colds.

As her eyes adjusted to the dark, Alexa glanced at the room. A table with two chairs occupied the center of the space. Candles flickered across the floor. Silk in deep shades of red, green, and purple floated from the ceiling to the floor and swayed in the breeze that accompanied her into the room. Alexa had never been in such a strange, but oddly comforting, room.

"Melina Odella?" Alexa held out the stitching.

The fortune-teller unrolled the cloth, and her eyes showed her surprise at the moving picture. She gestured Alexa to the table. "Come."

They slid into armless chairs. Fiona wiggled out of the pocket and perched in Alexa's lap with her front paws resting on the table where three piles of cards sat in ominous stacks. Melina Odella shuffled the cards before spreading them across the table in front of her.

"Choose one."

Alexa examined the elaborate red scrollwork designs across the white backs. As her hand hovered over a card near the middle, a tingle vibrated through her fingers. She tapped it.

Melina Odella moved it face up in front of her saying, "Another," and "Another." She placed the second and third cards on each side of the first.

A sudden panic rose in Alexa's throat, and she fought the urge to run from the room. She shouldn't have come. What if she didn't like what the cards told her? She started to rise, but curiosity won out, and she settled stiff-backed in the chair.

Studying the center card the fortune-teller stated, "What you ask will be achieved."

Alexa's shoulders softened, and she hid a grin. This was good. It was what she wanted to hear.

Melina Odella held the second card. "But it will come at a price. Alexa, you will learn you cannot control everything in your life."

A sudden chill swept the room, and Alexa shivered. Maybe she *didn't* want to know what the cards would predict.

The third card lay in the fortune-teller's hand. She raised her eyes. "You risk despair."

Fiona scurried into Alexa's pocket and hid, shivering.

As the chill deepened, Alexa's resolve hardened. She had a plan, and she wouldn't let fear sway her. She whispered, "I need a potion."

"You're too young for that potion."

"Many girls are betrothed after the quest."

"And many girls make that decision too early." Melina Odella studied the three cards. "Are you certain of what you ask?"

Alexa nodded, and the fortune-teller stood and drifted through the red curtain. She returned and placed a small brown bottle, plugged with a cork, on the table in front of Alexa. "Mix half in a drink. Be sure he gazes in your eyes as he partakes, and he will love only you."

"The other half?"

"So you, also, love only him."

CHAPTER ELEVEN

Zander

Zander was free. No quester lesson, and Father was at the market for his weekly fur sales. Sometimes Zander helped, but they were short on pelts. He would hunt. He searched the village land, but as usual, found nothing except for young boys with make-shift bows who made enough noise to scare off the already too few animals.

He hiked to the dividing line and vaulted over the fence. Shadow slipped through the split wood rails. Together, they headed deep into the forest until Zander ascertained it was Elder Warrin's land and not Elder Terrec's. Of the five elders whose lands bordered the village, Elder Terrec was the harshest and Elder Warrin the kindest. Still, Zander would be careful. None of them approved of poachers.

He snorted and said to Shadow, "How do they expect the villagers to survive on what they find on the fringes of town?" Meat was a luxury for most of the poor. "But not Odo and Kaiya's family, huh, Shadow? We make sure they eat well." He left meat and bread twice a week for them and hadn't been found out yet.

Zander caught a flash of red fur. A fox would make Father happy. He nocked an arrow and hesitated. The faint barking of dogs drifted from behind him. The fox disappeared. The elder who followed the hounds hunted it also. He scooped a fox token off the ground, knowing he didn't deserve it, and searched for a place to hide. He tucked Shadow under his jacket, hoping the dogs would stay with the scent of the fox and ignore his, but when the barking pitched into a frenzy, Zander panicked. Had they tracked him? The racket ceased, and shouts rang out.

"Hoy! Grab him!"

When he realized it wasn't him they were grabbing, Zander crept through the dried brush. Foxes didn't get grabbed. People did. He shuddered when he spied Cobie thrashing against three Protectors. One man remained on his horse. The elder's purple and gold tunic and fine saddle left no doubt to his status, but it was his demeanor Zander regarded. Elder Warrin sat relaxed in the saddle, chin high, and chest out. Confident.

On a black horse next to the elder, a boy smirked. It was Dharien. A random thought crossed Zander's mind. What was Dharien's patron? He'd seen all the others, but never Dharien's.

One of the men yanked Cobie's arms behind him and tied them with hemp. Another held his bow and quiver of arrows. "You won't like the jail cell I'll be taking you to for hunting Elder Warrin's estate."

Dharien snickered.

Zander fingered the wooden heart Melina Odella had given him the first day of class. He'd wrapped it with wire and run a plaited dried reed through it so he could wear the token hidden under his tunic. As he stroked it, calm seeped into his being. Taking a deep breath, Zander stepped into the clearing. The men turned toward him, but Zander sought the eyes of the man on horseback. He steeled himself for the secret, and then his stomach lurched. Elder Warrin's secret revolved around covert negotiations for a new horse. It gave Zander nothing to bargain with for Cobie's release. The elder's heart was pure.

A Protector lunged toward Zander. Instinctively, Zander drew his bow. Shadow slipped from his coat and stood next to him. The pup's hair bristled along his back.

With more bravery than he felt, Zander said, "Look at his clothes. He's in his time of magic. Let the quest be his judge."

The Protectors looked to Elder Warrin who turned to Dharien. "Is this true, Son?" Dharien nodded. The elder faced Zander. "Who are you, who also wears the clothes of a quester and appears to hunt as well?"

"I am Zander, son of Theron, the furrier." He lowered his bow, but kept the arrow nocked.

"Well, Zander, son of Theron, why should I not take you both to the court to be dealt with by the letter of the law?"

Lifting his bow, Zander aimed at Dharien, who paled. "If I am to lose my hand, I may as well lose my life, as hunting is my only pleasure."

To his surprise, the elder chuckled. "Put down your bow. You have my word. You and your friend will be released with your hands intact."

Thankful the elder hadn't called his bluff, Zander lowered his bow. Because he had seen Elder Warrin's heart, he trusted him. Zander tried not to laugh at the look of astonishment on Dharien's face.

"Father, you can't let them hunt our ground."

"The forest holds plenty for the hungry poor." Elder Warrin waved toward Cobie and ordered the men. "Unloose his hands, and return his bow." To Zander, he said, "I think we've lost our fox. For sport, let's see how you young men shoot."

The Protectors marked three trees as targets. Elder Warrin clapped Dharien's shoulder. "Don't show off too much, Son."

Dharien's chest puffed, and he smirked at Zander and Cobie. The three strode twenty paces from the trees, bows in hand.

Elder Warrin called, "Take your mark."

Confident in his aim, Zander shifted his bow to the left. He wouldn't let the elder know of his skill at shooting. Elder Warrin would be happier if Dharien won, and Zander wanted to stay in his good graces, no matter how much he would have enjoyed beating Dharien.

"Release your arrows!"

Dharien let out a whoop as his arrow struck truest to the mark, almost on spot. Cobie's hit two fingers to the right while Zander's hit one finger to the left, as he'd planned.

"Fetch your arrows, boys. We have a contest!"

Three rounds in, Dharien led in hits. After the fourth round, Elder Warrin strode to Zander and turned him, forcing him to look in his eyes.

"It serves no one for a man to pretend to be less than he is. Do you think these Protectors would be so cowardly?"

Zander blushed and shook his head. The elder was observant if he caught him throwing the contest.

Clapping Zander's shoulder, Elder Warrin declared, "The first four were practice rounds. Let the competition begin now."

For the next ten rounds, Zander's arrows flew true, hitting the mark dead on. With each hit, Dharien's countenance grew darker until hatred flew like sparks from his eyes. Cobie shot well, beating Dharien on some rounds, but still ending last. Peacock omens for pride, scorpions for envy, and hornets for hatred fell like rain around the boys.

Elder Warrin laughed. "It seems you boys will be busy earning tokens to counteract all these omens." He clapped Zander on the back. "I expect to watch you at the shooting match next month at the Festival of Victoria."

"Only elders' and Protectors' sons are allowed to compete with the bow," Zander responded. The rush of energy from winning pushed him to continue. "But maybe a man of your influence could arrange for two boys in their time of magic to join the competition?"

"Yes, I think I can arrange it." The elder gazed from Cobie to

Zander, and his face turned pensive. "You're welcome to hunt my lands, but Elder Terrec's lands adjoin mine. He will not be so generous. Stay far from his borders."

Zander bowed his head. "Thank you, Sir. You are most kind."

He left confident of two things. Elder Warrin respected his ability and maybe even liked him, and Dharien hated him more than ever.

CHAPTER TWELVE
Four and a Half Months until the Quest

Alexa

Clutching her bag, Alexa felt for the brown bottle nestled among the tokens and omens. The Festival of Victoria, the saint who sacrificed true love to save her people, would be the perfect time to use the potion, and although Alexa's heart feared, her will remained strong.

She joined the other questers at the Quinary, eager to enjoy the celebration, but when Melina Odella's gaze fell on Alexa, she remembered the warnings in the cards. *You can't control everything, it will come at a price, you risk despair.*

After the priest cautioned against earning omens, Alexa moved with the others to the festivities. It was time. If she didn't do it now, she might lose her nerve. Alexa lowered her lashes and smiled at Paal. "I'll find drinks."

Paal's face lit. "Thanks, Alexa."

As she crossed the market, the priest's laughter rang out from the sausage stand. Alexa skirted around the side to find the cider and carried two mugs to an empty table. She turned to hide the brown bottle she pulled from her bag. Holding her breath, she struggled with the cork. Carefully, so as not to spill the precious liquid, Alexa poured half of the potion into each drink. The warning of the cards whispered through her head, *you can't control.*

She dismissed the knot in the pit of her stomach. No matter how Alexa examined her circumstances, this was her chance for the life she wanted. She squared her shoulders and carried the drinks, weaving through the crowd, fearful of spilling.

The priest's shadow fell across her, and he reached for a mug. Alexa stepped back, holding tight to the handle. His flashing eyes bore into hers. "Greed, Alexa? Not an omen to wish for, Child."

He held out a snake omen, and Alexa stiffened. As he pulled the cup from her hand, his eyes narrowed at her shocked face. "Generosity cures greed," he spat. He tossed the omen at her feet and then drained the cup as he strode toward the fortune-teller. His voice called out, "Melina Odella?"

The fortune-teller gazed past the priest, and met Alexa's eyes. Alexa held up the single cup and shrugged. Melina Odella gasped.

Trembling, Alexa turned, unable to watch as the fortune-teller faced the priest. She hurried toward Paal. She could still give him the potion. She concentrated on the first card's message—*what you ask will be achieved.*

Paal stood talking with Zander. "Thanks, Alexa. You only brought one?"

"Uh, I gave one to the priest." *You can't control* flowed through her head.

Zander glanced at Alexa. A dark shadow crossed his face. Why did she feel Zander peered into her soul each time their eyes met?

He stepped in front of Paal. "No."

"Stay out of this, Zander," Alexa hissed. *It will come at a price.*

"I can't let you do this."

When Zander reached for the mug, she twisted and knocked into Dharien.

"Thanks, Alexa." Dharien smirked as he grabbed the mug from her hand and brought it to his lips.

"No!" Alexa yelled. *You risk despair.*

Zander pushed her from Dharien and grabbed for the mug.

Dharien turned and gulped the cider. His smug gaze softened at Alexa, and he beamed, reaching for her hand.

Alexa's eyes flashed at Zander. "This is your fault! I hate you!" She snatched the hornet omen at her feet and stomped off. *It will come at a price. You can't control. You risk despair.*

The premonition consumed Alexa. The cards had foretold she would achieve success, and an elder's son *had* fallen in love with her.

But he was the wrong boy.

CHAPTER THIRTEEN

Zander

Zander pushed away the confusion he felt about Alexa. He'd been unsettled since seeing her plan on the first day of class. He shouldn't care if she played games with Paal and Dharien. It wasn't his fault the wrong boy drank the potion.

He scrutinized his arrows, checking the quills once again for damage. He had yet to decide if he would shoot to win, but they must fly true. His heart desired the championship, but his gut warned of danger. If he won and gained the respect of the elders, it could help him realize his dream, but it could backfire if it angered them instead. Not listening to his gut usually ended in trouble.

Content with the state of the arrows, Zander strode to the competition with Shadow at his side. He and Cobie stood last in line at the check-in table. Zander's shaking legs threatened to betray his nervousness, but when he noticed the sweat on Cobie's forehead, he knew Cobie shared his fear. Never before had boys other than the elders' and Protectors' sons competed in the archery tournament. He didn't expect the other competitors to welcome them. Dharien certainly wouldn't. Zander spoke to reassure them both. "Elder Warrin gave his word we could compete."

Cobie whispered, "Look at the others. They've trained for this. We're illegal hunters."

"We belong here as much as they do." Zander reached down to

pat Shadow. Now if only he could believe it himself. Nerves wouldn't help him shoot straight.

The man at the registration table eyed them. "You're not the sons of an elder or Protector." He glared at Shadow. "No dogs allowed."

"Elder Warrin gave his permission." Zander pointed to the last two names scrawled on the list. "Our names are recorded there." He tucked Shadow into his pack and grinned. "And this is not a dog."

The man narrowed his eyes and waved them past. "Go on with you then." He muttered as they left, "Looks like a dog."

Zander trailed the others to the practice area where chaos slowly resolved into order. The younger boys, who had not yet completed the quest, moved into a group to the left of the viewing stands, while the older unmarried boys practiced behind. Zander set his pack in a shady corner and lifted the flap. "Stay boy," he said to Shadow, and because the pup had learned his commands easily, Zander felt confident he'd be safe.

As the stands filled, the proctor announced the rules. "Each boy takes ten shots, with points given for each hit. Bull's-eyes receive ten points with two points less for each circle away from the middle. One point's awarded for hitting any part of the target outside the circles. The top two marksmen in both age groups will advance to the finals."

The group of younger boys would compete first. The proctor called Zander's name.

"The worst luck," Zander muttered as he entered the arena. He flexed his hand to release the cramp from clenching his bow. As he glanced into the packed stands, the elders scowled. Zander took a swig of water to wet his mouth.

The proctor announced to the crowd, "Zander, son of Theron, in his time of magic, competes at Elder Warrin's request."

The villagers murmured their surprise. The elders glared at Elder Warrin. They didn't like change, and especially not if it meant two village boys would be competing against their sons. Zander grinned. Nope, not happy.

Elder Warrin caught Zander's eye and nodded. Zander had at least one person supporting him. Father was likely drunk in the mead tent. Zander hadn't told him he'd be competing. Now, it seemed foolish. Father was sure to hear of it.

The proctor motioned for Zander to shoot.

Beads of sweat popped up on Zander's forehead. His inner voice reminded him, *Calm down. Jittery hands make for a shaky bow.* He nocked his arrow, inhaled, and pulled back the string. He sighted along the arrow as he'd done hundreds of times since Father had taught him to hunt at the age of five. He could outshoot every boy there. Probably.

Willing himself to stillness, he tried to shut out everything but the target. The crowd disappeared. The chatter of the boys faded. The bull's-eye filled his vision.

As Zander released the arrow, Dharien yelled, "Low-lifes don't belong here."

Zander jerked the bow to the side, and the arrow struck the edge of the target. Zander's face burned at the laughter from the stands. He would begin the competition with one point.

As the next contestants shot, Zander pulled his energy into his gut and sent it deep into the earth imagining himself as a sturdy oak tree. Calm flowed into his body. Confidence replaced nerves. At his next turn, he stepped again into the arena. The target filled his vision, and he lifted his bow with relaxed shoulders. He sighted, breathed in, and released. The arrow flew true. Bull's-eye.

With that second shot, Zander's shoulders snapped back, and his chest thrust out. He stared into the stands, daring them to laugh now. He would overcome his first bad shot. He could still win and he would. He'd prove to Dharien and all the elders he deserved to be in the competition. He'd prove being a elder's son wasn't enough to cheat him from what he deserved. With a jolt, Zander realized he wasn't thinking of only this competition. On his next eight turns, Zander hit the bull's-eye. With each round, the applause from the stands grew. At his tenth and final attempt, the peasants and merchants stood hushed as he prepared to shoot. The elders and Protectors who filled the front rows remained seated. Tied with Paal, and Dharien one point behind, the last round would determine the winners. Zander's pulse raced. If he bull's-eyed the last shot, he'd advance to the finals. And if the other two boys shot less than a ten, Zander would win.

He strode to the arena and breathed deeply to slow the adrenaline racing through his blood. He couldn't let his nerves control him. Not now. Not with the chance of winning so close. He nodded to the proctor and faced the target. He wiped his palms on his pants.

Time slowed as he nocked the arrow and lifted the bow. Everything around him stilled. The pounding of his heart drowned out every other noise. He sighted, released, and followed the arrow as it flew.

Bull's-eye.

The arena came back into focus, and Zander turned to the wild cries of the audience. With a wide grin he couldn't conceal, Zander graciously acknowledged them and bowed. He had advanced to the finals. When the round ended, Zander had won. Paal finished second and Dharien third. Cobie seemed pleased with sixth.

After his adrenaline subsided, Zander tucked Shadow under his tunic and relaxed with Cobie in the shade. Zander couldn't stop thinking of his final shot and the cheers from the crowd. He'd done it. He'd proven himself to the elders, and more importantly, he'd given Fate a reason to grant his dream. He didn't even care when the peacock omen for pride formed next to him. He'd work on earning sparrow tokens later.

He enjoyed the older boys' competition. After a close contest,

Dharien's older brother Greydon finished first and Elder Terrec's son, Lash, finished second.

Cobie left to help his father in the market. "I'll cheer for you in the finals," he said with a backward wave.

While the crowd filtered from the stands for a break before the final competition, Zander inspected his arrows and pulled one with torn quills from his pouch. The rest remained perfect. As he slid his bow over his shoulder and across his back, Dharien punched his arm.

"I should have been in the finals. Not you! You don't belong in this competition"

"It was your father who gave permission," Zander shot back.

"You must have cheated. Magic helped you win. Did Moira give you the favor of shooting straight? I'll have you thrown out!" Dharien ran to the man in charge.

This could be trouble. The proctor was sure to side with an elder's son. Red-faced, Dharien shouted and pointed at Zander.

A shadow passed over the proctor's face. He strode toward Zander. "Is this true? Did magic help you win?"

Wondering how he could prove otherwise, Zander's pulse raced. No way would this man believe him after Dharien's accusation. Zander had one chance. He held the proctor's gaze long enough to see his secret. Suddenly, Zander laughed.

"You think this is funny? I disqualify you from the competition!" The proctor grabbed Zander's arm. "Come with me to the judge."

Standing behind the proctor, Dharien smirked. "I knew it. No peasant could win without magic."

Zander pulled away and held up his hand. He couldn't reveal his favor, but he could use the information he saw. He bent and whispered into the man's ear. "You steal from your land holder to gamble and drink. What do you think Elder Martin would say if I told him?"

Through clenched teeth the proctor muttered, "You lie. You cannot know this."

"And yet I do." Zander said. "It's no lie." He hoped the proctor wouldn't disqualify him for his boldness. Not many wanted their secrets known, and Zander didn't think he was brave enough to expose him to Elder Martin.

The proctor turned to Dharien. "No cheating has occurred. Zander moves to the finals!"

Dharien's mouth dropped and then his eyes narrowed. "You won't win." He pushed Zander against a corner post and held him. "You're nothing but a low-life furrier's son. You don't deserve to win. I'll see to it you lose in the next round." Dharien stomped on the scorpion omen that appeared next to his foot.

Zander jabbed his finger in Dharien's chest. "Empty threat, Dharien." He ducked under Dharien's arm and picked up the omen. He tossed it at Dharien before he sauntered away. For the first time, gratitude for his gift filled him. It might prove useful, after all.

CHAPTER FOURTEEN

Alexa

Alexa didn't care about the shooting competition, but thankfully, Dharien had to leave her to compete. He kept trying to hold her hand. Merindah had been disgusted with Dharien's puppy eyes and left with Kaiya to cheer for Zander and Cobie. At any other festival, Alexa would have been happy to join them, but she needed to talk to Melina Odella. With the crowd headed to the stands, the fortune-teller should be easy to find.

Despite the sun's warmth, Alexa clutched at her tunic, shivering. She wandered past a half-empty cart of copper kettles for sale. The grilled venison drifting from the next booth turned her stomach, even as it grumbled. She'd skipped breakfast, remembering all the treats the festival would offer. Now, nothing smelled good. She bought a small bag of roasted hickory nuts. Maybe they'd settle her stomach and her nerves.

Laughter and music drifted from a large tent. After the quest, Alexa would be old enough to enter. As she cracked a nut and popped it in her mouth, she peeked through the open door. From her pocket, Fiona begged for a treat and Alexa absently gave her a nut. In one corner of the tent, a Protector played a fiddle tucked under his chin. His foot vigorously tapped out the beat. Next to him, Eva, the midwife and healer, played a flute, her eyes sparkling. Alexa loved watching her. Eva was Mother's best friend and had helped birth Alexa. Kaiya's father beat a drum and sang a duet with Merindah's mother who tapped a tambourine against her leg. The potter played a recorder.

The music wound into Alexa's soul and her tension eased. The happy beat was contagious. Her eyes flitted to the couples dancing in the center. One of the men, already drunk, fell against a chair and landed flat on his back. His laughing wife pulled him up, and held him tight as they continued to dance.

Alexa wrinkled her nose. She hoped her future husband wouldn't drink. She shuddered. Would it be Dharien? She didn't know him well, but most of the elders enjoyed their mead. Zander's father sat alone in a corner with a pint clutched in both hands. He didn't look like he enjoyed the festivities.

She backed away from the tent. She'd check to see if Mother needed help. She could find Melina Odella later. When she reached the bakery, the door was closed and Mother was gone. The racks were empty. As usual, Mother's breads and cakes had sold out. There went her excuse not to find the fortune-teller.

She wandered down the market street and turned at the row with the jewelry. She ignored the call of the sparkling gems and instead purchased a copper leaf pin for her tunic. She passed the woven coverlets and stopped at the corner booth of games for the younger children. The sack races started and Alexa laughed with the others as a small boy fell and then wiggled to the finish line. It wasn't so long ago she'd played those games.

She turned the corner and her stomach lurched. Melina Odella stood in a booth and held out a coin for a bolt of purple silk. Alexa sighed. She had to talk to her sometime.

Melina Odella stepped into the sun and spied Alexa. Her eyes flashed. "How did the priest come to drink the potion?"

Fiona took one look at the fortune-teller's wolf and disappeared into Alexa's pocket, trembling.

"I don't know what happened." Alexa spread out her hands as she pleaded with the fortune-teller. "He took one cup, and Dharien drank the other. This isn't what I wanted. Can you make a potion to undo this one?"

"No, I cannot," the fortune-teller replied hoarsely. "We both have to deal with your mistake. The cards warned you, and yet, you ignored them."

Surprised at the fortune-teller's reproach, Alexa stammered, "But you said I'd achieve what I wanted."

"And you did. An elder's son is in love with you."

"It's the wrong one."

Melina Odella stared at Alexa. "The priest thinks he's in love with me."

"He can't…"

"Exactly."

The priest was forbidden to love one person. His love was sanctioned for the village as a whole. There had to be a way to undo the potion. For the priest and for Dharien. Alexa shaded her eyes as she squinted at Melina Odella. "What will happen?"

"What do you think? If the elders believe Chanse has broken his vows, he'll be removed from his position. Is that what you wanted when you gave him the potion? Was this always your plan, Alexa? To disgrace the priest?"

"No. I didn't give it to him. I tried to stop him, but he gave me an omen for greed and took it anyway. I promise, Melina Odella. I didn't want this."

Melina Odella stepped toward Alexa, until inches separated them. She gripped Alexa's arm. "You'd better hope nothing comes of it. I can make the quest difficult for you. You don't want to cross me, Alexa."

Alexa jerked her arm away and ran. She needed to talk to

Merindah. She found her with Kaiya in the stands where the two sat with their patrons on their shoulders.

"Can I talk to you?" she whispered to her best friend. "But not here, not with Kaiya."

Kaiya leaned across Merindah. "Zander shoots next. You should see him, Alexa. He's tied with Paal and Dharien." She bounced against the wooden seat. "Can you believe it? A peasant is winning. He's a hero!"

A hero? That seemed a little strong. Alexa glanced at the smiling faces of the villagers. If Zander won, each and every one of them would share in his celebration.

As Zander continued to hit bull's-eyes, she couldn't help herself. Alexa cheered and screamed with the rest of the villagers. They were peasants. If Zander could do it, if he could rise above his station and beat the elders, then they could. She could.

Zander won and the crowd roared. The elders sat quiet as if stunned. Dharien didn't seem happy to place third.

Alexa sat through the older boys' competition waiting to talk with Merindah. At the break she grabbed her friend's hand. "Kaiya? Can I talk to Merindah for a few minutes?"

Kaiya nodded. "I need to find Odo. I'll meet you here for the finals."

Alexa pulled Merindah to the top of the stands and waited for the arena to clear. She curled forward and wrapped her arms around her knees. She wasn't sure she wanted to confess.

Merindah blurted out, "What's going on with you and Dharien?"

"I think I made a mistake. I went to the fortune-teller for a potion."

"What are you talking about?" Merindah's eyes narrowed. "What have you done?"

After taking a deep breath, Alexa confided her secret and what happened with the mix-up and the priest. "But it didn't turn out as I wanted. What should I do?"

Merindah chewed a fingernail. "You have to tell Dharien."

"No! I couldn't!" Alexa hid her face in her hands.

"Does Zander know?"

"How could he? But it's his fault Paal didn't drink the cider."

"It's not fair to condemn him for your mistake." Merindah glared at her. "How could you think this would work?"

"You blame me too?" If Merindah was mad at her, she had no one on her side.

"Who else?" Merindah shrugged and her black curls bounced against her shoulders.

Alexa rubbed her arms. "I'll fix this. I have to! I can't have Dharien thinking he loves me." He didn't really love her, did he?

"And what of the priest?"

Remembering Melina Odella's anger, Alexa didn't care what happened to the priest. "The fortune-teller threatened me. She can deal with him."

Merindah snorted. "She's our teacher. She wouldn't threaten you. It's always about you, isn't it, Alexa?" She shook her head.

Alexa's face fell. "Is that what you think?"

"In your scheming, did you ever consider what Paal wants? Or what he would think of you tricking him?"

Alexa closed her eyes to calm her sudden anger, but before she could answer, Merindah stood. "I think you deserve Dharien."

The sting of Merindah's words cut through Alexa's anger and tears threatened. When Merindah rushed off, Alexa bent over her knees and pressed her palms into her eyes. How could she fix this?

She felt someone standing in front of her.

"Alexa?"

Dharien. He must have been waiting. She forced a smile as she glance up. "Congratulations. Third place is still good, isn't it?"

He scowled. "Third is terrible. Zander stole my place in the finals. He never should have been allowed to shoot."

She shrugged. What could she say. "There's always the next one."

Dharien's scowl turned to a smile. "Forget that low-life. Let's enjoy the festival. Let me buy you sweets."

If Zander was a low-life, what was she? Dharien wanted to spend time with her because of the potion. This was never going to work. She held back her tears. "I can't. I have to find Mother." It was a small lie. She did need Mother if she wanted to be rid of Dharien.

Dharien looked hopeful. "Maybe later?"

"Maybe."

Dharien took her hand as they walked down the steps. Alexa reminded herself it wasn't real. He was under the spell of the potion.

"Dharien!" Elder Warrin's voice boomed from the bottom steps.

Dharien jerked his hand from Alexa's. His cheeks reddened.

Elder Warrin frowned and ignored Alexa. "Your mother is looking for you. She wants to celebrate Greydon's win as a family." He spun on his heels and strode away. He commanded over his shoulder. "Come now."

Dharien pouted at his father's back before he turned to Alexa. "If it weren't for Zander, we'd be celebrating my win too."

"I'm sorry, Dharien." Not really, no, not sorry at all.

He leaned forward and kissed her cheek. Then he was gone, hurrying after his father.

Alexa's stomach lurched. Even if she liked Dharien, his family would never accept a peasant into their family. The look in Elder Warrin's eyes confirmed that little truth. No longer interested in the festivities, Alexa threaded through the crowd and stumbled to the bakery. She climbed the steps to her room, fell to the bed, and cried herself to sleep with Fiona tucked in her arms. The day had been a disaster.

As Alexa tossed in bed, she dreamed of potions and boys who

loved her and then hated her. When she woke, the last dream she remembered was Zander's face. His eyes were the blue of the sky while hers were the black of night.

CHAPTER FIFTEEN

Zander

Paal caught Zander as he left the arena. "Come on, champ. Let's find some food. I was too nervous to eat before the contest."

As Zander walked through the market, every villager smiled and offered congratulations. The men slapped his back, and the women touched his arm. It was that moment Zander realized every peasant shared in his win against the elders. His own smile grew larger, and he took the time to thank each one. "You'll be there to cheer me on in the finals, won't you?" he asked.

"Yes, yes," they replied and nodded their heads. "We'll be there."

Paal grumbled, "I'll die of starvation before we find the food."

Zander smiled. Paal was in no danger of starving. The smoky aroma of the fire pit drew them past the copper kettle vendors until Zander stood in front of a meat booth. He had enough money for one roasted leg of lamb. When Zander offered the coin, the vendor beamed and waved him away.

"You're one of us. No charge for the winner," he said.

After Paal paid for a slab of grilled goat and they both snagged cups of cider, they found an empty high-backed bench across from the music tent. Zander leaned against the smooth wood and tapped his foot to the drum beat. He pulled a piece of meat off the bone and shared it with Shadow. As an afterthought, he handed a piece to Paal's dog, Silk. What a strange name for a dog.

Inside the tent, a Protector played the fiddle and another danced with his wife. The men would compete with bows on the second day of the festival. Zander imagined how it would feel to win that competition. He hoped he'd impressed Moira. He could be a great Protector if she gave him the chance. For the first time in his life, Zander felt special. He was a winner. And he liked it. He liked it a lot. If he was a Protector, the villagers would always look up to him.

A peacock omen appeared at his feet. Blushing, Zander scooped the omen into his closed fist, hoping Paal didn't see. He grimaced. He'd have to earn another sparrow token.

Paal punched his arm and snickered. "My father says if I earn any more omens, I'll never make it back from the quest."

Confused, Zander pulled away. "You aren't worried?"

"Fate won't take me. She'll take someone like Odo or Kaiya. There's always another peasant to take their place in the fields."

Zander struggled to reply. Is that what it meant to be an elder? To disregard a person's worth because of how they were born? Is that what Paal thought of him? That he was expendable?

Paal leaned back and licked the spicy meat sauce off his fingers. "You're not worried, are you? You're strong, and you know your way around the gulch. You'll do fine."

Father was right. The elders were all alike. Zander couldn't stand to look at Paal.

Just then Father stumbled from the tent. Zander slouched, hoping he wouldn't see him, but his luck had run out. Father headed his way.

"Zander," he slurred. "Enjoying the festival?" He rubbed his eyes and stared at Paal, as if he couldn't believe what he saw. "You're Elder Rowan's son? What are you doing with my son?"

Paal's mouth dropped. "Don't you know? Zander won our division in the archery tournament. He's in the finals in an hour."

Zander's face flushed.

As he grabbed at the top of the bench to keep his balance, Father sneered. "You aspire too high, Son. You'll never be a Protector." He patted Zander's head and lurched back. "Don't forget your place in this world." He left, shuffling past the bakery and disappearing around the corner.

"What's wrong with your father?"

"You mean besides being drunk?" Zander could recite a whole list of things wrong with his father.

"He didn't watch you shoot?"

"I didn't tell him I was competing." No way would he have told him. Father would have shown up drunk and embarrassed him.

"Why not?"

"You saw him. He started drinking before the festival began. He's a jerk when he drinks."

"Is he always like that?"

"He's not so bad when he's sober." Zander muttered, "He's just not sober often." He stood. "Sorry you had to see him. Let's take Shadow and Silk for a run."

As they walked to the open area behind the arena, Zander was glad Paal dropped the conversation. Father was right about one thing. He had no business hanging out with an elder's son. Paal wasn't his friend, and he didn't know why he'd confessed about Father's drinking. He shook his head. As if it was a secret. The whole village had to have seen Father stumbling through the market.

At the clearing, Paal grabbed a stick. "Let's see whether a dog or a coyote fetches better."

A contest was just what Zander needed to take his mind off Father. He motioned Shadow to his side. "Sit." Shadow sat at attention. It took Paal three tries to get Silk settled at his side.

Paal waved the stick in the air. "One, two, three, go!" He threw it overhand and the patrons raced off.

"Run, Shadow!" Zander grinned as his patron forged ahead of Silk.

At the last second, Silk leaped into the air, snagged the stick and whipped around to race back to Paal with Shadow on his tail. It seemed his patron needed more practice.

Each time, Silk beat Shadow by seconds. On the last throw, both dog and coyote jumped and each caught an end of the stick. They tumbled when they hit the ground, but neither let go and they raced back together. Zander laughed with Paal, but he couldn't help wondering if there was a message in there for him. Maybe it didn't matter if Paal outranked him. Maybe they could be friends.

With two tired patrons, Zander and Paal headed to the arena and spent time practicing while Greydon and Lash shot at a second target. Zander studied Greydon. Someone in his lineage had been Chahda. He'd let his dark blond curls twist into long dreadlocks. His blue eyes contrasted with Dharien's brown ones. Would Greydon's heart be pure like Elder Warrin's or dark like Dharien's? Drawn from his thoughts by Lash's laughter, Zander scowled at Elder Terrec's son.

"Hey, little boys. You can't beat us," Lash taunted. He pointed at Zander. "Especially you, scum. You got lucky and luck doesn't last." Lash snorted and turned to Greydon, who stood eyebrows drawn, tapping an arrow against the ground.

Zander met Greydon's eyes and found him nothing like his brother. Greydon possessed a pure heart. His secret shocked Zander, but he didn't have time to ponder what it meant.

"I haven't had serious competition for many festivals." Greydon grinned. "Let's see what you can do, Zander, son of the furrier." He clapped Zander's shoulder. "It's time to prove your worth."

The crowd was still trickling into the arena when the proctor called the contestants to the front. He bellowed over the excited chattering crowd. "Finals begin in five minutes."

Confident he could shoot as well as any elder's son, Zander spent that five minutes centering himself. As the other three contestants chatted with their families, he stood alone facing the stands, aware only of his breath. Then he spread his awareness to the villagers in the stands who supported him. He pulled their excitement into his body, tempering it with control. When the proctor announced the competition's start, he was ready.

Paal was called to shoot first. Relief flooded his face as the arrow hit a finger's breadth off center, and he slung his bow over his shoulder before he jaunted to the sidelines.

Lash shot second and hit the bull's-eye. "Beat that, low life," he said as he shouldered past Zander, knocking his quiver to the ground and scattering the arrows.

Stooping to help gather Zander's arrows, Greydon muttered, "Ignore Lash. He's always been an arse."

Remembering the times he'd hunted Elder Terrec's land without permission, Zander smirked. At his turn, he sighted. His aim was sure, and his body calm. The arrow hit dead center. He started the competition with ten points.

Greydon shot a matching bull's eye.

On his second turn, as he walked to the target area, Zander glanced at the elders in the front row of the stands. Elder Warrin appeared unperturbed, but Zander wondered what he truly thought now that Zander competed against his first-born son. He might be wishing he hadn't asked Zander to participate.

When Zander pulled back the string, someone yelled, "You don't deserve to be here."

His heart thudded as Father's words echoed back at him. He lowered his bow and peered into the stands. Was Father watching?

Elder Terrec laughed and shouted, "You're a peasant." The Odwa's trait of red hair made him easy to spot in the stands.

Zander blushed, but he'd rather have Elder Terrec yelling at him than his drunken father. One by one, the peasants stood to show their support. He nodded to the crowd as their pride soaked into his soul. He would win for them. He couldn't let the elder bother him. When he shot, he hit the bull's-eye. For them and for him.

After the fourth round, Greydon and Zander were tied with forty-points. Lash followed with thirty-eight, and Paal trailed with thirty-six.

Dharien strode from the sidelines and glared at Zander. He called out, "Greydon, my brother. Looking for another championship? No doubt you'll win the lucky seventh."

Greydon's eyes danced. "I have competition this time."

Dharien spat. "Zander? A peasant? He can't beat you!"

"He had no trouble beating you, little brother."

Holding his laugh, Zander removed an arrow from his quiver and leaned the leather holder against a post. After he shot his fifth bull's-eye, he pulled the arrow from the target. The tip pulled away, but Zander was unconcerned. He still had plenty of good arrows left.

As he passed Greydon, the older boy congratulated him. "Zander, you push me to my best."

When Zander returned to the sidelines, Dharien had gone. Before his next turn, Zander pulled an arrow and glanced at the fletching. He gaped at the torn feathers. He pulled another and another, each one damaged. Only one person would have destroyed his chance at winning. Dharien! But who would believe him? The proctor would think he was trying to avenge Dharien's earlier accusation. Zander glanced at the stands where Elder Warrin leaned forward as he watched Greydon shoot. Zander respected the man too much to accuse his son without proof.

When the proctor called his name a second time, Zander snatched a damaged arrow and trudged to the arena, his mind roiling. He'd shot bad arrows before, but never with so much depending upon a perfect shot.

He sighted, calculated, and adjusted his aim to compensate for an arrow that wouldn't fly true. When he loosed the arrow, it zipped to the target and hit one circle from the center. The crowd gasped, and Zander's dream slipped away. Greydon wouldn't miss, and Zander had four more rounds with damaged arrows. His father's words whispered through his head. *You aspire too high.* Maybe this was Fate's way of agreeing with Father.

Greydon grimaced as he passed Zander. After he shot another bull's-eye, the elders leaped to their feet applauding. When Greydon reached the sideline he pushed aside Lash's congratulations and shoved Zander's shoulder. "Are you throwing the competition? I watched you change your aim."

What could he say? Zander reached into his quiver and pulled out his arrows.

Greydon scowled at the damaged feathers.

Zander uttered one word. "Dharien."

At his brother's name, Greydon's face reddened, but he didn't argue. He reached into his own quiver and pulled out four arrows. He handed them to Zander. "I want a fair match."

Zander nodded his thanks, unable to speak. Greydon could have used the damaged arrows to his advantage. He surely wanted to win as badly as Zander. It took a good heart to do what Greydon did.

After Zander's next bull's-eye, Greydon intentionally shot to the left, putting him in a three-way tie with Zander and Lash. "I want it fair," he avowed to Zander.

In the eighth round the three still tied, and Paal trailed by six points. On his ninth shot, Lash missed his mark but Zander and Greydon shot true. And when the four each hit the bull's-eye in the final round, Zander and Greydon tied for first.

The proctor checked the rule book before announcing to the excited crowd, "In the case of a tie, each contestant will shoot progressively farther from the target until we have a winner at the end of a round."

When Greydon handed him five fresh arrows, Zander shook his head. "The others are still good."

Greydon pressed the arrows into his hand. "I want it fair. I have new arrows, you'll have new arrows."

After the fourth bonus round, they were tied with four bull's-eyes each. At his fifth turn, Zander glanced into the stands. Dharien hunched in the front seats glaring at him. Next to him Elder Warrin appeared thoughtful, fingertips stroking his chin. He probably hadn't expected Zander to challenge Greydon for the championship. Zander had proven himself. Maybe he *should* throw the match and allow Greydon to win. Then he remembered Elder Warrin's words spoken that day in the woods. "*It serves no one for a man to pretend to be less than he is.*" Zander took a deep breath and resolved to do his best. On his fifth shot, the arrow flew true and struck the center.

When Greydon took his turn, Zander scanned the crowd. Merindah and Kaiya waved at him, and he smiled in return. He heard Greydon's arrow hit the target with a thud.

The stunned crowd fell silent, and all eyes turned to Zander. As one, they stood and cheered.

Shocked, Zander spun around. Greydon pulled him to the center. As the crowd roared, the proctor presented Zander with a longbow and two dozen arrows worthy of any Protector.

Lash refused to shake Zander's hand, which caused Zander a pang of regret. He'd seen Lash's secret. Elder Terrec would take the rod to his son for his loss. Only winning would have prevented a beating. It was a secret he'd rather not have seen.

Greydon clasped Zander's hand. In the moment where he should have let go, Zander held longer and said, "Greydon, you will make a fine and fair elder." It was all he could say without revealing his favor.

Greydon's grin faded.

The secret Zander had seen revolved around Greydon's fear of living up to his father's image. Greydon worried he wouldn't measure up as the eldest son. And more than that, he would be expected to produce an heir. It would be unlikely.

Greydon liked boys.

CHAPTER SIXTEEN

Alexa

On the second day of the festival, Alexa stayed home. After the mess of the day before, she didn't want to see anyone. Especially not Dharien. Mother asked her plans, and Alexa said, "I'm going to fast today to earn a butterfly token."

Drinks were allowed on a fast. Mother brewed Alexa a pot of chamomile tea with honey. She kissed Alexa's cheek. "I'm sorry you're missing the festival. If you need me, I'll be with Eva in the music tent."

What Alexa needed was time to think. As she sipped the tea, the scent of the flowers calmed her jittery nerves. She was on her own to fix the mix-up with Dharien. He believed he loved her, but he didn't really. And it wouldn't be any better if it was Paal. Seeing the way Dharien had acted under the effects of the potion made her know one thing for certain. She didn't want a husband who didn't truly love her. Merindah was always so level-headed. Why hadn't she talked to her best friend before she went to the fortune-teller? If she had, Dharien wouldn't think he loved her, Melina Odella wouldn't be angry, and Alexa wouldn't be alone in her room during one of her favorite festivals.

She didn't dare confide in Mother. Alexa wouldn't be able to stand the disappointment Mother would feel with her. And what could Mother do? No, it was hers alone to fix. There had to be a way.

While Fiona curled on her pillow, softly snoring, Alexa picked through her fabric and chose a blank cloth. She threaded purple into the needle she kept in her tunic hem. The tension in her stomach dissolved as she chain stitched around the border and then sprinkled dainty yellow French knots here and there. Zander had tried to keep her from giving the cup of cider to either of the boys, but he couldn't have known she'd added a potion to it. She stitched his likeness and clothed him in white. She added Dharien dressed in red and Paal in yellow. Merindah brought violet to mind, and Alexa stitched her in a lovely dress with a flower ring in her dark hair.

Her tea grew cold and the hours flew by. Afternoon shadows fell across the floor as she stitched herself clothed in black—the color that matched her mood. After all, Melina Odella had given her the word "night" at the first day ceremony.

As she knotted the last thread of her signature in the border, the embroidered figures moved around the cloth, and she wondered— could she control their actions in life if she controlled them on the cloth? She threaded her needle with thick black cord and connected Zander to Dharien. She was still upset Zander had interfered with her plans. If this worked, maybe forcing him to stay close to Dharien would teach him a lesson. Changing colors, she created a white criss-crossed fence between Dharien and herself. She added a pale pink thread connecting her heart to Merindah's.

On the cloth, Zander and Dharien struggled, unable to move far from the other. Alexa grinned at her revenge and hoped the fence would keep Dharien away from her. The pink thread cheered Alexa, knowing even with Merindah's anger, they remained connected. Paal alone roamed free.

As she fell asleep, a butterfly fluttered across the room and dropped onto her pillow as a wooden token. If nothing else, Alexa had accomplished that. She left it out so Mother would see it before going to bed.

The next morning, Alexa fretted over going out for the last day of the festival. It wouldn't hurt to earn another butterfly token, and if she could find a way to earn a turtle to counteract the hornet omens she'd earned for anger, it would be good. Not going meant she'd miss playing skittles. Mother had probably left to help set up the lanes with the nine pins. The women would roll heavy balls to try to knock them over amid lots of laughing. Mother always teamed with Eva and sometimes they won a purple ribbon. Alexa and Merindah always teamed up.

She thought of Dharien. If he found her, and she was sure he would, he'd want to buy her sweets or hold her hand. And then there was Merindah. She was probably with Kaiya. It wouldn't be any fun without Merindah to laugh with and eat candies until they earned a pig omen for overindulgence.

She wandered downstairs to the kitchen. She was right, Mother had gone, but her yellow canary serenaded Alexa from the cage that hung next to the front window. Alexa wasn't sure how the patron helped Mother with her baking. Maybe the bird's singing inspired her.

Alexa's stomach grumbled from fasting the day before. She wasn't going to earn a butterfly that day. She slathered butter on a roll, and remembered the red-haired boy who had helped her find Melina Odella's house. If he hadn't shown up, she wouldn't have found it, and she wouldn't be in the mess she was in now.

A knock at the door startled her. Maybe Merindah had come to find her. When she yanked the door open, an old crone with sparkling emerald eyes, stood outside.

She handed Alexa a brown wooden spider. "Don't blame others for your mistakes, Alexa."

As Alexa stood gaping, the old woman disappeared. Moira. Alexa's stomach lurched. She wasn't doing a good job of staying on Fate's good side when twice she'd personally delivered an omen.

Her appetite left with Moira. Alexa tossed what was left of the roll in the trash bin. She remembered how thin Zeph had been and the gleam in his eyes when she'd given him one roll. She'd forgotten her pledge to take bread to the kids in the shack houses. None of those kids would have any coins to spend at the festival. She didn't have time to make yeast rolls, but she could bake biscuits. It wouldn't take much flour, and she was sure Mother wouldn't mind. She'd make sugar biscuits with a little bit of cinnamon. She didn't have to be an elder's wife to do that.

Fiona chased round stones across the floor as Alexa added wood to the coals in the oven and fanned them to flames. Then she measured out flour, sugar, baking soda, and salt. She cut in lard and stirred in goat's milk until the ingredients stuck together. She dumped the dough out on a floured counter and kneaded the lump for three turns before she rolled it to a one-inch thick slab. She used a metal ring to cut out circles of dough, placed them on baking sheets, and sprinkled a mix of cinnamon and sugar across the top. She couldn't stop smiling, imagining the surprise she'd bring to those kids.

As she cleaned the kitchen and waited for the fire to die down in the oven, a carved turtle token appeared on the table. In this case, patience did pay off.

Alexa baked four dozen biscuits to a light golden brown and hoped it would be enough. For the first time in a long time, she enjoyed the smell of bread. When they cooled, she layered them in a basket, pulled on a hooded tunic, and slipped out the back door, away from the festival.

The first person she found at the shacks was Zeph.

"Hey, I remember you," he said. "Did you find what you wanted with the fortune-teller?"

"Kind of." Alexa held out a biscuit. "I brought treats. Will you help me pass them out?"

He shoved half the biscuit in his mouth and mumbled, "Sure." He stopped with Alexa at the first house.

"Hey, Lorna. Want a biscuit?"

A little girl with stringy blond hair peeked out the doorway. Her face lit when Zeph handed her the treat. A younger brother stood behind her clutching her legs.

Alexa knelt. "Here's one for you too."

He tucked his head into his sister's back, but held out a hand. When Alexa laid a biscuit in it he disappeared into the dark of the house.

It didn't take long to pass out the treats. After the final shack, three remained in Alexa's basket.

"Here, Zeph. You can have the rest."

He stepped back and stared at Alexa. "Why'd you bring them?"

"I . . . I thought you'd like them. With the festival and all, I didn't think you probably got to go."

Zeph reached in the basket and took out the biscuits. "I'll share these with Lorna. They never have enough to eat." He headed to the first house and then turned to Alexa. "I forgot to say thanks."

A lump formed in Alexa's throat. She managed to croak out, "You're welcome, Zeph," before she ducked her head to hide her tears. Zeph had to be hungry too and yet he was willing to share. She had to do this again. And soon.

As Alexa walked the path home, another joined her.

"This," an old woman rasped, "is why I designed the quest. You've learned to use your talents to help others." Moira tapped the basket. "Look inside." And then she was gone.

When Alexa checked the basket, a dove and four small bread tokens nestled in a pile. The dove would vanquish the spider she earned earlier, and the bread meant she wouldn't go hungry in the quest. When she needed them, each would turn into a real loaf of bread. She smiled. That was good, but the way her heart filled with happiness was better yet.

That night, Moira's words haunted Alexa. She had a talent besides baking. She slept that night with her newest stitching beneath her pillow. When she woke, she folded the scene and placed it in her bag. Anxious to see if the cloth would affect the actions of the others as she hoped, she hurried to the church. If it worked, what else could she do with her favor?

At the church, Alexa slipped into a seat around a wooden table new to the room. Dharien sauntered towards her and then stopped. His eyebrows pulled together, and he appeared puzzled. He tried to step closer, but the fence she'd stitched appeared to be working. He gave up and sulked to a seat at the far side of the table.

Merindah entered with the peasant cousins and slid into a seat next to Alexa. She whispered,

"I missed you at the festival. I'm sorry I got mad."

For the first time, Zander didn't barge in last. He plopped into a seat next to Dharien and then seemed surprised to be sitting next to him. Paal wandered around the room before taking the final seat. Alexa couldn't hide her smile. Her stitching worked.

The priest began. "Pull out your tokens and omens. Today we'll study your possible scenarios."

Zander dumped his bag, and the rest of the class grew silent. He had the most thorns, but they wouldn't kill him in the quest. His pile of tokens dwarfed everyone else's. When Zander blushed and fiddled with his journal, Alexa wondered how he'd earned so many. She wasn't alone. Kaiya and Odo gazed at his tokens and exchanged whispers behind their hands.

Melina Odella surveyed the group. "Today, we'll practice with what you've earned. Consider your omens, and choose tokens you think can counteract them."

Alexa arranged her omens and tokens as best she could. Melina Odella had said the butterfly would banish the pig. She sniffed. She couldn't imagine how it would work. She set the turtle token next to the three hornet omens. "Father? Will the turtle eat more than one hornet?"

He walked over and pulled two of the hornets to the side. "One turtle, one hornet, Alexa. It seems you need to practice patience." He patted her head and smiled. "You have plenty of time to earn more."

He must not know about the potion. At least he wasn't mad at her. Melina Odella was still shooting darts from her eyes. Patience wasn't Alexa's best trait, but she would try to earn more turtles. She hated being stung. One dove and two scorpions. She could be kind. It shouldn't be hard to earn another dove or two. She needed to earn more butterflies. A shudder ran down her spine at the thought of fighting a pig without help. She set a goal to fast one day a week. It wouldn't be easy since she lived in a bakery. The bread tokens she set aside. Food would help her stay strong during the quest.

Dharien scowled across the table. His pile held multiple scorpions, peacocks, and hornets. She spied at least four pigs, but no butterflies. The tokens he had now wouldn't come close to fighting his omens. Maybe the quest would take care of her problem with Dharien. She gasped at her thought. She didn't want him to die. She'd figure out another way to fix the mess. She didn't want any of them to die in the quest.

Dharien noticed her stare and cocked his head at Zander's tokens. "He cheats even at this." he muttered.

Zander ignored him, but his cheeks flushed.

For the remainder of the morning, Alexa discussed potential strategies with Merindah and wrote the possibilities in her journal. Merindah had few omens and all the tokens she needed to fight them. Typical.

Her head pounded from the scenarios, and relief filled her when the noon bell rang. Alexa smiled as Zander bolted from the room and Dharien followed as if pulled by an invisible string.

Merindah touched her sleeve. "Still friends?"

Nodding, Alexa kept her embroidery hidden. Merindah wouldn't approve, and Alexa didn't want to jeopardize their shaky friendship. They discussed their tokens as they strolled through the market. Alexa spent the afternoon helping her mother in the bakery before she sought her room. She earned another turtle token by caring for a crying baby while his frazzled mother chose her bread. Alexa wasn't sure she wanted to be a mother. Babies required a lot of patience.

With the success of the stitchery, she had another idea. She selected a large ivory cloth and cut a circle. In the quiet of her mind, Alexa began to stitch, starting with the brown and gray Quinary in the middle and then beginning the green forest around the edges. This project would take awhile. She aimed to stitch a likeness of the village and add each student. She didn't know her intention yet, but she felt it would be useful. Moira told Alexa to use her talents to help others. Maybe she could control the quest so no one would die this year. She might even help Dharien.

CHAPTER SEVENTEEN

Zander

After class, Zander bolted from the church. Exhausted from the morning games of strategy, he grabbed his new bow and hiked into the forest. He didn't like everyone in class seeing his tokens and omens. He was surprised no one earned a scorpion for envy. Dharien scowled at him all through class and then followed him after dismissal as if he couldn't help himself.

Anger danced through his thoughts like flames licking at wet wood. If he wasn't careful, it could consume him, and he needed a clear head. He tried stuffing the anger deep into the hollow of his gut, but it wouldn't stay. The hornet omen that flew into his chest only made him angrier. Rubbing the heart token hidden under his tunic didn't calm him. Neither did Shadow.

During the festival, he'd learned that Dharien, as a second son, would apprentice with the Protectors. Could he train beside a boy who hated him for no other reason than Zander being a peasant?

Zander didn't know what to think of Greydon's secret. Zander respected him and would enjoy having him as a friend, but what if Greydon liked him for more? Zander's favor for seeing secrets had been helpful, but he'd be better off if he didn't know them. He still couldn't look Father in the eye, and Zander had no idea who the woman was he'd seen in the vision.

Finding no game, Zander pushed deeper into the forest.

Thoughts rolled unbidden through his head, distracting him as he trailed a deer. He felt like ants crawled over his body. Alexa had stared at him during class. Was she still blaming him because Dharien had taken the potion? What was Alexa thinking? She was pretty enough to find a boyfriend without tricking him. Now that Zander knew Paal better, he didn't think Dharien or Paal were good enough for Alexa, but she'd wanted Paal. Zander would have to fix his mistake.

His head pounded. Father was right to live away from the villagers. Zander was happier when he didn't have to spend time with the questers and their secrets. Even Melina Odella had been in a bad mood all morning. Next to her, the priest had seemed nice, and it had been one of the rare days he hadn't given Zander a thorn omen. Maybe he'd seen the pile Zander already had and realized Zander had enough.

As he shook his head to push away the thoughts, rustling leaves made Zander turn, expecting to see a deer. Instead, Dharien, Lash, and Elder Terrec glared at him from their horses.

Zander swung around. He must have wandered out of Elder Warrin's land.

The man scowled. Short in statue and pocked in the face, his thinning red hair showed his age. When he spoke, his voice rang out deep and accusing. "You know the consequences of hunting my land."

Grateful for the lack of prey, Zander lifted his arms to show no carcasses at his side. "I have no game. I'm practicing with my new bow." He whispered to Shadow, "Go home, boy and stay." The coyote obeyed immediately and disappeared into the trees.

Anger twisted Elder Terrec's face. "You hold a bow you don't deserve." He sneered. "I know full well you intend to hunt. Dharien tells me you traipse across his father's land. Elder Warrin is a fool to allow it. I am no fool."

In his eyes, Zander noted Elder Terrec delighted in cruelty. The elder's men grabbed Zander's arms and stripped him of the bow. As he struggled, one of the men clubbed him in the head. Zander fell to his knees, and his face scraped across the dirt.

Elder Terrec's deep laugh echoed across the gulch as the men yanked Zander's hands behind him and tied them with thick hemp rope. One man handed Zander's bow and arrows to the Terrec, who passed them to Lash.

"You won't need this when you've only one hand," Terrec spat.

As the men dragged Zander away, he glanced behind him. Elder Terrec and Lash gloated. Dharien's face darkened in confusion. Zander puzzled over it, even as he feared what came next.

At the jail, the men handed Zander over to the guard who tossed him into the dark cell. Zander gasped at the ragged clothes and gaunt bodies of the other men. They appeared to have been imprisoned for a long time.

As he stood between a dirt wall and the iron gate, trying to avoid the stink of unwashed bodies mixed with wet earth, Zander pressed his face against the bars. Elder Terrec would push for the full extent of the law, and the courts would not go easy on him. He could lose his hand. If he didn't bleed out, he still might not heal before the quest. And even if he did heal, could he survive the quest without it?

Oddly, in the dark cell, Zander found what he had sought in the forest. His mind became clear. If he survived with his hand, he would strive to become a Protector. He'd make peace with Dharien, if needed, to achieve his goal. No matter how long it took, he'd work his way to the top of the order. He'd practice harder and longer, and he'd cultivate Greydon's friendship. One day, Greydon would rule in Elder Warrin's place. Changes needed to be made in how the peasants were treated. As a Protector, Zander would work to make life better for the poor. Maybe Puck's ghost spoke the truth. Maybe he could unite the tribes.

What he could do for Alexa was still cloudy. He could ask Melina

Odella for help. She made potions and spells. The fortune-teller liked him. He'd work to get the priest on his side too—if he got out of jail before the quest. He could end up like the men surrounding him.

Hours later, his head pounded from thinking. When he could no longer ignore the moans of a man hunched in the corner, Zander covered his nose with his sleeve and inched towards him. He eyed the man sitting across the cell, whose vacant eyes stared at nothing. Zander knelt and lifted the sick man's head. He shared water from the flask on his belt. A tiny replica token appeared at his feet.

After he drank, the man grabbed Zander's tunic and wrenched him close to his face. The man trembled as he spoke. "Secrets surround you." Zander stared into dark eyes belying any sanity, and the man wheezed. "Beware the person you trust." Released from the compulsion to share the prophecy, the man collapsed.

Scrambling across the cell, Zander tried to still the adrenaline racing through his body. He rubbed the heart token Melina Odella gave him the first day of class until his racing blood slowed. Near dawn, he heard a yip. "Shadow!" The pup squeezed between the bars and licked at Zander's face. Zander laughed and hugged the coyote. With the comfort of his patron, Zander fell into a fitful sleep. He woke to shouting in the alley.

"Bring me the boy or you'll regret your miserable life!"

Keys rattled and the iron door clanked open. Burly arms grabbed him, pulled him down the dark alley, and shoved him into the street. Zander slumped to his knees, while closing his eyes against the assault of the sunlight. He whispered to Shadow, "Go home."

Elder Warrin barked at the jailer. "Here are the papers. Release this boy into my custody. I've paid his bail."

The jailer pulled Zander to his feet and left him standing in front of the elder.

"Sir?" Zander asked, removing his hand from his eyes, but still squinting. "How did you find me?"

"I overheard Dharien bragging about leading Terrec to you. Greydon would have come himself if I hadn't stopped him. I left him to deal with Dharien. Didn't I warn you of Elder Terrec?"

"Yes, Sir, I'm sorry you've been troubled. I will repay you, Sir."

"You're right. You will repay me by serving in my house." Elder Warrin crossed his arms over his chest and smiled.

Zander stepped back, stunned. Even a servant in an elder's house had a better life than his, but he had no plans to serve. There had to be another way to repay him.

"Don't look so alarmed, Zander." Elder Warrin chuckled. "You'll find your duties to your liking. I need someone with your shooting skill to accompany me on my hunts. I'll use your talents well."

As his shoulders relaxed, Zander unclenched fists he didn't realize were tight.

"Come, we'll talk to your father. I'm sure he'll agree to my proposal."

They trekked in silence to Zander's home. How would his crude hut appear to someone who lived in a manor?

Father stood open-mouthed as Elder Warrin explained how he had paid Zander's bail and the charges were dropped. Elder Warrin must have bribed the sheriff, for bail money did not dismiss charges. How long would it take to pay the debt? Even if his duties were pleasurable, he would still be bound as a servant.

After he agreed to Elder Warrin's offer, his father helped Zander pack his few possessions. As the elder waited outside, Father whispered, "Do what he requires. This is your chance at a better life than I could give you."

"Don't you want me to be a furrier?" Hadn't Father accused Zander of aspiring too high? Then it hit him. Father wasn't drunk.

"This is better. Maybe Elder Warrin can protect you where I can't."

"Protect me from what?"

"The quest. Maybe Moira will respect an elder's wishes better than mine. There." Father handed Zander's pack to him.

"But, Father," Zander hesitated.

"Don't question me, Zander. Do this one thing. Be valuable to him. Become a son to him."

Become a son to Elder Warrin? A brother to Greydon and Dharien? That would never work. "You need me to hunt for you. I'll still bring you pelts when I can." Zander's chest tightened. Was Father glad he was leaving?

He stroked the wooden heart as he left the only home he knew. As the calm filled him, he sensed his life shifting. He gave a sharp whistle, and Shadow crept from behind the house to slink at his side. Zander glanced sideways at Elder Warrin to see if he minded. Zander wouldn't leave his pup with Father. When the elder didn't comment, Zander let out his breath. Shadow would come.

At his estate, Elder Warrin led Zander to a room in the stable. Zander threw his clothes on the small bed with a faded blue coverlet, and Shadow disappeared underneath. A dusty window let in the afternoon light. It was small, but a room of his own, and more than he had with Father.

Zander scratched his head. "I don't understand. I'll be living in the stables?"

"Have you ridden?"

"No." He ran his tongue over his chipped tooth, remembering his only experience on a horse. When he was seven, he'd pestered a Protector into lifting him onto his horse. When a wagon of kettles spilled nearby, the horse reared, and Zander flew into a post. The man's kindness had planted Zander's dream to become one of the protectors. He didn't think it counted as riding.

"As I thought." Elder Warrin leaned against the door frame. "You'll be riding with me, and I want you trained."

Zander's heart raced. Was his dream to come true? "Will I be trained as a Protector?"

Elder Warrin burst into laughter. "No, Zander. The son of a furrier does not become a Protector. Only those born to it receive that honor. You'll be my hunter."

Heat flushed through his body, and Zander turned so the elder wouldn't see his red face. He stroked the wooden heart and regained control before facing the elder.

While nodding to a door across the hall, Elder Warrin studied Zander. "My marshal, Fulk, lives there. He manages the stable, and he'll teach you to ride. I want you to spend as much time with the horses as you can. Your meals will be brought here. You aren't afraid of the horses, are you?"

"No, Sir." Not afraid of horses, just terrified of riding one. Zander shuddered. "Am I restricted to the stables then?"

"You're not my slave, Zander. You're free to come and go as you like. It's to your advantage to stay. It'll take a while to repay me. The more time you spend helping Fulk, the faster you'll start earning your own money."

"Sir? Why would you do this for me?"

Elder Warrin grinned. "You're the best marksman I've seen in a long while. You honor my house with your talent. And Fulk can use your help in the stable."

"Thank you, Sir. I'm sorry to have caused you trouble."

Zander settled into his room. Could he overcome his fear of riding? What kind of man was Fulk? He didn't have to wonder long.

"Boy!"

He whirled to find the largest man he'd seen filling his doorway.

CHAPTER EIGHTEEN

Alexa

Alexa twisted the hem of her tunic. Zander wasn't at their lesson, and Father Chanse wasn't happy.

"Anyone seen Zander?" the priest asked as he stood behind the empty seat.

The other questers shook their heads, but Dharien stared at his hands. He'd come in with a swollen eye. Dharien didn't like Zander. Had they fought? If Zander had given Dharien a black eye, what had Dharien done to Zander? Something was wrong, she could feel it.

"He's obviously not coming," Melina Odella said. "Chanse, it won't hurt Zander to miss a little history." She lowered herself into Zander's chair. "The quest is a part of our tradition. Although we have very little contact with others, we think we're the only village whose young people are tested this way. Perhaps because of our isolation and the way we must depend on each other, Moira devised a way to ensure our youth will grow into productive and strong adults."

The priest paced behind the circle of chairs. "When the gulch was first settled, Moira appeared to the fortune-teller and the priest in a vision. She explained the quest and set out the rules. Throughout the centuries, there have been few changes. Every child who is sixteen on the first day of the New Year begins their time of magic, which culminates in the quest six months later. The earning of tokens and omens determines who will survive."

"Not always," interjected Melina Odella.

"What?" The priest frowned.

The fortune-teller stared at Alexa and then glanced at the priest. "It's been years since we've had twins in the quest. Do you forget, Chanse?"

The priest growled at the fortune-teller. "Melina Odella, there's no reason to talk of the curse of the twins."

The curse of twins? What was he talking about? There were no twins in the village.

"Chanse," Melina Odella continued, "it is merely a history lesson." She crossed her legs and leaned back in the chair. "Only once in our history have twins both survived the quest. Twins are rare, but a few of our villagers had a twin before they went through the quest. Ask the cobbler."

"Melina Odella! That's enough." The priest scowled. "George needs no reminder of his quest or the brother he lost."

"That's why George acted sad when I told him I was questing this year," Merindah said softly. "What happened? Why does one twin die?"

"While the quest is meant to be undergone alone, the bond between twins seems to draw them together during the challenge. One sacrifices their life to save the other. In the past, parents of twins have tried many ways to prevent this disaster." Melina Odella glanced at Alexa and a smug smile appeared. "It appears Moira frowns upon twins, and we all know Fate cannot be cheated."

A sudden chill made Alexa wrap her arms around her chest. "How did that one set of twins survive?"

The priest blushed. "They were elders' sons. Moira evidently found them worth saving. It's nothing to worry about this year." The priest glared at Melina Odella. "We have no twins."

He continued with the history, but Alexa had stopped listening. Melina Odella had made a point of staring at Alexa when she talked about the curse. The fortune-teller was still angry with her, so maybe she was trying to scare her, but why? Alexa wasn't a twin.

Images started playing through her mind. Mother never talking about Alexa's father. The way Mother worried excessively about Alexa surviving the quest, and how Alexa suspected Mother hid a secret. What if she was a twin?

She glanced around the table. Could one be her twin and she wouldn't know? A shiver ran through her. Paal looked like her. Maybe Mother had an affair with Elder Rowan and when she birthed twins, he'd taken the son and left the daughter with Mother. It was true Elder Rowan's wife didn't care for Mother, and always sent her servants to buy bread. What if Paal was her brother?

She had a horrible thought. What if Paal had drunk the potion? Zander may have done her a favor when he prevented it. She studied Paal. He couldn't know either. Their parents were keeping it a secret until after the quest. Alexa didn't need Dharien as a boyfriend. She was an elder's child. She would be sure to stay far away from Paal in the quest. They wouldn't fall to the curse.

After class, Alexa walked with Merindah to the market. Her mind whirled. She was a twin and Paal was her brother. Would Elder Rowan claim her as his daughter after the quest?

Merindah touched Alexa's arm. "You're quiet. Are you worried about the quest?"

It would be better if no one, not even Merindah, knew of her suspicions until after the quest. "I hate to think about anyone not surviving."

Merindah shivered. "I'm glad we don't have twins this year. How awful it would be to know one would die in the quest."

Alexa blushed. "Yeah, terrible. I've got to hurry to the bakery. I promised Mother I'd come home right after class. See you tomorrow?"

She sprinted home, and her heart wasn't thumping from the run.

CHAPTER NINETEEN

Four Months until the Quest

Zander

According to Cobie, all Zander had missed in class was a history lesson. He'd survive the quest without it. He settled into a routine at the stables and found that, even with Fulk's unpredictable moods, he enjoyed his time with the gruff man. He rose at dawn each day to clean stalls, and slowly came to enjoy the horses. He still shuddered at the idea of riding, but he'd have to learn soon.

One horse in particular became his favorite. Helios, a black stallion, and the only destrier, had yet to be ridden. When Zander first met Elder Warrin, he'd seen his secret which centered on this special horse. Elder Warrin paid more for the war horse than for the rest of the horses combined. The horse was intended for Greydon.

To Zander's surprise, Greydon worked at the stables before breakfast each morning and had been happy to hand over the mucking out to Zander. They cleaned stalls, and fed and groomed the horses together. Fulk was a little hard of hearing, and Greydon and Zander frequently joked about him when they didn't think he could hear them. It was easy for Zander to forget Greydon was a first-born.

One morning they ate breakfast perched on the wall of Helios's stall. Shadow sat alert below them, waiting for bits of dropped food.

Greydon's eyes shone when he gazed at Helios. "He's a beauty, isn't he?"

Zander nodded. "When do you think he'll be ready to ride?"

His grin faded. "Father's worried I'll be thrown. Someone else will ride him and make sure he's broken before I'm allowed." He leaned over and bumped Zander's shoulder. "Maybe you'll be the lucky one. Fulk tells Father you have a way with animals. He brags about how well you've trained Shadow."

Shadow looked up at the sound of his name, and Zander tossed him a piece of sausage. The coyote had been easy to train. Fulk had a soft spot for him. Shadow stayed with the marshal while Zander attended his lessons.

"So what do you think? We're about the same size. Want to be the first to ride Helios?"

"Um," Zander's cheeks burned, but he trusted Greydon not to ridicule him. "I've never ridden. Maybe I should start out on one of the palfreys?"

To Zander's relief, Greydon laughed. "Good idea. This weekend, let's take out the two bays. Star and Lady are as easy to ride as any of them. If you can't ride Star, you'll never ride anything."

Zander's stomach flipped. He hoped Greydon's words weren't prophetic.

After he fed Shadow, Zander bolted from the stables at the last moment to avoid walking with Dharien, who'd taken to following him to class. He slipped in at the last moment and dropped into a chair.

The priest lectured on the purpose of the guilds. Zander had no interest in the various apprenticeships. If he could gain enough tokens to impress Moira, he still believed it possible she would allow him his dream of becoming a Protector.

After hiding yawns all morning, Zander perked up when the

priest spoke of the nunnery. Merindah pulled her journal close and clutched her pencil. Blushing, she focused on the priest. Her deepest desire was to be a nun. Now, maybe he'd learn why she hid it.

"Nuns serve the church through prayer and caring for the poor. Currently, we have two aging nuns serving our village. Perhaps with this quest, Moira will assign us a new one."

The priest glanced at Merindah before he continued. "Much of the nun's time is spent in meditation, as well as chores and upkeep of the church." Father Chanse appeared pensive. "Rarely, a nun is called to be an anchoress. We've not had an anchoress at our church for more than one-hundred years. The anchoress lives and dies in a brick cell connected to the church. One small window, called the squint, opens to the sanctuary so the anchoress can attend services. An outside window allows people to seek her advice and prayers. A third window is used to bring in food and water and remove waste."

Merindah's face burned. That was her secret? She wanted to be an anchoress? He'd been locked in a cell for three days and thought he'd go mad. How could Merindah desire that?

When the noon bell rang, Zander darted for the door hoping to avoid Dharien, but the priest blocked him. He seldom met Zander's gaze, appearing as troubled as Zander when their eyes met.

Thrusting out his hand to receive whatever omen the priest deemed necessary for his sins of the day, Zander stared at the floor.

Instead of dropping a thorn in Zander's hand, the priest asked, "Did you receive an omen for hunting Elder Terrec's lands?"

Zander gasped in surprise that the priest was aware of his offense. He averted his eyes. "No."

"And in jail? Did you receive omens?"

"No, only a dove and water token for helping a man who was ill." What did the priest want?

Father Chanse tapped his fingertips together in front of his chest. "I don't understand you, Zander. You've never attended church, you're always late, and yet you amass more tokens than anyone I've known. And outside of the ones I've given you, you have few omens. Has Moira given you a favor that affects this?"

"No, Sir. I have no favor like you ask."

"But you do have an early favor?"

Blushing, Zander dipped his head.

The priest scratched his cheek. "What is it?"

Melina Odella interrupted, "Chanse, his favor is his alone and needs no telling."

Anger colored the priest's cheeks. "Why do you undermine me at every opportunity, Melina Odella?"

"Only when you overstep your boundaries." She motioned for Zander to leave, and as he crossed the doorstep the priest's voice rose.

"Who are you to decide my boundaries? A fortune-teller? I serve a higher purpose than concocting spells and potions, Melina Odella!"

He didn't wait to hear more. As he sprinted out the door, Zander noticed Dharien leaning on the other side of the door, listening in the shadows.

CHAPTER TWENTY

Zander

Zander had never heard Melina Odella and Father Chanse argue, and it appeared they fought now because the fortune-teller didn't want the priest to know about Zander's favor. He worried over it all the way to Elder Warrin's estate. When he reached the hedge separating the elder's land from the village, Shadow raced toward him and ran in circles until Zander dropped to his knees. He pressed his face into Shadow's neck.

"I missed you too, boy." Zander grabbed a stick and tossed it high in the air. Shadow ran and leaped to catch it. They played the rest of the way to the stables. When they both arrived breathless at the gate to the corral, Greydon was saddling Lady.

He grinned at Zander. "Fulk's waiting for you."

Zander's stomach flip-flopped as he entered the hall and threw his pack on his bed. He made his way to the stalls where he found Fulk with a grin matching Greydon's.

"Saddle Star. It's time you learned to ride."

Zander's heart almost stopped. "N-now?"

While leading his own horse, Tipper, out the door, Fulk said, "Now, as in today, as in get her saddled and outside."

With trembling hands, Zander blanketed the brown mare before centering the saddle and tightening the cinch. He checked the girth, as Fulk had taught him, fitting two fingers between the strap and the horse. He flipped the reins over Star's head to rest on the horn. Rolling his shoulders, Zander patted the mare. She skittered sideways, reacting to his nerves, but Zander led her outside.

Fulk chuckled atop his bay, "You're not scared, are you?"

With Fulk and Greydon watching, Zander faced the saddle, took a deep breath, and placed his left foot in the stirrup. He grabbed the horn, jerked himself up, and swung his right leg over Star's rump. Adrenaline rushed from his chest. He made it.

Star trotted behind Lady and Tipper out the gate. Once in the meadow, she settled into the ambling gait palfreys excelled at. Zander's heart nearly burst. He clenched his legs around her middle until his muscles burned. Maybe he could do this.

Fulk pulled Tipper next to Star, and demonstrated using his knees to control his horse. "You need trust between the horse and the rider, boy. The horse needs to understand you're in control even when the reins aren't tight. Get her steady."

Zander practiced until Star responded to the pressure of his legs. When he had the bay quiet, his heart finally stopped trying to jump out of his chest.

"Now Greydon's going to show you how to shoot from the saddle," Fulk said.

Greydon wrapped the reins loosely around the pommel. Zander had a death grip on his, but he loosened his fingers and tried to look relaxed. He had to ride to earn Elder Warrin's respect and pay off his debt. Greydon aimed at a nearby ash tree. At the thunk of the arrow hitting the bark, Star's head jerked up. Zander grabbed for the reins and pulled them to the left. Star turned and Zander pulled tighter until they spun in a circle.

Fulk laughed, distracting Zander even more, and he pulled hard on the reins which caused Star to rear. Zander's throat closed as he flailed forward, desperate to stay in the saddle. Star kicked her heels, and Zander flew to the ground. His breath slammed from his chest.

He skidded across the rough ground, slicing his cheek on a rock. When he glanced up, he caught Star's backside as she disappeared into the woods. Fulk leaned over Tipper, chortling good-naturedly.

Greydon raced after Star, and Zander soon glimpsed him returning with Star walking docilely beside Lady.

Still on the ground, Zander held his head. He had a killer headache and his cheek throbbed.

Fulk reached out and pulled Zander to his feet. "You better hope Star's not hurt, or you'll be working the rest of your life to pay for her." Fulk wiped the sweat off his forehead. "But I swear, that was the funniest thing I've seen in a long time."

"It wasn't my fault! And look at my face," Zander protested as he rubbed blood from his cheek. "She startled and threw me before I could control her."

"Bah! If you're riding her, she's your responsibility."

There was no sense arguing. Fulk was right. Zander flushed as Greydon handed over the reins for Star. No way was he getting back in the saddle, no matter how hard Fulk and Greydon tried to convince him. Finally, they gave up and trotted away.

After Zander limped into the stable with Star ambling behind, he rubbed down the bay and checked her for injuries. Fulk and Greydon were gone and that was fine with Zander. He didn't need Fulk's teasing or Greydon's glances of sympathy. Shadow skulked under Zander's bed, peering out as Zander went about his chores.

He dumped a scoop of oats in Star's trough, and when she ate, relief spread through Zander. He relaxed muscles he didn't realize he'd been tensing. She would be all right. He pressed his forehead against the mare's neck and calmed to the crunch of her teeth as she ground the grain. Why couldn't he overcome his fear of riding? Greydon was right. If Zander couldn't ride Star, he couldn't ride.

He mucked the stalls, and the stench of manure burned his throat as shame burned his gut. One fact wound through his mind, repeating until Zander thought he'd never think anything else. If he couldn't ride, Moira would never allow him to be a Protector.

After he finished his chores, Zander grabbed his bow. "Come on Shadow. Let's hunt."

He opened the door. Odo and Kaiya were walking up the path to the stable. Odo had a bow slung over his shoulder. His yellow kitten, Boo, trailed behind. Kaiya carried six arrows with tattered fletches. Her crow, Korble, soared high above in lazy circles, riding the thermals.

"Hoy!" Odo hollered at Zander.

Zander jogged out to meet them.

Boo arched his back and hissed when Shadow bounded up to sniff him. Zander held his hand between the two patrons. "Friends."

Shadow sat and the kitten's tail curled over his back. Boo rubbed his nose against the coyote's neck. Shadow licked Boo from his head to his tail as the cat purred.

Zander grinned. "Good boy." He turned to the cousins. "What are you doing here?"

Kaiya stared at the ground. "We know you've been hunting for us." She knelt to pet Shadow and glanced up. "Thank you."

Zander reached for the heart token under his tunic to calm him. He didn't know they'd figured out he was the one leaving food. "You don't need to be hungry."

Odo's eyes danced. "Will you teach us to hunt, so we can find our own meat?"

Zander arched his left eyebrow. "We?"

A smile lit Kaiya's face. "Both of us."

"Let me see the bow," Zander said. After Odo handed it over, Zander stood it on end next to Kaiya. "This one's too long for you." He handed it back to Odo. "Wait here." He disappeared into the stable and returned with a shorter bow. "I've outgrown this one. You can have it."

Kaiya placed it over her shoulder and accepted the quiver of arrows Zander held out. He handed a second quiver to Odo. "We'll use yours for practice, but you need better arrows to hunt."

Zander led them to Elder Warrin's practice field and demonstrated how to hold the bow, nock the arrow, and draw the string. He shot a bull's-eye. "See?" He grinned and rubbed his tongue over his chipped tooth. "Easy."

Odo elbowed Zander. "Easy for you. How long have you been shooting?"

"Since I was five." He'd practiced for hours before he got it right. Maybe that meant there was still hope he could learn to ride.

The cousins spent the next hour shooting arrow after arrow before either came close to hitting the target. The tension from earlier disappeared in the laughter Zander shared with Odo and Kaiya. Even Shadow perked up from Zander's better mood and enjoyed the extra attention from their guests.

Zander moved between Odo and Kaiya as he corrected Odo's stance and touched Kaiya's shoulder to remind her to keep it relaxed. Once, he stood behind Kaiya and wrapped his arms around her to correct her aim. Lavender drifted from her hair, and Zander found himself distracted as he breathed in her scent. With that shot, she hit the target for the first time. She turned to Zander with a huge grin and gave him a hug.

He blinked in surprise. "Uh, good job, Kaiya. You're shooting better than Odo." He blushed. It was a dumb thing to say to a girl who hugged you.

But Kaiya didn't notice as she danced over to Odo and said, "Told you I'd hit the target first."

Odo shrugged and kept shooting until he tagged the corner. Soon, they were both hitting the target more often than not, although Kaiya outshot Odo and teased him mercilessly. It was the most fun Zander had had in a long time.

When it was obvious by the sloppy shots the cousins were tiring, Zander called a stop to the practice. "Keep working on it, and I'll take you hunting soon," he promised.

They relaxed together in the grass. Zander threw sticks for Shadow. Boo chased white butterflies while Odo reclined on his elbows. Kaiya fed Korble dried apples. None felt inclined to talk, and Zander felt more comfortable with the cousins than he did with anyone.

The sun had moved several hands to the west by the time Odo stood and scooped Boo into his arms. "Time to go."

"You're a great teacher." Kaiya said. "Thanks for the bow."

Her smile made Zander forget all about being thrown by Star.

CHAPTER TWENTY-ONE

Alexa

It was Mother's birthday, but it was a market day. They'd celebrate that evening. As Alexa sold bread, she studied her mother and wished she could see her secrets. Then she'd know if Paal was her brother. She wanted proof, but she didn't dare ask. She chewed on a fingernail.

After the market cleared, Alexa rushed to her bedroom and unfolded her embroidery cloth. She'd stitched the forest in vibrant greens on the edges of the round cloth. Sparrows, hawks, and owls flew across the trees. Gray doves nestled on the roof of the Quinary. In her mind, she mapped out the important landmarks. She would add the bakery and the church. She debated the importance of stitching the other questers' homes and chose to include them. She knew where they all lived except Zander, who resided somewhere outside the village.

Merindah would help Alexa if she didn't suspect her motive, and Alexa was determined to keep her embroidery a secret. She thought of a plausible plan as she trudged the short walk to Merindah's home.

"Mother's birthday is today. I'm going to Zander's father to see if he'll trade a small fur for bread. Will you go with me?" She held up a sack of almond bread.

They asked directions and found themselves on the far side of the village in front of a hut made of mud and straw tucked into the forest. Alexa glanced at Merindah. It appeared deserted except for the hides hanging around the side and the stink of lye from the tanning pit in back.

"Maybe we should leave." Merindah pulled at Alexa's arm.

Alexa started to agree. Maybe this wasn't her best idea. Before she could reply, a man stepped around the corner of the house. He glared at them and then dropped the wire brush he held. He took his time before he stooped to pick it up.

"Excuse me, Sir? We're questers with Zander, and I want to trade for a pelt for my mother's birthday."

The man grunted his reply. "What kind are you after?"

Alexa swallowed. "What will you trade for this bread?"

She held out the sack, and he reached for it with shaking hands. Glancing inside, he muttered. "I have a red fox. Zander hunted it himself."

She expected a rabbit pelt or a small ermine, not something as nice as a fox. "Mother would love a fox. Thank you."

Zander's father turned and strode to a thatched hut behind the house. He returned with the pelt. "For your mother." His eyes met Alexa's.

Merindah gasped and then clapped her hand over her mouth.

"Th-thank you, Sir. It's perfect." Alexa folded the pelt into her bag.

Once Alexa and Merindah left the wooded path, they sprinted the rest of the way to the bakery, paying no attention to the late afternoon shoppers they dodged as they entered the market.

Safely in Alexa's room, they collapsed on the bed, giggling at their fright. "Did you see how rough he was?" Alexa remarked. "No wonder Zander is backward."

Merindah added, "And the way he fumbled with the sack of bread? How does he make any profit trading a fox for so little?"

"I think we made him nervous. Maybe he's not used to dealing with girls." Alexa rolled to her side to peer at Merindah. "Why did you gasp when he handed me the pelt?"

Suddenly serious, Merindah hesitated. "Did you see his eyes?"

A sudden knot in her throat silenced Alexa. She nodded.

Merindah whispered, "Your eyes are like his."

After her friend left, Merindah's words tumbled round and round in Alexa's head. "*Your eyes are like his.*" She pushed her confusion deep into her gut, telling herself the words meant nothing. Lots of people in the village had dark eyes.

She wrapped the fur in a deep purple cloth she'd traded for a piece of embroidery. Mother would be pleased with the gift. Alexa carried it downstairs and laid it on the serving table in the dining room. Her mood lightened when she spied her mother's oldest friend. "Eva!"

The midwife pulled Alexa in for a long hug. "It seems like yesterday I helped your mother birth you, and now you're a beautiful young lady."

Alexa grinned. "Mother says you're busy since Beatrice has gotten too old to midwife." A chill ran through her. Eva would know if Paal was her twin.

Eva laughed. "This is true. I'm busy with babies. That and gathering herbs in the forest leave me little time for social visits." Eva plucked Fiona from Alexa's pocket. "Look at this cutie. If I'd known you had a ferret patron, I would have brought Pixie. Nothing's cuter than two ferrets playing."

Alexa stilled. Would she be a healer like Eva? The village needed more than one. Taking Eva's arm, Alexa led her to the dining table they seldom used. During their meal of roasted duck and potatoes, Alexa chatted about her studies and the quest.

She abruptly turned to Eva. "We learned about the curse of twins in the quest. Have you delivered many twins?"

Her mother gasped.

Eva startled and then exhaled before answering. "I've birthed two sets. Why do you ask?"

"Was the cobbler one of them? Melina Odella said his twin sacrificed his life for George."

"Yes, that's true." Eva pursed her lips and glanced at Alexa's mother. "I don't believe it's a curse to be a twin in the quest. Elder Rowan is a twin, and they both survived."

Paal's father was a twin. It had to be true then. He was her father. "Where's his twin now? I've never seen him."

"Their father's estate was too small for two sons. He left to find a wife in a village near the sea."

Alexa bit her lip. Dare she ask? With her blood racing, she took a deep breath. "Who are the other twins?"

A mug of cider hit the floor.

Alexa jumped from her chair and rushed to her mother. As Alexa wiped at the mess, Mother trembled. "What's wrong?" Alexa asked, although she knew the answer. Mother didn't want Alexa to know she was a twin.

Rubbing her eyes with the back of her hand, her mother hesitated. "It's this talk of the quest. You know I'm nervous with you going into the gulch alone."

Alexa tried not to shudder. She hated the gulch and the rumors of Puck haunting it. "I'll be fine, Mother. I have more tokens than omens, and the priest and fortune-teller are preparing us well." She disliked seeing Mother upset. She wouldn't ask any more questions.

"I know, Alexa." She twisted her napkin. "You'll return to me."

Eva cleared the table and returned with a small cake. Trying to lighten the mood, she teased, "So Alexa, are there any cute boys in your class?"

Blushing, Alexa glanced at her mother who stared back with interest. "Well, there is one boy. His name is Dharien, but he's an elder's son."

"Ah, you can dream, can't you?" Eva grinned as she handed Alexa a slice of walnut carrot cake.

Alexa wasn't sure she wanted that dream anymore. "Eva? Are you sad you didn't marry and have a family?"

Laughing, Eva spread her arms. "With the babies I deliver, I have plenty of family. And leaving in the middle of the night to care for the ill wouldn't leave me time to care for my own. I have Pixie for company."

"But wouldn't you like a husband to take care of you?"

Searching Alexa's face, Eva shook her head. "A strong woman can take care of herself." She nodded toward Alexa's mother. "Your mother's done all right by herself."

Alexa twisted her mouth. She'd never thought of her mother as strong, but Mother had no other choice but to be tough. She managed the bakery without a husband's help, rising before dawn to bake. She provided well for Alexa. A pang of guilt coursed through her for wanting to leave.

As she ate cake, Alexa contemplated Eva's assertion she didn't need a husband. She almost forgot the fox pelt. "Mother, I have a present for you."

Her mother's eyes lit at the beautiful purple cloth, and she fingered its rich softness. Her eyes held a question her mouth did not speak.

"Open it!" She couldn't wait to see Mother's face when she unwrapped the pelt.

When Mother untied the cord and glimpsed the fox pelt, she clutched the table. She closed her eyes and took several deep breaths as if to calm herself before she stared expressionless at Alexa.

It wasn't the reaction Alexa expected. Even more perplexing was Eva's smile.

With a ragged voice, her mother whispered, "Where did you buy this?"

"Zander is in my class. His father is a furrier. I traded bread for it."

Peering intently at Alexa, her mother asked, "You traded with Zander or his father?"

"With his father."

"You are never to go to him again. Promise me, Alexa!"

Not trusting her voice, Alexa nodded. Never had Mother forbidden her to see anyone in the village. What was it about the furrier that frightened her so? He'd seemed rough mannered, but not dangerous.

Mother calmed at Alexa's agreement. "Thank you for the gift. Eva and I will clear the dishes. It's late. Go on to bed."

Alexa hugged Eva and went up the stairs to her room. As Alexa pulled her door shut she heard Eva.

"Lark, you need to tell her. It's not a curse to be a twin. Explain how she needs to complete the quest alone. She's a good girl. She'll be fine."

She sagged against the door frame. It was true. Paal was her twin. Alexa stepped quietly into the hall and hoped they couldn't hear her heart thudding. She had to catch Mother's reply.

"Theron wants to tell them, but I can't take a chance, Eva. I can't. The village has kept the secret for sixteen years. Why would Melina Odella talk about it in class?"

Who was Theron?

"Who knows why the fortune-teller does what she does."

"You don't know how hard it's been, Eva. Every time I look at her and see Theron's eyes staring back at me, I want to tell her everything."

Merindah's words slammed into Alexa's gut. *Your eyes are like his.*

Alexa choked back sobs. Was the furrier her father? If he was, Paal wasn't her twin.

Zander was.

CHAPTER TWENTY-TWO

Zander

After the cousins left, Zander was anxious to get away from the stable. He skipped dinner to hunt for his father. With Shadow as his retriever, Zander caught four rabbits, an ermine, and a prized fox. When he approached the hut, Zander found Father still working at the pit, tanning a deer hide. Zander hadn't caught one lately, so it must be from an elder's hunt. The harsh stink of lye drifted over. His nose burned and he coughed.

Father looked up and Zander's insides lurched. He'd hoped Father would be happy to see him, but the frown crossing Father's face made Zander nervous. He dropped his catch on the work table, and together, they skinned the animals, falling into the quiet pattern they had shared for years.

Breaking the silence, Father glanced at Shadow. "How's the training?"

A grin lit Zander's face. "Shadow's smart. He knows my commands, and he's learning hand signals."

"He's about big enough for a pelt."

Anger blocked Zander's throat until he spotted the grin his father tried to hide. As quickly as it rose, the anger disappeared. He joked back, "He'd make a fine pair of gloves."

Father snorted. "Barely." He threw his arm around Zander's shoulder. "You'll stay for dinner?"

Zander nodded and ducked, blushing. He couldn't remember the last time his father had come close to hugging him. Maybe being apart had been good for both of them, and Father hadn't been upset to see him. Of course, it helped that Father was sober.

They relaxed in comfortable silence at the table and made a meal of roasted rabbit and stewed parsnips. Zander was surprised when Father snuck a piece of meat to Shadow, who lurked under the table.

Shifting in his chair, Father asked, "That elder treating you right?"

"Yes."

"Not working you too hard?"

"No."

"What happened to your face?"

"I'm learning to ride." Zander glanced at his father and shrugged. "I fell off." Reliving the embarrassment made his heart thump.

"Why? When will you need to ride?"

Zander started to speak and then shook his head, unable to explain his dream. Father wouldn't understand, and Zander didn't want to hear why it would never happen. What did his father know of dreams? He pelted. No one dreamed of pelting.

Instead, he said, "Elder Warrin's all right, and his son, Greydon, works in the stables with me. But the other son, Dharien, takes every opportunity to annoy me."

Father snorted. "Zander, you might as well understand. Elders and Protectors are men, and men can have good hearts or bad hearts. Having wealth or position doesn't give you honor."

Zander nodded, and they finished their meal in silence. When Zander stood to leave, his father reached for his shoulder. Searching Zander's eyes, he said, "Sit a minute, Son. I appreciate the pelts today, but it's not your responsibility to take care of me. Your life is with Elder Warrin now. Spend your time pleasing him and be a good servant. Pay off your debt and hope Moira will assign a good apprenticeship for you."

"But Father, I don't mind hunting for you."

"No, Zander. You don't understand. It's better for you at the stables. He doesn't know anything about you. You'll be safer when you quest."

"What are you talking about?"

"Trust me. We'll talk after the quest, but until then, stay with Elder Warrin. I don't want you hunting for me."

Shocked, Zander nodded and said, "All right, Father, if that's what you want." He stood. "Come on, Shadow."

When he and the pup reached the comfort of the woods, Zander slumped against a tree, and the hard bark pressed into his shoulders. Father was talking crazy, and he hadn't been drinking. Zander hadn't always been happy at home, but Father was his only family. Tonight he'd made it clear he didn't want Zander.

As the calm from the tree seeped into Zander, his distress resolved into determination, and his mind cleared. In Father's eyes, Zander had once again seen the secret woman. If Zander knew the truth of who she was, he might understand Father's decision.

Before Zander could leave, Father stepped outside and headed to the back of the house. Zander followed in the dark. Father packed the rabbit meat in his bag and threw it over his shoulder. Then he disappeared down the path the led to the village.

Zander followed. He'd find out where Father took the meat and maybe find out about the woman he hid in his thoughts. He stalked Father to the market and the back of the bakery where Alexa lived. After Father knocked, a woman opened the door, and Father handed her the bag. She threw her arms around him.

This was the woman Zander had seen in the vision. As he crept closer, she said, "Theron, we'll be together soon."

"I hope so, Lark," Father replied, his voice muffled.

The woman pulled away and wiped at her eyes. "Can you come in?"

The door closed and shut Zander out, alone in the dark. His father loved Alexa's mother? He stumbled backwards into a cart and shoved it. Copper pans crashed against the brick wall. He shot away, but his anger propelled him straight into the path of the Protectors.

"Hoy, we have a thief!"

A club smashed into his stomach and Zander collapsed to the street. Two men grabbed his arms and jerked him to his feet. Zander swung blindly and connected with the side of a head, but six against one were not good odds. Thrown face-first against the wall, Zander struggled until his wrists were tied behind him. He hung limp as two men dragged him down the alley. They shoved him into the same dark cell he'd been in not many days before.

"What do I do with the coyote?" the jailer asked.

"Put him in with the boy,"

Sliding down the dirt wall, Zander gathered Shadow onto his lap and cried for the first time since he was five.

CHAPTER TWENTY-THREE

Alexa

When Zander wasn't in class, Alexa nearly wept with frustration. Where was he? She needed to talk to him, although the idea of confronting him about his father made her stomach knot up. Could Zander be her twin?

She paid no attention as the priest's voice rose and fell in boring crescendos, warning of omens. Her mother's words jumbled over and over. Alexa had her father's eyes. Merindah had been right. She had the eyes of Zander's father.

Mother said the village was keeping their secret. Alexa spent a sleepless night puzzled until Melina Odella's words came to her. Twins didn't both survive the quest because one almost always sacrificed their life for the other. Mother and Father had separated her and Zander so they wouldn't know they had a twin during the quest. And the whole village was in on it. They all wanted her and Zander to survive. Alexa thought she'd cried out all her tears, but her eyes grew blurry and she pressed her palms into them. She needed to talk to Zander, but would it be better if he didn't know?

Next to her, Merindah whispered, "What's wrong?"

Alexa shook her head and mouthed, "I'll tell you later."

Dharien cocked his head at her, and Alexa had an idea. He might know where Zander was. After all, Zander lived at Dharien's estate. She'd been avoiding him, but now she needed Dharien's help. He'd know if Zander was sick or injured. Or maybe he'd been sent home. Alexa's mind churned her fears over and over. She hardly noticed when the priest dropped a thorn omen on the table in front of her when class dismissed. She snatched it and chased after Dharien before Merindah had stuffed her journal in her bag.

She stumbled out the church door and glimpsed Dharien as he mingled with the villagers on the path to the market. "Dharien!" she yelled as she sprinted to catch him.

He turned to glare. "You're talking to me now?"

She took a minute to catch her breath. "Where's Zander?"

He snapped, "Why would I know?"

"He lives with you."

Dharien snorted. "He lives in the stables because of the idiocy of my father."

Alexa hated what she would have to do next. She fluttered her lashes and reached for him. He stood rooted, but allowed her to take his hand.

"You're kind to look after him." Alexa pulled him closer and whispered. "I'm worried. Could you find him?" She hoped he didn't feel her hand shaking. She was taking advantage of him, but Dharien was her best chance to find Zander.

He blinked without speaking.

"Please?" Alexa searched his eyes. He appeared shocked, but when his eyes softened, she knew he'd decided to help.

"Uh, I guess I could try."

"Thank you, Dharien." Alexa leaned in and kissed his cheek. He blushed bright red. "I trust you to find him."

After Dharien bolted, Alexa turned to find Merindah standing behind her with crossed arms.

"What was that?" Merindah asked.

"I'm worried about Zander. I asked Dharien to find him."

"When did you start worrying over Zander?"

Alexa stared at Merindah and tipped her chin up. "When I found out he might be my brother." Her voice dropped to a whisper. "You have to keep this a secret. I think Zander and I are twins."

Merindah gave Alexa a satisfying gasp.

CHAPTER TWENTY-FOUR

Zander

In the dark cell, Zander slumped with his back to the earth wall. A dank smell wound up from the ground, and he sneezed. He didn't expect a rescue. Elder Warrin wouldn't use his influence again. And if he did, Zander would never be able to work off the additional debt.

He dozed and woke to the revelation that he was on his own. His father had dismissed him, probably glad to be rid of him, so he could be with Alexa's mother. Was Alexa his half-sister? Nothing made sense. Too many questions rattled through his head, and he had no answers. Well, he had one. He knew where the bread had come from. The coins Zander believed went for fancy bread probably had bought more mead. Or maybe Father had given them to Alexa's mother. It was one more unanswered question that no longer mattered.

The noon bells rang, reminding Zander he'd missed another morning of class. And breakfast, but he wasn't hungry enough to eat the slop the guard brought for the noon meal. He poured a little in each of the men's bowls he shared the cell with. He slept again, curled around Shadow, dreaming of carrot cake and warm oat bread.

The iron door clanked open, waking him. The jailer called out, "Zander, son of Theron, come forward. Your charges are cleared." The man grabbed Zander's shoulder and guided him through the dark passageway. When they emerged at the end, the late afternoon sun created deep shadows in the street.

Unable to believe who stood in front of him, Zander rubbed at his eyes and sputtered, "Dharien?"

Dharien spat at Zander's feet, but motioned for him to follow. As they traipsed through the village, Dharien broke the silence. "I still hate you."

Zander's head jerked up. "Then why did you come?"

"Alexa asked me to find you."

"I thought she hated me too." Zander grimaced. Why would she send Dharien to rescue him? Did she pity him?

Dharien shrugged. "I thought she hated both of us." He blushed deep red. "But then she kissed me."

Alexa had kissed Dharien? Zander suddenly felt protective. He shook his head. "Well, thanks for getting me out."

"I did it for Alexa." He glared at Zander and added, "You know she'd choose me."

"What?"

"Alexa. If I asked her, she'd pick me over you."

Zander started. "What makes you think I want her as a girlfriend?"

"You're always watching her. You lie if you say you don't."

That was true. He did watch her. "Having money doesn't mean she wants you. Alexa's better than that."

"I could give her a better life than you could." Dharien kicked at a rock. "When I'm a Protector, you'll still be living in Father's stable paying off your debt to him."

"What will it take to repay you?" Even as he asked, Zander feared the answer.

"Stay away from Alexa."

Zander nodded, but somehow he didn't think it would be

possible. He glanced at Dharien puzzled. "What's your patron? I never see you with it."

Dharien's face darkened. He reached into his pocket. "If you make fun of him, I'll kill you." He opened his hand.

It was all Zander could do not to laugh. Dharien's patron was a mouse. A black mouse with a cute white face. He sputtered, "Nice, Dharien. A very handy patron."

"Mice are smarter than you think." He scrunched his eyebrows. "I've taught him to sit up and beg."

After he hid the mouse in his pocket, Dharien sped up. The boys matched each other stride for stride as they trekked to the estate. They parted at the path to the stable. Zander slipped in the back door and reached for the door of his room. Fulk's heavy footsteps stomped in the hall.

"Not so fast." Fulk eyed Zander up and down and muttered, "You look like death." He hesitated and his forehead wrinkled. "You can skip your chores tonight. Get cleaned up and ready for dinner."

Grateful for Fulk's tact, Zander ducked into his room. After a quick wash, he downed a plate of roasted venison and apple cobbler. Then he fell into bed where he tossed through the night. Visions of Alexa flitted through his dreams. In the haze between sleep and wakefulness, Zander recalled a memory long buried. He was young and he chased a girl his size. As he caught her, they tumbled together laughing. The warm yeasty smell of bread wafted through his memory as it often did in his dreams. When the girl gazed at him it was through the dark eyes of Alexa. The same eyes his father had.

Zander's heart raced, and he stroked the wooden heart token to calm himself. It didn't work. Bless the fates. Alexa wasn't his half-sister. She was his twin.

CHAPTER TWENTY-FIVE

Three Months until the Quest

Alexa

The next day, Zander walked into class with a nasty bruise on his cheek. Alexa hoped she could gather the courage to talk to him after they dismissed. The more often she snuck glances at Zander, the more Dharien scowled. Zander looked up once and caught her eyes before he blushed and appeared to find his hands more interesting.

She needed to know the truth. If they were twins, they needed a plan. The embroidery she stitched of the village hung at the fringes of her thoughts, unclear in meaning, but heavy with promise.

She caught Melina Odella's stare, obviously still angry, but why did the priest glance at Alexa and then drop his eyes?

When Melina Odella told them to dump their bags, Alexa complied without thinking. She automatically matched tokens with omens. She'd done this a dozen times. The priest and fortune-teller strolled around the room commenting here and there to help a quester who appeared puzzled over which token to use. They encouraged good deeds to gain the tokens needed, but warned only actions done with a pure heart would earn them. The same words they always said.

As usual, Zander's tokens outnumbered everyone else's. He

blushed as the others teased him about his pile. Dharien scowled and tapped his fingers on the table, as if deep in thought.

Near the end of class the priest announced, "I need the day and month of your birth. It determines where you enter the forest for the quest."

The fortune-teller wrote as the questers called out their dates. Merindah, "First of February."

Paal, "Twenty-eighth of April."

Alexa blushed. If she'd thought to ask Paal his birth date, she would have known they weren't twins.

Dharien smirked. "The village celebrates my birthday. It's the first of May, the same as the May Day Festival."

Mulling over what she wanted to say to Zander, Alexa stopped listening. At her turn, she called out, "Eleventh of November."

Alexa glanced up at the silence as the class waited for Zander to respond.

He hesitated and then blurted out, "Twelfth of November."

She blinked confused. Did they not share a birthday? Was she wrong to think they were twins?

The noon bells rang, and Zander dashed for the door before Alexa could stop him. When she stepped from the church, he'd disappeared into the market-goers.

"Have you talked to him?" Merindah asked at her side.

"No, and it seems I won't find him today." Alexa kicked at a rock and sent it scudding against the side of the church.

After she parted from Merindah, Alexa meandered toward the market lost in thought. As she passed an empty booth, Zander reached out and pulled her into the stall his father used on Saturdays. With the cloth overhang pulled over the opening, they were hidden from the crowd.

"We have to talk." Zander's eyes searched Alexa's. Dizziness washed over her, and Alexa grabbed at the side of the stall.

"I think my father . . ." Zander started.

". . . is also my father." Alexa finished.

Zander collapsed against the wall of the booth. "My birthday isn't November 12, it's November 11."

"I remember you!" Alexa had a vision of Zander chasing her through the house, their father laughing, with Mother on his lap. Her knees buckled. "We're twins. Dear fate, by the graces, we *are* twins!" She felt the energy tying her to Zander. Memories flooded through her and filled her with joy.

They sat cross-legged on the dirt floor, as if the village surrounding them didn't exist. The voices outside disappeared, and the darkened booth seemed their world.

Alexa glanced up at her brother and stared back at the floor. "I . . ." she started and then couldn't find the words to continue.

Seemingly equally tongue-tied, Zander twisted his hands. After a few moments, he said, "Tell me about our mother. I don't remember her."

Alexa hesitated. "She's the best baker in our village."

"No, I mean what's she like? Does she kiss you goodnight? Does she talk with you at meals?"

Blinking back tears, Alexa confessed, "She works hard, and she's tired at night. She doesn't have much time. What about Father?"

Zander shrugged. "The same, I guess. He works hard, and he drinks too much. He hardly ever talks to me. I thought it would be different if I had a mother."

She reached for his hand. "We have each other now. It'll be enough." She searched his eyes. "We can't tell our parents we know. We need to keep the secret until after the quest."

"But why did they separate us? Why the secret?"

Zander had missed the class when Melina Odella explained the curse. After Alexa repeated it, she said, "We'll be fine if we complete the quest alone." But even as she said it, she wondered—wouldn't their chances be better if they worked together?

"We have three months until the quest." Zander appeared unsure. "Can we keep the secret until then?"

"We have to fool the whole village. Everyone has kept the secret, hoping we beat the curse."

"We can do it." Zander reached over and gave Alexa a quick hug. "I have to hurry to the stables, or Fulk will yell at me for being late."

She nodded. "I need to help Mother at the bakery."

He hesitated. "I'm glad we found each other before the quest, in case . . . well, you know, in case one of us doesn't return."

When Zander uttered those words, Alexa's heart split open. She'd do anything to make sure they both survived.

CHAPTER TWENTY-SIX

Two Months until the Quest

Zander

Partly sunny, partly cloudy skies greeted the villagers as they rushed to the Quinary for the beginning of the May Day Festival. Traveling bands of Raskan performers had been arriving for a week, and their joyful singing teased at the hint of summer for the villagers weary of the drab mud of spring. The Raskans were the one tribe not represented in their village. Zander often wondered what it would be like to not have a permanent home. He couldn't imagine a life spent traveling from one remote village to another.

Jugglers, dancers, and storytellers came like the spring birds and drew visitors from other far-off villages. Puck's Gulch population doubled for three days.

Painted wagons had settled around the market, seeming out of place next to the daily stalls. Their fine metalwork and sturdy horses attracted buyers with plenty of coins. Colorful tents sprang up on the outskirts while children, who had been confined in small wagons for the long journey, squealed their joy and danced in the sun. Temporary stables housed weary horses and donkeys.

In past years, the May Day festival had been Zander's favorite celebration, but that morning filled him with dread. Although lessons were cancelled for three days, the relief didn't counteract the anger threatening his happiness at finding Alexa. If he wasn't careful, it would spill over and ruin the calm he cultivated, the facade he wore for others.

Spending time with his twin had opened something in his heart he didn't know how to contain. He'd spent his life shutting off his emotions. They hurt. When his drunken father had collapsed into bed before dinner, Zander had learned to take care of himself. Anger didn't cook for him. It wasn't his way to let himself feel. Not anger, not hurt, and not love. Alexa had cracked open his heart, but as it opened, the anger he had stuffed deep snuck out and wound its way from his gut to his heart. He was having trouble holding onto this new feeling of love, as old feelings of anger threatened to overcome it.

Living at Elder Warrin's estate hadn't made his life easier as he'd hoped. As if to make up for getting him out of jail, Dharien had turned crueler. He mocked him during lessons, and it seemed with the priest's blessing. When Zander retired at night, he frequently found his room in shambles or muck in his bed. He kept his tokens tied in a bag hidden under his tunic even as he slept. He knew Fulk had suspicions, but Zander wouldn't give Dharien the satisfaction of denying his accusations. He kept the bullying to himself.

Under his false calm, Zander experienced a rage he barely controlled. He hated his father for being a drunk, and he hated the mother who had deserted him. He hated the priest, and he hated Dharien. A war waged in his head, and a hornet omen appeared at his feet.

Although thrilled to find his twin, he now feared the quest. He recalled his shock when she had told him of the curse of only one twin returning from the quest. Alexa believed they'd be fine if they stayed away from each other in the quest, but Zander's view of Moira didn't lead him to think she could be fooled. What if he lost Alexa?

His father's words echoed in his ears. *"There's no cheating Fate, Son. She's a foul mistress."* For the first time in his life, Zander cursed

Fate and hated her for the control she held over his life. When the second hornet omen appeared, he threw it against the wall.

His thoughts turned to the festival. The wrestling tourney started after the noon bells, and Zander couldn't wait to fight. There, he'd use his anger to his advantage.

He remembered when Moira first came to him. She'd said his favor would be useful. Maybe he could use it in the tournament. He'd learned secrets changed with situations. He dismissed the nagging idea that a Protector wouldn't use his favor to gain an advantage over his opponent. He'd only do it this one time. Moira had given it to him. He would use it.

The priest had requested the students meet at the beginning of the celebration, but Zander stayed at the stables. When Fulk questioned him, Zander lied. "I don't need to go until the wrestling at noon." He snatched the snake omen from the ground and grimaced when he noted Fulk's recognition of the lie.

But Fulk didn't care. He threw his arm around Zander's shoulder. "Everyone from the estate is gone to celebrate. Let's see how Helios takes to the saddle. You've spent more hours with him than anyone but Greydon, and Elder Warrin won't let his first-born ride until Helios is gentled. If he'll let anyone sit on him, it would be you." He squinted at Zander. "You're not going to ride Helios. Just sit in the saddle."

Fear seized Zander, and then as quickly, his destiny opened to him. This was his chance to prove he was capable of being a Protector. He didn't have to ride, just sit on Helios. He'd let the outcome choose if he used his favor in the tourney. If Helios allowed Zander to stay seated, then Zander wouldn't have to prove himself in the games.

And if he didn't? Then it would be up to Zander to make his dream come true.

"By the stars, yes!" For the first time in days, Zander's anger receded.

"I'm ready."

Helios pawed at the ground, and his nostrils flared when Zander laid the blanket across his back. He'd worn the saddle, but now the whites of his eyes showed as Zander ran his hands under his belly checking the girth.

Fulk held the lead as Zander took a deep breath, slipped his foot into the stirrup, and in one smooth movement, mounted. Zander clenched his knees against Helios's flanks.

The horse skittered sideways.

Fear consumed him, and Zander hated his weakness. Anger bloomed in his gut and spread through his chest.

Helios tensed and lowered his head. He bucked and sent his rider flying over his head. Zander rolled as he hit the dirt.

Fulk swore while Zander scrambled out of the way. As he walked the horse, Fulk glanced at Zander, who moaned and rubbed his backside.

Fulk scratched at his stubby beard. "Guess old Helios isn't ready for a ride."

With his body already beginning to ache, Zander felt his dream to be a Protector die. A darker desire settled over him. If Dharien could lie and steal without punishment because he was an elder's son, then Zander could use his favor for his own gain.

He would use it, and he would win the tourney.

Zander's gut clenched and warned him to stay at the stables. Nothing good would come of going to the festival. He shook away the warning. He had to go. He had to win.

As he sat on the ground, a tiny black horse materialized at his feet. Glaring, he grabbed it. Was it an omen or a token? What had he done to deserve it? Helios stamped his foot and neighed.

When Zander glanced up, he swore the horse smirked.

An hour later, Zander limped to the festival and registered for the wrestling tournament. Shadow had grown too large to carry in his pack, so he'd left him asleep on the bed. He glanced at the other boys waiting and waved at Greydon. All the young men in the village were encouraged to enter—supposedly, wrestling skills could aid in the unlikely event of an attack on the village.

The registrar eyed Zander and assigned him to a group based on his size. Dharien would be in his group, and Zander could think of no boy he'd rather beat than Dharien. Anger flushed Zander's cheeks when he spied him warming up.

"Hoy, Zander!" Cobie clapped him on the shoulder.

Zander spun and raised his hand to strike.

Alarmed, Cobie stumbled backwards.

"Sorry," Zander muttered. "I'm a little jumpy."

They practiced holds and take downs. Evenly matched, Zander hoped not to wrestle Cobie. He didn't want to cheat against his friend.

Six rings were scattered across the grounds to accommodate the differing classes. The boys lined up in front of the stands as the proctor announced the rules. "Two will wrestle until one pins the other, with both shoulders to the ground, for the count of three. Winners advance to the championship round. The defeated wrestlers go to the loser's bracket where they can earn their way to the finals by winning every match thereafter. Two losses and you're out. At the championship match, the undefeated wrestler is the champion after one win. The wrestler from the loser's bracket will have to beat his opponent twice to win the purse." The proctor jingled the coins in a green velvet bag.

Zander checked the post for his first opponent. It wouldn't be an easy win, but he'd beaten Waku in the last tournament. Waku would fight hard. Winning would mean his peasant family had enough food for the coming year. Even the second place purse provided enough money for half a year of food.

Nervous energy charged through Zander as he paced the sidelines. The calm he craved eluded him. Images of Alexa, his father, and the mother he didn't know flashed through his head. Hatred warred with love until his body trembled.

"Zander?"

Yanked from his thoughts, Zander blinked at Alexa, who stood against the fence. The pounding in his chest slowed as he focused on her anxious face.

She came forward to touch his arm. "I wanted to say good luck."

Zander pulled her behind a corner. "Alexa, we have to be careful no one sees us."

"Mother's still at the bakery. Is Father here?"

"No, he's likely lost in his cup of mead."

Alexa glanced around. "No one's watching."

Zander's eyes traveled past her to where Dharien lurked in the shadows. Hatred flashed between them. Zander cocked his head toward the shade. "Dharien noticed."

"Don't worry about Dharien. I'll talk to him."

Zander didn't think talking would help. He'd show Dharien by winning the championship. "I fight for both of us, Alexa."

She nodded. "Never again will we be apart."

"Never. I'll talk to you after the match."

He watched as Alexa wound through the stands and sat next to Merindah and Kaiya.

At the call of his name, Zander strode to the ring, ready to fight.

CHAPTER TWENTY-SEVEN

Alexa

"I'm nervous. Zander's different today." Alexa chewed on the hem of her sleeve.

"He looks angry." Merindah stroked a strand of rose colored prayer beads. "I'll pray for him."

Kaiya leaned forward. "Hurry. He wrestles next."

With Angel snuggled on her shoulder, Merindah chanted the prayer of protection.

Zander faced Waku and shook his hand. When the referee lowered his arm, Alexa's heart thumped out of sync and then found a rhythm with Merindah's chanting. She wanted Zander to win, but the menace in his eyes frightened her. Today he wasn't the gentle boy she thought she knew.

Zander rushed in and grabbed Waku. He slammed him to the ground and struggled to press his shoulders down. Alexa caught her breath. Zander's cheeks were flushed and his eyes wild.

She yelled, "Go Zander!"

Zander glanced at her and when he hesitated, Waku flipped him to his back, hooked one arm behind Zander's knees, and lifted. With his other arm he pressed his elbow and palm against Zander's upper chest.

"One, two, three!" the referee yelled and slapped his hand against the ground.

Waku jumped up victorious while Zander lay as if stunned.

"What have I done?" Alexa cried to Merindah. "I distracted him. It's my fault he lost. He's going to hate me."

Alexa stumbled from the stands, bolted for the bakery, and flew up the steps to her bedroom. With trembling hands she cut a square cloth, quickly stitched a faceless figure lying on his back, shoulders pressed against the cloth, and then added Zander, large and strong, with his arm raised in victory. She grabbed thread and a pair of scissors and stuffed them with the cloth into her bag. Breathless, she raced to the stands and slipped into her seat next to Merindah.

"Zander came to find you."

"Does he hate me?"

Running her fingers over her beads, Merindah frowned. "No, he said to tell you he's sorry."

"When does he wrestle again?"

Pointing to the far ring, Kaiya squinted. "Now."

With sure fingers, Alexa stitched the blond hair and blue shirt of Zander's opponent on the cloth. As the referee lowered his hand, she added his blue eyes and stitched a large black X holding him to the ground.

Merindah spat, "What are you doing?"

With steely eyes, Alexa stared at her friend. "Your prayers didn't work, Merindah." She pulled the cloth to her heart. "I'll help him. Zander *will* win."

CHAPTER TWENTY-EIGHT

Zander

Zander strode to his second match. As a loser, he had to win every contest to reach the championship. He had to use his favor.

When he'd glanced at Alexa earlier, she'd seemed frightened, and he'd lost his concentration. He couldn't let it happen again.

As Zander shook his opponent's hand he peered into the boy's eyes. Zander detected his plan to rush for his left side.

The referee's arm dropped, and the boy lunged for Zander, who stepped back and to the right. As his opponent faltered off balance, Zander flipped him and pinned the helpless boy.

"One. Two. Three." The ref grabbed Zander's hand, raising it high amid cheers from the crowd.

Match after match, Zander exploited his favor to read his opponents' moves. And match after match, he won. Some easily, some not, but all wins.

With some time before his next bout, Zander relaxed with Alexa under the stands where they could talk unseen.

"Where's Merindah?"

Alexa shrugged. "She left after your second match."

"What about Kaiya?"

Alexa gave him a funny look, and Zander felt heat creep up his neck.

"She's sitting with Bindi and Tarni."

They stood in the shadows and followed Dharien's match.

"I hope he loses." Alexa tossed her hair. "He's too smug."

"No, I want him to keep winning. I want to face him for the championship."

"That would be perfect." Alexa glanced sideways at Zander. "I know you can beat him."

Dharien continued to win, as did Zander. Between matches, Zander scanned the crowd for Alexa. He frowned as she cut threads from a cloth and quickly re-stitched them. What was she doing?

By the end of the afternoon, Zander had wrestled his way through the loser's bracket, and Dharien remained undefeated. They would fight for the championship, but Zander would have to win twice.

During the long break, Zander and Alexa meandered through the crowd, avoiding villagers who might recognize them. With the extra people in for the festival, they blended with the crowd. They stopped first at a booth selling quince pie and bought one to share. As they turned to the cider table, Zander remembered the festival when he'd tried to prevent Alexa from giving the potion to Paal. He scowled as he recalled the results. Dharien had drunk it, and now he believed he loved Alexa.

When they headed toward the colorful trinket wagons, Alexa skipped to keep up with Zander's longer legs. "You're going to beat Dharien. I know it!"

Zander grinned at Alexa's enthusiasm. "I'll make him regret getting to the championship."

They moved with the flow of the crowd toward the row of amusements where the Raskans had booth after booth of games and contests.

"Let's play a game, Zander, please?"

They passed by the marbles, ring toss, and shuffleboard before

Alexa clapped her hands together and dragged Zander to the Wheel of Fortune.

A red-haired girl not much older than Zander smiled and beckoned to him. Unable to resist, he drifted over to stand in front of the large wooden circle divided into twelve pie pieces. A black arrow pointed out from the middle.

"For a bronze, win a prize, and learn your future." The girl leaned into Zander, and an exotic spice he couldn't place filled his nose. Patchouli, perhaps, but he couldn't say for sure, only that he felt light-headed and weak in the knees.

"I'm Sophia," she whispered.

The Raskan women were known for their enchantments. Each year after the festival at least one young man left with the wagons, dreaming of love and faraway adventures. For a moment, Zander considered how easy it would be to leave with the red-headed girl before the quest. No worries about tokens or pleasing Moira. As Sophia held his eyes, he decided. He'd go.

"Zander?" Alexa clutched his arm. "Are you all right?"

As if released from a dream, Zander stumbled back a step. He couldn't leave Alexa. He'd just found her. "Uh, I don't want to play. You do it, Alexa."

The disappointed look on Sophia's face almost made him change his mind. He dug in his pocket and pulled out one bronze. As he handed it to Sophia, he whispered, "For my sister."

Her smile returned, and she trailed a finger down his cheek. "Your sister. Not your girlfriend?"

He gulped and shook his head.

Sophia turned to Alexa. "Spin the wheel. Learn your fortune."

Alexa used both hands to pull down the peg and set the wheel in motion. It spun round and round, mesmerizing Zander, before it stopped at a red wedge.

"Fire." Sophia shrugged. "It appears turmoil will enter your life." She handed Alexa a small metal star. "For good luck." She frowned and added, "Moira says you may use it in your quest."

Zander's throat tightened. Moira talked to Sophia? He thought Fate only oversaw Puck's Gulch.

Alexa grabbed his hand. "It's my second star. Zander, I can use it for light."

As they moved away, Sophia called, "When you're ready to see your future, you know where I am."

Alexa chattered on as Zander played a game of marbles and a round of darts. He gave her the trinkets he'd won, and they moved from the games and into the Raskan market where he admired the horses and laughed with Alexa over the antics of the goats. A Raskan child dressed in multi-colored skirts, danced and sang a lyrical song in a language Zander didn't recognize. When she bowed at the end, he hauled out his last coin and gladly dropped it in her palm. She ran away giggling. It was only then that Sophia's charms lost their hold.

As they strolled past a black tent with red symbols painted on the side, a woman stepped in front of them. Her dark skin contrasted with her pale blue eyes. A tunic embroidered with snakes hung over a black velvet skirt swirling around her ankles.

She searched their faces. "Come," she beckoned to the tent and pulled aside the cloth door.

Zander balked. "Not another fortune, Alexa."

She tugged his hand. "This is different. The other was for play. This is what Melina Odella does."

"I've never had a fortune-teller read me," he whispered. "I don't know if I want it."

Alexa's eyes twinkled. "It'll be fun. Let's see if she knows we're twins."

As his eyes adjusted to the candle light, only Alexa's firm grip on his hand kept him from running. A black panther squatted on its haunches next to a table covered by a purple cloth. Its glowing green eyes tracked Zander's movements.

The fortune-teller tucked Alexa's offered coin into a hidden pocket in her sleeve. "I am Tshilaba, the seeker of knowledge."

She studied Zander. "Great power lies in your name, defender of all."

Defender of all? Melina Odella had told him to find the meaning of his name. What did it mean?

Tshilaba searched their faces. "Names are important. They're meant to guide you."

Alexa asked eagerly, "What does my name mean?"

Tshilaba smiled. "You'll learn soon enough." Her gaze moved to stare beyond them and she grew stern. "Danger surrounds you. Your auras are clouded with it." She examined Alexa. "You are as the night." Turning to Zander she added, "And you are the day." Taking their hands, she closed her eyes. "One cannot exist without the other. Your destinies are entwined, but I cannot see the outcome." She shuddered as if coming from a trance and motioned them to the table. "Sit." She shuffled a deck of cards and spread them in a line. "Let's see what the cards say. You will each choose three."

Alexa picked first and left her cards face down on the table. Zander's hand hovered over the cards before drawing three from the middle.

The fortune-teller turned their first cards face up, side by side. She turned to Alexa and held up the Tower card. "You have a choice before you. You can continue to try to control your circumstances or you can trust Fate."

Alexa's hand clutched Zander's. He glanced at her solemn face.

As the fortune-teller bent toward Zander, his heart quickened. Tshilaba's stare seemed to penetrate his soul, and although he longed to look away, he could not, even as he feared she discerned his secrets.

"The Hermit warns not to search outside yourself for what is real. Truth lies within your heart. When you release what you think you know, the truth will arise gently as smoke rises from a well-tended fire."

Zander wiped his free hand on his tunic. What did that mean?

Tshilaba pressed the second cards on top of the first ones. To Alexa she said, "The Nine of Wands. You are not where you will be. Do not be deceived that this," the fortune-teller swept her hand through the air, "is your destination. The life you live now will soon change in a way you cannot yet understand." She hesitated and murmured, "If I could stay longer . . . I would be of help to you."

She tapped Zander's card. "The Seven of Swords warns of bad luck. You may soon learn that life is not always fair."

Zander almost laughed. He'd learned that lesson a long time ago. Tshilaba studied him. "Beware a theft."

A jolt shot through his gut. Shadow was the only thing he feared stolen. Surely Moira wouldn't allow a patron to be taken. As he stroked the heart token Melina Odella had given him, the calm energy filled him. It was the only way he stayed seated.

Grasping Alexa's final card, Tshilaba closed her eyes, and held it to her chest. She whispered, "The card of the Master." She opened her eyes and placed her right palm on Alexa's forehead between her eyebrows. "You are the master of your own destiny, but not in the manner you now seek." She shuddered. "It was right I read for you. If you heed my advice it could save your life."

Apprehension filled Zander as Tshilaba turned his final card. A man hung upside down chained by one foot to a circle. Zander started to shake.

"Do not fear the Hanging Man." Tshilaba rested her hand on his. "It will be through silence you will understand. You will choose this, for it will bring you great wisdom."

The fortune-teller swept the cards from the table and returned them to the deck. She fumbled in a pouch at her waist and pulled out a stone half-red and half-black. She folded Zander's fingers around the stone. "When the silence comes, hold this to your heart."

Trembling, Zander reached for his bag to add it to his tokens. She shook her head. "No, not there."

Zander nodded and slipped it into his pocket instead.

As they stood, Tshilaba placed her hands upon Zander's and Alexa's shoulders. "A dark night is upon you. As an arrow flies to its target, so fly you to the blackness. Nothing I say will change your path, for you have chosen. Fate will ensure you fly true to your destinies."

As Zander stumbled from the tent, he blinked in the sun. "What was she talking about?" he whispered.

Alexa shook her head. "I'm not sure. What did she mean, the dark night?"

He shivered. "That panther. And the stone she gave me. She scared me."

They didn't speak again until they reached the stands. Alexa twisted her hands. "Are you ready to wrestle Dharien?"

"Yes—two wins to be the champion." He stuck his hand in his pocket, and when he clasped the red and black stone, a vibration moved through his chest. He frowned. What kind of magic did it hold? He didn't want it interfering with his favor when he wrestled, so he held it out to Alexa. "Would you hold the stone Tshilaba gave me?"

After placing it in her sewing bag, Alexa clutched Zander's arm. "Good luck. I know you can win."

As Zander hurried to the rings, he twisted to glance at Alexa. She bent over a cloth and the sun flashed from a needle as she stitched.

Tshilaba's words nagged at him. Was he cheating when he used his favor to win, or was it his right to use it? Moira gave it to him early. What was its purpose if not to help him? He couldn't think clearly with her warnings in his head. But even with the questions, Zander remained sure of one thing. He had to beat Dharien. Twice. And he would do whatever it took to win.

Cobie helped him warm up. "Dharien's bragging how he's going to beat you in one match. You have to win."

"I will."

The championship matches would be played one at a time. His and Dharien's would be third. Zander couldn't focus. What did Tshilaba mean about the silence? And the dark night?

Greydon wrestled a peasant in the second match. Zander pulled his thoughts away from the fortune-teller's words to watch. Greydon had become a friend, and Zander wanted him to win, but the boy he wrestled needed the money. Greydon competed for glory. For the peasant it meant his family could move from the alley. Zander hadn't given any thought to the money. He'd never come this close. He just wanted to tromp Dharien.

Dharien cheered for his brother. Not that it mattered, but Zander wondered who Greydon would root for in his match with Dharien.

Cheers from the audience brought Zander's mind back to the match as Greydon pressed his opponent's shoulders to the ground, and the ref declared him the winner. Greydon jumped to his feet, and Zander experienced Greydon's excitement as if it were his own.

After Greydon accepted the purse, he pulled Dharien to his chest. "Make our father proud, brother. Give us two champions in the family."

He no longer wondered who Greydon would root for, but as Zander glanced at Alexa he understood. He would choose her over a friend always. Warmth filled him when he spotted Greydon sprint after the loser. In the shadows, his friend pressed the winnings into the hand of the surprised peasant. Dharien would never be so noble.

He and Greydon were brothers, but as different as night and day. He shook his head. Both fortune-tellers had told him and Alexa the same, but Alexa was nothing like Dharien.

Determined to win his match, Zander strode to the ring, leaving his bag of tokens and omens tucked safely inside his tunic in the shadows of the stands. Crouched across from Dharien, Zander realized how similar they were. Same height, same build. Both had straight dark hair, but Zander's eyes were a clear blue while Dharien's were dark, and now those brown eyes flashed with anger.

As confident as Dharien appeared, when Zander stared in his eyes he glimpsed fear mixed with hatred and a determination matching his own. Zander's own anger rushed to the surface, and he steeled himself. He couldn't wait to take Dharien down.

They shook hands, and the referee lowered his arm. The cheers of the crowd barely registered over the pounding of the blood in his ears. He locked his gaze on Dharien's eyes and spied what he needed. When Dharien rushed him, Zander countered, but missed grabbing him when his opponent rolled to the side. Zander barely recovered his balance before Dharien lunged for his legs and knocked him to his stomach. Zander scrambled on hands and knees with Dharien clinging to his back. Zander managed to stand. Dharien released him. They stood panting with eyes locked.

Dharien shot head first and butted Zander's chest. Zander landed on his back with the wind knocked from him.

Dharien went for the pin, and the ref started to count.

"One, two . . ."

He wouldn't lose. Not to Dharien. Zander caught his breath and flipped Dharien over his head in one quick move. Positions reversed, Zander struggled to pin Dharien's shoulders. Dharien's legs wrapped around Zander and threw him to the side. They scrambled to stand.

Once again they faced each other. Zander grinned when he

studied Dharien's eyes. When Dharien lunged, Zander jumped over him, twisted and landed on Dharien's back.

While Dharien scrambled to stand, Zander swept his legs and flipped him over. As he pressed Dharien's shoulders to the ground the crowd roared.

In three seconds it was over. Zander had won the first match.

Shaking from exhaustion, Zander headed to the sidelines. Sweat soaked through his shirt.

Alexa flew from the shadows. "That was amazing! I knew you could beat him!"

Zander accepted her hug and reached for his tunic. "My bag! Where's my bag?"

Alexa searched with Zander, as his excitement turned to fear.

The bag was gone. And all of his tokens with it. Why hadn't he listened to Tshilaba's warning?

CHAPTER TWENTY-NINE

Zander

Despair settled into Zander's stomach, making it a quagmire of churning quince pie. They searched the ground and the piles of clothes around them. His bag was gone.

"The only one who would steal them is Dharien, but he couldn't have. Who else would?"

"Are you sure your bag was here when you left for the match?"

Zander ran his hands through his hair. "It was here."

"We can report it to the priest and fortune-teller. Maybe they can do something." Alexa tried to console him. "You still have two months to gain tokens."

When his name was called for the final match with Dharien, Zander bent over his knees. "I can't wrestle now. Not like this." His mind whirled. The omens would still challenge him in the quest, and now he had no tokens to fight with.

Alexa grabbed his arm and willed him to stare in her eyes. "You can wrestle, and you will win. You must!"

What Zander spied in her eyes shook him more than the loss of his tokens. She held a new secret. Somehow, she cheated for him. He grimaced, trying to understand, when she glanced to the side and blushed.

"Go. Win." Alexa pushed him toward the arena. "For both of us."

He sprinted to the ring as the proctor called his name for the third and final time. Before he could calm his racing heart, the ref's arm dropped, and the match began.

Zander leaned in and sought Dharien's eyes. Dharien knew where his tokens were! Stunned, Zander hesitated. His opponent lunged for his legs, and Zander found himself on his back. Dharien scrambled to press his shoulders to the ground. For a second Zander accepted defeat, but as the ref counted two, his anger took over. Adrenaline surged through his body, and he threw Dharien to the side. His elbow connected with Dharien's nose. Blood spurted through the air.

The ref stopped the fight long enough to shove a plug of wool up Dharien's nose and warn Zander to watch his elbows. As they faced off, waves of hatred rolled off Dharien. Zander returned them with his own.

Dharien's eyes dared Zander to make the first move, but Zander waited. The crowd booed. They wanted action. Zander didn't care what the spectators thought of him, but he knew Dharien's pride would overrule his plan to wait for Zander's move.

Seeming unnerved by the jeers, Dharien stumbled to Zander's left. Zander stepped to the side. Flustered, Dharien feinted to one side and then another. Each time, Zander reacted in time to stay out of reach.

In desperation, Dharien launched himself at Zander's chest. Zander stepped to the side, swept Dharien's legs, and fell with him. As they rolled, the crowd jumped to their feet, roaring approval.

Zander fought to stay on top. Dharien ducked his head and flipped Zander to the side. When Dharien pounced, Zander rolled and scrambled to stand. Dharien jumped to his feet. They locked arms with sweaty foreheads touching. Dharien was involved with Zander's missing tokens, and Zander would make him regret it.

Staring past Dharien's shoulder, Zander focused in on Alexa standing with her embroidery cloth pressed to her heart. She straightened and nodded once.

He twisted away and waited to see Dharien's next move. After a moment of confusion, Dharien's eyes hardened, and he gave Zander the information he needed. When Dharien stepped back, Zander followed and pushed his opponent off balance. Dharien fell to his back with a thud. Zander landed on Dharien's chest and knocked the air from him.

As Zander pressed Dharien's shoulders to the ground, the ref hollered, "One. Two. Three." He slapped his hand on the ground, and it was over. The ref raised Zander's arm while the crowd exploded. With a pat on the back, the ref handed Zander a bag of coins.

Stunned, Zander accepted the prize. He'd never had so much money. He could repay Elder Warrin. He could help Father. Fear fell like a stone in his stomach. Coins wouldn't help in the quest. His tokens were still gone, and beating Dharien didn't bring them back.

When Zander returned to the sidelines, away from the view of the spectators, Alexa threw herself at him. "You won! I knew you could do it."

He hugged her and then pulled away. "Winning doesn't mean anything if I die in the quest. I've let you down, Alexa. I was careless to leave my tokens where Dharien could steal them."

"You don't know Dharien stole them. Cobie might have seen them and kept them safe for you."

Zander's face darkened. "Dharien knows where they are."

"The cheating twins."

Zander twirled to find Moira standing behind him. She came as the crone; wrinkled and stooped, but with emerald eyes. She held out clenched hands and opened her fingers to reveal a black panther omen in each palm.

"It always happens." She scowled. "Every single time. Twins try to save each other."

"You gave me your favor," Zander stammered. "I used it to have an advantage." Even as he said it, he heard the lie of it. He'd used it to win. To beat Dharien, because he hated him.

Moira cackled and the sound made Zander shrink back. Alexa grabbed his arm.

"You think to fool me? No human fools me. Not you, not your sister, not your parents. What is meant to happen, will happen. I see to it." She dropped the omens to the ground. "Take them or not. They will challenge you in the quest, regardless." In an instant, she was gone.

Zander stooped to grab the omens. He turned them over in his palm before he squinted at Alexa.

They asked together, "What did you do?"

"Never mind. Let's get out of here." Zander gripped Alexa's elbow. "Come to the stable with me." As they stumbled from the arena, Zander remembered Tshilaba's warning. Was this the blackness she spoke of? He had chosen to cheat, and he'd seen in his twin's eyes she also cheated.

They hiked in silence to Elder Warrin's estate. When Zander opened the door to the stable, Shadow raced from Zander's room and leaped into his arms. "Whoa, boy. Did you sleep all day? I wish I'd stayed home with you." If he'd paid attention to his gut, he'd still have his tokens, and he and Alexa wouldn't have the dangerous black panther omens. The bag of coins hung heavy from his belt. It hadn't been a good trade. Not at all.

He carried Shadow to Helios's stall. "I should have listened when Helios threw me this morning."

"Helios threw you? What does that have to do with losing your tokens?"

"I didn't lose them, Alexa. Dharien stole them."

"But that's not your fault."

"Wasn't it? My gut told me to stay away from the festival today, but I didn't listen. Helios felt it in me. That's why he tossed me off." He held out slices of apple on his open palm and waited while Helios sniffed the fruit and then chomped them. He scratched Helios's nose. "Now you like me, huh?"

Alexa climbed onto the rail to brush Helios's mane. "How did you cheat? Why did Moira give you the panther?"

Blushing, Zander stared at the ground. "Moira gave me an early favor. When I stare into someone's eyes, I see their secrets." He glanced at Alexa's stunned face. "In wrestling, your next move is a secret. I used it to win."

"You see everyone's secrets?"

Zander hid his smile. He could tell by her face Alexa knew he'd seen her plan for Paal. "It's not as much fun as it seems." He brushed dirt off his tunic. "I saw in your eyes you cheated for me."

Alexa picked at her fingernails to avoid his eyes. "She gave me my favor early too. I can control people with my embroidery. What I stitch, happens. Remember last month when you and Dharien couldn't stay apart?"

"You did that?" Zander grimaced. "Why?"

She shrugged. "Revenge. I thought you deserved each other. But I cut the thread." She glanced up, but avoided letting Zander look into her eyes. "When you lost your first match, I knew I could help."

"So you stitched me winning and it worked?"

"Between your favor of seeing and mine of controlling, I guess we both earned our omens. But we had to do it. You needed to win."

"And now we have the hardest omen to fight in the quest. I don't know of a token that will beat the black panther. Yeah, that was worth it." He strode to his room and brought back his quiver of arrows, which he dumped in the straw. He picked out the fox, the mountain lion, and the black horse. Those and the wood heart he wore around his neck were the only tokens he possessed.

"The mountain lion might fight off one panther, but not two." He handed it to Alexa. "You take it. I can fight another way."

She shrank back. "No, I have time to figure out something else."

Alexa handed Zander the red and black stone she'd held for him. He stared at the stone and stuffed it in his pocket before Alexa could notice it was now more black than red. What made it change?

Alexa opened her bag of tokens. "I have plenty. I'll share."

"No, you're right. I have time. I'll earn more in the next two months." His voice shook as he held out the black panther omen. "But Alexa. This . . ." He gulped. "It may be impossible to defend against."

"What about Shadow? He could kill a panther."

Zander felt like he'd been punched in the stomach. "Never!" He sagged against the stall. But would he need to sacrifice Shadow to save his twin?

CHAPTER THIRTY

Alexa

Alexa walked outside with Zander, and they sat on the stone fence leading to the estate. Fiona scampered along the wall, teasing Shadow, who tried repeatedly to jump on the fence to join her. Alexa laughed when he tumbled backwards.

She stared at the estate she once wanted to live in. She pulled her knees up to sit cross-legged and rested her chin in her hand. What a foolish dream. Now, she had more important things to consider.

How could they defend against the most dangerous omen? Alexa pondered the round embroidery cloth she kept secret. In her mind she schemed. If she stitched two panthers and enclosed them in a cage, they wouldn't be able to harm her or Zander in the quest, but would she risk another omen?

Her twin nudged her knee. "What are you thinking? Worried about the omen?"

She hesitated, knowing he wouldn't like her thoughts. "Zander, I can use my favor to control the quest."

Zander's head jerked. "No, Alexa. It's not worth getting another omen."

She recalled the fortune-teller's words. "Tshilaba said I was the master of my destiny. We can't allow Moira to win. Our parents have sacrificed their happiness to keep us alive."

With the sun sinking in the west, lightning flashed in the clouds looming in the east. Alexa stood and stretched her legs. "I have to go. Mother will worry."

Zander studied the sky. "The storm will hit around midnight. Come on, I'll walk you to the border." As they trekked, Zander begged her. "Please, Alexa, don't use your favor for the quest. I can earn more tokens."

After a late dinner, Alexa kissed Mother goodnight and climbed the stairs to her room. She lit her lamp, closed her door, and dug the stitching out from under her dresser. After changing to a pale yellow nightshirt, she leaned against her headboard and out of habit, reached for her basket of thread. She smiled as she lifted Fiona out of the basket and unwound silver thread from around her ears. She gave her patron a tummy tickle and settled Fiona in her lap.

Lost in thought, Alexa hesitated for a few moments before she stitched the panthers, black in the forest. With shaking hands, she threaded the needle with a fine metallic thread and enclosed them in a golden cage. She closed her eyes. If it would only work.

As thunder rumbled against her windows, she considered other items that might help them survive the quest. She stitched brown loaves of bread scattered through the gulch and clear ponds with tin cups littering the banks. She stitched bows with arrows and long knives.

The wind howled as she stitched herbs growing throughout the forest; deep purple lavender for calming and pain relief, green mint for upset stomachs, twiggy rosemary for sprains and clear thinking, and broad-leafed comfrey for cuts and insect bites.

Near midnight, as Zander had predicted, the storm hit in full force. Deafening peals of thunder shook the house, sending Fiona cowering under the covers. Lightning flashed and rain beat at the window while Alexa stitched the final questers with each of their patrons. Thirteen figures poised at the edge of the forest ready to enter for the quest. She stitched her name, but didn't tie the knot. It wasn't yet time to set the cloth in motion.

As she slept, the storm invaded her troubled dreams. In the early morning, when she woke to a quiet village of downed trees and overturned market stalls, one thing was certain; she *would* control her own destiny. She would not allow Moira to decide for her. Not now.

CHAPTER THIRTY-ONE

Zander

Zander tied his winnings around his neck. He found owning that much money a worry. Even after he paid Elder Warrin the debt he owed and they had agreed on a weekly salary for Zander's work in the stable, the weight pulled at his neck. The clinking coins spooked the horses. And though he trusted Fulk, he declined the marshal's offer to lock the coins in his room. He didn't trust Dharien.

He took one coin from the bag and returned to the festival. A sword had caught his eye when he and Alexa had wandered through the Raskan tents. Then he didn't have money—now he did. After finding the sword fit his hand perfectly with a weight he could heft, Zander gladly handed over the coin without haggling. Hiding it under his long leather coat, he returned to the stable and shoved the blade under his bed. It was impulsive and he didn't know how to fight with it, but he felt safer.

Even with the blade, that night he barely slept, and he clutched the bag with both hands. When he woke, drenched in sweat, his first thought was of the coins. Each night after was the same torment, and a week later, he trudged to his father's house. As he slumped at the door, memories flooded Zander, and he grabbed at the handle to steady himself. He was the son of a furrier. What was he doing pretending to be something he wasn't?

He jumped when Father opened the door.

"I watched you win the championship," Father said.

Shocked, Zander met his eyes. "You went to the festival?"

"I was selling pelts to the Raskans, and I heard you were wrestling for the purse." His father surprised him when he pulled Zander into his chest and hugged him hard. "I'm so proud of you, Son. After the quest you can build a house or start a business. Moira may be fickle, but she does what's best for the village. She'll assign you a good job."

Zander couldn't tell Father about Moira's latest visit. Father might not be so optimistic if he knew of the omen Zander carried. Instead, he stuttered, "I . . . I paid off my debt to Elder Warrin, but I don't know what to do with the rest of the money."

"He won't help?"

"You're my father. I don't trust anyone else." Zander sought his father's eyes and found them clear and unclouded from mead. He ignored the secret.

Father straightened his shoulders. "What do you want?"

"Would you keep it for me until after the quest? And if I don't return," Zander swallowed, "it's yours to do as you like."

"You'll return, Son. You have to return."

Zander nodded. He wanted to admit he knew Father's secret, and how he'd found Alexa and their plan for the quest, but the words refused to come. Maybe after the quest, if he and Alexa survived, they could be a family again.

After Father promised to keep the money safe, Zander headed back to the stables. Unable to reconcile his feelings, he felt out of control, and it wasn't a feeling he enjoyed. He loved Alexa and was grateful he'd found her before the quest, but his life had turned upside down since they first talked in the market stall. He couldn't keep his old hurts locked away. They rose to the surface of his mind at inopportune moments.

Today, Father had been sober and concerned. Exactly what

Zander had hoped for and yet as he left, memories of Father drunk drifted in and swirled around Zander's feelings of abandonment as a child. He'd grown up with no mother, and Father, lost in mead, who wasn't even a father most of the time. The two conflicting emotions left Zander feeling off-center and unbalanced. He'd been stuck in class or at the stable too often lately. He needed time alone.

"You and me, Shadow," he said to the pup.

Zander clutched at the red heart hanging from his neck, and the calm it brought seeped through his body. He dug in his pocket for the red and black stone. As he rolled it between his fingers, he puzzled that the black had taken over even more of the red as the hate in his chest pulsed against the love in his heart. Something in his life needed to change, and soon, or the hate was likely to win.

The next day in class, Zander slouched next to Alexa. He glared back at Dharien's dark stare. Even after a week, purple surrounded one eye from the elbow punch when Zander had bloodied Dharien's nose. Still, Dharien had appeared smug all week.

Melina Odella paced the room, as if trying to rid herself of nervous energy. "Let's talk of the rules of the quest. It lasts five days. You'll enter the forest after the noon meal on day one. You may take your journal, a water skin, your bag of tokens and omens, and the clothes you wear. Your tokens can be used at any time, but the challenges begin at dawn on the second day and end at dusk on day four. That gives you three days to fight your omens. Most of you have earned bread tokens. Use those to keep your strength along with the food you forage. Moira gives you your nights free of threats, but there are natural dangers in the forest to guard against. During the last night, Moira will appear in your dreams to offer her congratulations, bestow your favor, and assign your apprenticeship. When you wake on the fifth day, you'll make your way to the village.

Your families will spend the time of the quest in prayer at the church and meet you at the Quinary when you return."

The grave look on the priest's face sent a shiver down Zander's back. "If any do not return, the families will search the gulch for the body. For those who do, the noon celebration will be your time of choosing. You'll announce your calling to the village and go with the guild Moira has chosen for you."

Alexa raised her hand. "Do we have no voice in our apprenticeship? What if we don't want what Moira chooses?"

From across the room, Melina Odella shrugged. "Sometimes she gives you a choice. Many times she doesn't. Moira knows better than you what the village needs."

Zander held his smile when Alexa continued to argue. "But what if I don't like her decision?"

Melina Odella narrowed her eyes. "Save your complaints for Moira. See if it gets you anywhere."

Merindah whispered, "Let it go, Alexa. Please?"

The priest rapped the table. "Today we're going to help you identify the wild foods safe to eat in the gulch."

Zander frowned. Something was wrong. Dharien should have been in a bad mood since he lost. Instead, he gloated at Zander from across the table. Melina Odella was nervous and avoided looking at him. Even the priest had been jumpy and hadn't bothered to give Zander a thorn omen since the festival.

Alexa asked, "Is it true Puck's ghost haunts the gulch? I've never gone to the bottom."

Zander snorted. "Of course it's true. He talks at me every time I'm there."

Silence fell over the room. Even Dharien looked shocked. The other teens looked at each other nervously.

The priest's mouth dropped open, and he blinked several times. "Uh . . ." he stuttered as if at a loss for words.

"What?" Zander's eyebrows shot up. "You've never heard him?"
Everyone shook their heads.

Huh, that was weird.

He thought Puck talked to anyone who went into the gulch.

Melina Odella sashayed across the room to stand behind Zander.
"You don't need to fear Puck's ghost. Even if he speaks to you, he
can't harm you. Let's go."

Zander trailed with Alexa and Merindah behind the others.
Merindah stopped to pick a bouquet of irises and chattered about
their meaning; something about the three petals representing faith,
valor, and wisdom. Alexa kept glancing at him, but she didn't ask
about his hearing ghosts.

The other questers wrote notes as Melina Odella pointed out
edible greens, safe mushrooms, and berries they could eat during
the quest, but Zander didn't need notes. He knew the gulch—what
was safe to eat and what wasn't. Father had taught him when he was
five. Instead, he observed the teachers. Father Chanse's eyes darted
everywhere but at Zander, and Melina Odella spoke curtly, as if
afraid to use too many words.

After the lesson, Zander intended to ask the fortune-teller
about his stolen tokens. His gut told him she couldn't help, but his
heart held hope. When they returned to the classroom, the priest
dismissed them before the noon bells.

Zander whispered to Alexa, "I'm going to speak to Melina
Odella. Wait for me outside?"

Alexa nodded and left with Merindah.

Hoping the priest would leave so he could talk privately to
Melina Odella, Zander fidgeted with his journal and token bag.
When it appeared the priest was staying, Zander stood.

Unable to meet his eyes, Father Chanse spat, "Zander, what
do you want?"

He hesitated. "My tokens were stolen at the wrestling tourney."

Zander searched Melina Odella's face, expecting sympathy. When she met his gaze, he viewed one secret that pushed the others away, and slammed into his gut.

She had betrayed him! She was the one who stole his tokens.

The words of the man in jail raced back to him. *Beware the one you trust.* He'd never guessed it would be Melina Odella. Heat flushed through him as he fumbled under his tunic for the heart. He yanked it from his neck and threw it to the floor as he bolted from the room. She'd given him the red heart. Maybe it wasn't the token he'd believed. He couldn't depend on it now.

Dharien slouched, laughing, at the door. Dharien and Melina Odella had worked together to steal Zander's tokens. What Zander didn't understand was why. Dharien hated him, but Melina Odella had always been friendly. He'd never trust a fortune-teller again.

When Zander stumbled from the church, Alexa grabbed his arm.

"What's wrong?"

"Melina Odella stole my tokens!"

CHAPTER THIRTY-TWO

Alexa

Alexa's shock at the fortune-teller's betrayal quickly turned to anger. Adrenaline propelled her into the church. She would confront Melina Odella and force her to return her twin's tokens.

As she approached the classroom, angry voices spilled into the hall. Curious, she pressed herself against the stone wall next to the open door and listened.

Melina Odella's terse voice flowed from the room. "I stole the tokens, and now you have them. We did what you wanted. What more do you ask?"

Dharien's voice sounded like steel. "Promise me Zander will die during the quest, or I'll tell Father that you and the priest are in love. I watched you kiss, you can't deny it."

Alexa's heart thudded. Why did he want her brother to die? And why did he threaten the priest? Father Chanse would be thrown out of the church if the elders found out he loved the fortune-teller. She strained to hear the fortune-teller's soft words.

"Zander and Alexa are twins. One of them will not survive." Melina Odella laughed raggedly.

"They're twins?" Dharien sounded confused. "I thought Zander—nevermind what I thought. I love Alexa. I don't want her to die. If this is true, it changes everything."

Why had she asked for the potion? Alexa dropped her head as Melina Odella continued.

"It changes nothing. What you've set in motion cannot be undone."

"But the curse of the twins. You said one always sacrifices for the other. What if Alexa dies?"

"Zander's the one without any tokens." Melina Odella hesitated. "Do you want the truth? Most of your group will not survive. Moira loves the number thirteen. The last time there were thirteen questers, only six returned. You have Zander's tokens. Your chances are better than the others. It's in Moira's hands. What is to happen, will happen."

Dharien's voice sounded desperate. "I have one more demand."

Alexa bolted down the hall. She had to tell Zander that Dharien had his tokens. Maybe Zander could steal them back. And with the news that half may not return, Alexa's plan became more important.

When she burst from the church, Zander was gone, and Merindah stood next to the wall crying.

"Is it true? Did Melina Odella steal Zander's tokens?"

"Yes, and it's worse. We're all in trouble, Merindah."

Alexa searched for Zander in the stables and then ran to his— no, their—father's house. He wasn't there either. She found Cobie with the peasant cousins at the market. No one had seen him.

Feeling defeated, Alexa returned to her room where she found Zander and Shadow asleep on her bed. Alexa hated to shatter his peace with the news.

CHAPTER THIRTY-THREE

Zander

After the shock of Melina Odella's betrayal, Zander hadn't been surprised to learn of Dharien's involvement. As Alexa shared the news, he slumped on her bed.

"I'm not going back to class. I can't sit there and pretend I don't know what they're planning." Zander hated the sympathy he caught in his twin's eyes. He didn't want anyone feeling sorry for him, not even his sister. "I'm going to the stables to pack my things. I've paid my debt, and I don't want the job anymore. I don't belong there and after the quest, Moira will put me where she wants. I can't stay there with Dharien plotting against me."

"Where will you go? To our father's house?"

Zander shook his head. "I'll camp in the forest for awhile. I feel safe there."

"You could stay here."

"No." Zander flashed a wry grin and rubbed his tongue over the chipped tooth. "I need time to think. I do best in the forest." Out of habit, Zander reached for the heart token, patting at his chest where it usually hung under his tunic. When he realized his mistake, anger replaced the calm he sought.

Alexa knelt at her dresser. She stuck her hand deep beneath it and pulled out a large cloth. When she unfolded it on the bed, Zander gasped at the stitched scene. It was beautiful. He traced the green trees in the forest around the edges, and couldn't help but grin at the blue ponds that didn't belong.

He turned the cloth in a circle as he recognized each quester poised to enter the gulch. Thirteen of them. Would they be unlucky as Melina Odella predicted?

Anger seized him when he saw Shadow stitched on the cloth. He jabbed his finger at the likeness. "Take him out. Now, Alexa. I won't use him." He shoved the cloth at her. "Cut the stitches."

His twin's eyes flared in fear, but she quickly cut the stitches and pulled them out. "I didn't mean you would use him. But it might be helpful to know where our patrons are."

He took a deep breath. He hadn't meant to scare her. "It doesn't matter where they are. They have to come if called. And I won't call Shadow." He picked up Fiona and held her in Alexa's face. "Will you call Fiona? Knowing she'll die?"

Alexa jerked back. She straightened her shoulders and glared at him. "If it's the only way to live, then yes. I'll call her." She blinked back tears. "I can't lose you. Please call for Shadow if it's your only hope."

Guilt stabbed at Zander's heart. "I'm sorry, Alexa. I can't do it. Not even to save my life." He pressed his palms over his eyes. But he would do it to save hers. He hoped he didn't have to choose Alexa's life over Shadow's.

Alexa sniffed and knotted a loose thread from her signature. Birds flew through the sky, wind rustled the trees, and the questers moved. The black panthers threw themselves against the gold bars of the cage. It stopped when Alexa unknotted the thread.

She quietly explained, "I'm not ready to set it in motion. Not until the quest starts."

"How will you use it?"

"I'm still thinking, but if we all work together and the panthers stay locked in the cage, we should be fine. The rest of us can help you fight the omens you don't have tokens for."

"I don't know." Zander rubbed the back of his neck. "We risk Moira's ire if we cheat again. We're to go alone to the quest. That's the rule."

Alexa's eyes gleamed. "We *will* go alone into the gulch, but then we'll have a meeting place. I'll use the cloth to find anyone who's lost. There's no rule against that."

"Let me think about it, all right? I'm not sure you and I should work together. There's still the curse of twins."

"If you don't earn enough tokens, it's your only hope, Zander."

Zander caught his twin's eyes. Her secret had changed. Her greatest desire now was his survival. Disturbed at what he'd learned, Zander stood. "Alexa, I need to go. Don't worry about me. I'm safe in the gulch even with Puck whispering his nonsense to me." He wiggled his left eyebrow up and down, and Alexa giggled. "As long as I have my bow and no omens to fight, I'll be fine." He gave her a one-armed hug and tugged at one of her braids. "I'll return in a week. We can talk more about this plan of yours then."

One thing he would never agree to—he wouldn't allow her to be in danger for him. Not ever. Even if it meant using Shadow to save her. Even if that meant his heart would break.

At the stables, Zander packed his bag. He'd come with little and hadn't added anything but the sword. He shoved it far under the bed against the wall. It had been a foolish purchase. It would be of no use to him. Everything else fit. He threaded his bow over his shoulder and hooked his quiver to his belt, next to his almost empty bag of tokens.

"Where are you going?" Fulk leaned against the door frame.

Zander met the marshal's eyes. No secret hid behind them. Only respect.

"I've paid my debt to Elder Warrin. It's best I go."

"And let the twerp win?"

"What?"

"Dharien. I've seen the way he bullies you. Muck in your bed and tearing apart your room. I overheard him brag to Lash about stealing your tokens. I'd say something to Warrin, but he turns a blind eye to his son's escapades." Fulk spat at the floor. "At least stay until the quest, and let Fate sort it out. You can earn tokens here as well as anywhere else."

"I need time to think. I can't do it here."

"I'll give you seven days before I say anything to Elder Warrin."

Zander held out his hand, and Fulk grasped it.

"Thanks, Fulk. I'll let you know."

Zander stopped at Helios's stall and offered him a carrot. "You let Greydon ride you, you hear me?"

Helios whinnied and pushed his nose in Zander's chest. Zander scratched the horse's head and whispered in his ear, "I'll miss you, you rotten excuse for a horse."

Time to go. "Come on, Shadow."

Zander walked out the door, not knowing if he'd ever be back.

CHAPTER THIRTY-FOUR

Six Weeks until the Quest

Alexa

Alexa sat in class and glared at Melina Odella. No one mentioned Zander's absence. Not the fortune-teller, not the priest, and not one of the questers.

Her mind drifted as the priest lectured yet again on the importance of gaining tokens. Was the fortune-teller right? Would Moira allow only six to survive? She glanced at each quester. They weren't all her friends, but she didn't want them to die. She shuddered. If Merindah didn't make it, what would she do?

The priest rapped his knuckles against the table. Startled, Alexa glanced up and caught the fortune-teller's eyes on her. She glimpsed sympathy until the fortune-teller's gaze hardened.

The priest cleared his throat, and then he stammered. The priest never stammered. "I . . . I have some news."

Across the table, Dharien tapped his fingers against the table and kept his eyes glued on the priest.

A sheen of sweat appeared on the priest's forehead. "The date of the quest has been moved up. You will enter the forest next Tuesday at noon and return Saturday morning. This Sunday we will have the blessing of the questers during morning service."

Alexa stumbled to her feet. "No!"

Stepping back in surprise, the priest's face darkened. "Sometimes Moira makes changes to the rules of the quest."

Melina Odella's skirts swished as she paced the room. "Moira has chosen this year to test your resiliency by surprising you with this change. You have a few days yet to earn tokens. You'll be ready."

As she stared at the shocked faces of the other questers, heat flushed through Alexa's body. She sucked in her breath. "Zander won't be fine, will he, Melina Odella?" She scowled at the fortune-teller. "Not since you stole his tokens and gave them to Dharien."

Dharien's face twisted in rage. "You lie."

When disbelief colored the other questers' faces, Alexa realized she'd have to be careful with what she said next. With her heart racing, she stood and faced Melina Odella. "Tell the class what I overheard you say to Dharien. The part about Fate taking half of us because we're unlucky to have thirteen in our class." She stepped closer and whispered, "Tell them, Melina Odella, or I'll share the secret you're so desperate to hide."

Resolve hardened on the fortune-teller's face. "Sit down, Alexa." A long, low sigh escaped her. "The last time there were thirteen was the year Father Chanse and I quested. Only six returned. It doesn't mean it will happen this year."

Merindah burst into tears while the others sat in stunned silence.

"We're not prepared." Alexa searched each quester's eyes. "But I have a plan. Come to the bakery when the market closes today if you want to survive. Bring your patrons." She rushed out the door without waiting for an answer.

As she raced from the building, Alexa chose not only to control her own destiny, but the destinies of every other quester. She had a plan for Zander's safety. She would expand it to include the others. But first, she had to find her twin. He needed to know the quest started next week.

Since she'd left class early, Mother wasn't expecting Alexa's help yet. She snuck up the back staircase. Safe in her room, she pulled out her embroidery and knotted the loose thread. Zander's figure moved deep in the forest. Even if she could find him, she wouldn't return in time for the meeting.

She helped in the bakery while her mind whirled with questions. Could she control the quest? Would the others attend the meeting? What would they think of her plan? She made so many mistakes, Mother dismissed her early.

As she waited in her room for the other questers, Alexa stitched on the gulch scene. Lost in thought, Alexa startled at the knock on her bedroom door. She pricked her finger and scowled as a drop of blood fell on Zander's figure and the cloth absorbed it. What did that portend?

When she opened her door, Merindah stood with the other questers lined behind her. Alexa motioned them in. They sprawled across the bed and sat on the floor. Eleven teens filled the space in her small room. Odo's kitten hissed at the dogs. Bindi's cat stared hungrily at Merindah's sparrow. Maybe bringing the patrons wasn't such a great idea.

Paal leaned against the door as if ready to bolt at any time and stated, "Dharien said he doesn't need your plan. He's not coming."

"What *is* the plan?" Kaiya asked. "Odo and I need to know more before we decide."

The others nodded.

"It's easier if I show you something first. Did Moira give any of you your favor early?" After they shook their heads, Alexa tied the knot on her embroidery. The teens studied the cloth and recognition flicked through their eyes as they followed Dharien's figure moving around his estate. Zander trekked across the gulch. Eyes widened as the scene continued to change until all their figures crowded together in the bakery.

Merindah gasped. "You're using your favor to control the quest?"

"I don't know if I can control it, but I'm doing what I can to help us."

Odo pointed at the black panthers. "Why did you stitch those?"

"Zander and I both have one. I hope the cage will hold them during the quest." She held out the black panther omen. Their stricken faces told her they understood the danger.

With a quiet voice Cobie asked, "Why would Melina Odella steal Zander's tokens and give them to Dharien?"

"Dharien knows a secret about the fortune-teller and the priest. He's blackmailing them. I think it's why they changed the quest."

Paal crossed his arms over his chest.

"Why would Dharien do that?"

"He hates Zander and wants him to go into the quest without his tokens." Alexa's eyes swept the room. "Zander has three tokens. That's all. If you have any you can spare . . ." She wiped at sudden tears before continuing. "There's something else that makes this quest more dangerous for Zander and me, but you have to keep it a secret. We're not supposed to know." She swallowed hard before continuing. "He's my twin."

Kaiya gasped while the others sat in stunned silence. One by one they pulled out their bags and cautiously contributed tokens they believed they could do without. None of the tokens would fight the more dangerous omens, but loaves of bread, a dove, and a tiny silver star dropped in a pile on the bed.

"Thank you." Alexa pointed to Zander's figure in the gulch. "Cobie? I need to find Zander. Do you think you can help me? He doesn't know the quest starts next week."

Studying the embroidery, Cobie appeared thoughtful. "Yes, I think I know where he is, but it's too late to start today. I'll go first thing in the morning."

Paal left his post at the door to stare at the cloth. "It's too far to walk. I'll take you. My father will let us ride our horses."

Grateful for their concern, Alexa nodded. "Come here first, and I'll check the cloth in case he moves."

Searching her eyes, Paal said, "Alexa, I think you need to come too. Our chances of finding him are better if we have the cloth."

Her heart softened at Paal's concern. She was glad he hadn't drunk the potion. She no longer wanted to trick him into falling in love with her.

Paal turned to Cobie. "Meet me here at sunrise."

They clasped hands.

"Can I go?" Kaiya asked so softly, Alexa almost didn't hear her.

Surprised that Kaiya cared, Alexa hesitated before agreeing. "Can you bring four horses, Paal, or is that too many?"

"Father's hunting with the Protectors tomorrow. If you'll ride with me, Alexa, she can come."

After seeing Kaiya's hopeful face, Alexa couldn't say no. "It's settled then. Now, let me tell you my plan." She stood at the door next to Paal. "On the day of the quest, they'll send us in into the gulch at different points. After we go in, we have to find each other. If we work together, we have a better chance to survive." She pointed to a large oak tree she'd stitched with bright yellow flags flapping in the breeze across the branches. "This is the tree due north of the market. We'll meet there. I'll have my cloth, so I can see where you are if you get lost. Those who go in closest to the tree can help find the others."

Merindah whispered, "You can't take the cloth with you. You heard the priest. We can take our clothes, our journals, a water skin, and our bags of tokens and omens."

Alexa grabbed her scissors and slit the embroidery to the middle, careful not to cut through any stitching. She cut a circle from the center, wrapped the cloth around her waist, and pinned it. When she pulled her tunic down, the embroidery was hidden. "I'll wear it."

"Alexa? Is it cheating?" Merindah paled. "I can't cheat."

As she thought of the black panther omen, Alexa hesitated. "I'm not sure, but if it is cheating, then it's my responsibility. I'll accept the consequences." She hoped it wouldn't be another panther.

"I'm not convinced we need to work together." Paal chewed his lip. "I'm not worried about surviving the quest. Why should I share my tokens?"

"Remember last year when Saul died the first morning of the quest?" Alexa glanced around her room and made eye contact with each of the questers. "He had plenty of tokens, but the snake struck him before he could throw one out. If he'd had help, he might have survived."

"Saul was my friend. He didn't deserve to die." Cobie took a deep breath. "I say we work together."

"What about Moira?" Merindah asked. "Won't she keep us from changing the rules?"

"I don't know." Alexa chewed on a fingernail. "I don't see any other way. We have to try something."

Odo scratched his forehead. "My uncle says once we begin the quest, we're on our own. We won't earn tokens or omens, and Moira only watches. She won't get involved."

"Father says you can't cheat her," piped up Bindi.

Waku, who hardly ever spoke said, "My granny says Moira's already chosen who lives and who dies."

"Stop." Alexa crossed her arms. "There are lots of stories about Moira. We have to do the best we can to survive. Melina Odella called us the unlucky thirteen. We have to help each other. There's one other thing." She glanced around nervously and felt for Fiona in her pocket. "We all love our patrons, but if it means the difference between living and dying then we have to call for them. Do we agree on that?

They each pulled their patron closer, but one by one, they

nodded. The teens stood and linked arms. Paal joined last. "We'll fight together," he said.

Somber faces stared at each other around the circle, and all of their hearts thumped as loud as Alexa's.

"Together," they each repeated as they filed from the room.

Alexa woke before dawn and checked her embroidery, pleased to see Zander's figure remained still. She stitched lavender and mint in the open patch next to him and smiled at the idea of him waking to the fragrance of the herbs. She folded the cloth, grabbed the bag of tokens the others had donated for Zander, and hurried down the stairs to the bakery.

Fresh loaves of oat bread sat cooling on racks. Alexa carried a tray of rolls to the counter and brushed them with butter.

"You're awake early." Mother shaped balls of dough into small, round loaves. She sprinkled them with rosemary and used a knife to slice an X across the tops.

"I'm going on a picnic. Can I make sandwiches?"

After loading the tray of bread into the oven, Mother leaned against the counter and wiped the flour off her hands. "Who are you going with and where?"

"Paal, Cobie, and Kaiya, from class." Alexa used her mother's weakness. "We thought it would help us in the quest if we spent time in the gulch."

"Are you interested in one of these boys?"

Alexa's cheeks warmed. She hadn't expected that question, but at least she could answer honestly.

"No, Mother. We're friends. That's all."

Mother pushed away from the counter. "I have a carrot cake that rose unevenly. While you make sandwiches, I'll ice it and you can take it too."

"Thanks, Mother." After Alexa packed a basket with sandwiches and apples, she sat the cake on top. She kissed her mother's cheek. "Don't worry. I'll be home this afternoon."

While she waited outside for the others, Alexa watched her mother through the bakery window as she pushed back sweaty hair and struggled with heavy trays of dough. A pang of guilt ran through her that she wasn't staying in the bakery when the quest completed. She might not marry an elder's son, but she wasn't going to be a baker.

Cobie startled Alexa when he appeared silently next to her. His chameleon clung to the front of his tunic. Cobie whispered, "I've never ridden. Have you?"

Alexa held out shaking hands. "No, and I'm nervous. Don't tell Paal, but I'm afraid of horses. And Cobie? I hate the gulch. I don't know what I'll do if Puck talks to me."

In the dimmest of light, Kaiya arrived with her bow over one shoulder and Korble riding on the other. Paal followed leading a horse and two ponies. Silk trotted behind. "The ponies are easier to ride. They'll follow my horse without your guidance." He took Alexa's hand. "Come, I'll help you mount."

Alexa flushed. Paal sat so close behind her his breath felt warm on her neck. Cobie and Kaiya looked terrified on the ponies, but Kaiya hid it better. She sat straight in the saddle as she took long slow breaths.

Cobie paled under his dark skin, and he kept patting the pony's neck, saying, "Good girl, good girl."

As the sun peeked over a clear horizon, the four entered the gulch.

CHAPTER THIRTY-FIVE

Two Months Three Days until the Quest

Zander

Shadow curled at his side when Zander woke to the smell of mint. Plants had sprouted overnight in the rich soil between the gully stream and the stand of trees he'd slept in. As he stretched, he detected the soothing fragrance of lavender, as well. He added kindling to the embers left from last night's fire, poked at it until it blazed, and then set a tin mug of water on one of the rough granite stones that ringed the fire pit. He'd make herb tea to go with his breakfast of apple cake that Alexa had insisted he bring.

It was his third day in the gulch. He'd spent his time in silence and hunting as necessary. Even Puck had been silent, as if leaving Zander to his own musings. As he savored the morning stillness, he examined his situation.

Although Dharien had stolen his tokens, Zander had time to earn new ones before the quest began in two months. He didn't understand why Dharien had hated him since the day they met, but he knew now how far his adversary would go to cause him troubles. He could never trust him.

Melina Odella had betrayed him. Better to know now than later. Another person not to trust. And the priest? Also on the "do not trust" list.

Knowing the reason for his father's pain, he understood why he drank, but it made him unpredictable. Untrustworthy.

For the first time in his life, he had friends, but Greydon, Cobie, Odo, and Kaiya had not been his companions long. Their friendship remained untested.

He trusted Alexa, and only her. It was as if his heart had been a half until they met. Now, it had become whole.

Anger still wrestled with the love in his heart, but it no longer overcame it. The time had come to use the black and red stone.

Reflecting on Tshilaba's whispered words, he turned inward. She said his name meant defender of all. She'd said his answers were in his heart, to let go of what he thought he understood, and when the silence came, to hold the stone to his heart.

As the sun began to warm him, Zander relaxed against the rough bark of an oak tree. He crossed his legs and laid his bow and quiver on the ground in front of him. Shadow kept guard at his side. Ready at last to find his answers, Zander released a long breath.

Opening the gray bag he carried at his waist, Zander poured the trinkets into his palm. The gold fox and mountain lion tokens sparkled in the light against the black of the panther and horse. He still didn't know if the horse would help or challenge him. And the magic of the red and black stone tingled in his palm, neither token nor omen. He dropped the animals in the bag and tucked it under his tunic.

Zander rubbed the round stone between his thumb and fingers and puzzled over the change. When Tshilaba had given it to him the red and black shared equal space. Now the black had crept across the surface until only a bit of red remained at the tip.

Uncertain how to use the stone, Zander held it in his right hand and closed his eyes. He took in a breath, and released it slowly, continuing with the measured breaths until his shoulders relaxed and the knot in his stomach released. After three more breaths, the sounds of the forest filled his being.

Oak leaves rustled like the wings of birds in flight.

A duck swam downstream with a subtle splash.

He cocked his head at a woodpecker's sharp cry as it searched for insects.

As he inhaled the tangy green life, a whisper of a breeze ruffled his hair.

With his eyes closed, Zander experienced the gulch differently. He needed to approach life in a new way too. Before he brought the stone to his heart, he mulled over what he needed to let go.

Anger. It threatened his relationship with the one person he trusted. His twin.

He'd been foolish to dream of becoming a Protector. It was time to let it go.

Sweeping his hand across his chest, Zander held the stone at his heart.

He waited.

He had no concept of how long he sat, but gradually a tingle started in his heart and spread throughout his chest. The energy encompassed his neck and head. It traveled through his legs and into his arms. When the vibration returned to the stone, it grew stronger and journeyed again through his body.

Still, he waited.

On the third wave of energy, Zander stepped away from his body. He observed himself sitting under the tree, eyes closed, hand clutched at his heart.

He witnessed the anger and the love at war over his heart. Black and red mist swirled around his body; sometimes more black, sometimes more red.

He ached for the little boy who felt unloved and for the older boy who was bullied and betrayed.

After long moments, Zander opened his heart. He held enough love to overcome the pain he'd endured.

His spirit eased back into his body. As he adjusted to sight, Zander studied the stone in his hand. The black was gone. Only the red remained.

For an hour, maybe for two, Zander sat under the tree, reluctant to lose the peace. He thought he imagined voices calling his name, until he recognized Alexa's.

When he stood, calm settled deep into his bones. It was part of him now and would be there when needed, like drawing cool water from a well.

A whinny drew Zander's attention. A horse and two ponies appeared through the trees, picked their way across the stream, and trotted to his side. Paal helped Alexa from the horse. Zander couldn't hide his smile. He couldn't stay on a horse, but it seemed his sister could.

She ran to hug him and then pulled away. "What happened to you? I can feel it. You're different."

"It's hard to explain. I'm not sure I understand it myself." Zander gazed across at the others, and Kaiya's shy smile filled him with warmth. "What are you all doing here?"

Cobie slid from the saddle. "Alexa asked us to help find you."

"We have news," Paal added. "It's not good."

Alexa hesitated. "The quest begins in three days." She explained what had happened since he'd left.

"So Dharien is still calling the shots and willing to risk everyone's lives because he hates me?"

"We've chosen to work together." Kaiya touched him arm. "We won't lose you in the quest, Zander."

"With the help of the embroidery, we're going to survive." Alexa pulled out a green velvet bag. "And each of the others have shared a few of their tokens with you."

Solemn faces focused on Zander as he gazed from Alexa to Paal to Cobie, and last to Kaiya. He ducked his head and slipped the bag around his neck.

"Tell them thanks. I'll return before the quest."

"Won't you come with us now?" Alexa's face fell. "Tomorrow is the blessing of the questers at church."

Zander laughed. "As if I'd let Father Chanse bless me? Melina Odella would probably curse me instead." He leaned close and whispered, "I'm not ready to return. I need a little more time here."

"Will you be all right?" Alexa searched his face.

He smiled. "I promise I will be."

"Zander, we'll work together, and we *will* survive the quest."

His smile faded. "I hope so, my sister, I hope so."

She glanced around nervously. "Has Puck spoken to you?"

"Not a whisper."

Her shoulders relaxed and she patted his arm. "Are you hungry? I brought lunch. For now, we can forget about the quest." She untied the basket from Cobie's pony and spread a red-and-white checked cloth on the ground next to the tree.

They sat under the oak. Zander's calm spread to the others as they shared sandwiches made with cold rabbit and goat cheese on rye bread. He noticed Kaiya's bow.

"How's the practice coming?" Zander asked and grinned when she blushed.

"We're both getting better, but I still beat Odo. And I'm not bragging, it's the truth."

"I bet you can. You're a fast learner. Show me?"

He studied Kaiya's stance as she shot and once stood behind her with his hands on her arms to improve her aim. He felt muscles that weren't there the first time he'd taught her. She also had a new confidence, and strangely, Zander's heart filled with pride for her.

When they walked to the others, Alexa looked at him

questioning, but he ignored it when he spied the carrot cake. His eyes gleamed. "This is my favorite cake of Mother's."

"When have you eaten Mother's cakes?"

"Father used to bring bread and sweets home late at night. I wondered where they came from until I followed him to the bakery that night." He stuck his nose close to the cake. "I love the smell of baking."

Alexa wrinkled her nose. "Try living above the kitchen and see how much you love it."

"I'd like that," he said. "I'd like that a lot."

They spent another hour enjoying the sun and each other's company, sharing light hearts and peace while their patrons napped. In a moment of quiet, a moan whispered across the gulch.

"Zander."

He stiffened. No one else seemed to hear it. Why did he?

"Unite the tribes. Save the village."

"Shut up, Puck," he muttered.

Alexa's eyes widened. "Do you hear him?"

Zander rubbed the back of his neck. "How do you not?" His eyes searched the other's. "No one?"

They all shook their heads.

"Four now convene. Add the fifth."

Zander cocked his head. That was new. He blanched as he understood. Sitting here were members of the Kharok, Chaphta, Yapi, and Dakta tribes. The only Odwa he could think of were Father Chanse and Elder Terrec. Neither were likely to join his group. He shook Puck's voice out of his head. He was sixteen. It wasn't his job to unite the tribes.

When he scrubbed his face and looked around, four sets of worried eyes confronted him.

Kaiya touched his arm. "Are you all right?"

"I am." He laughed. "Puck's a fool ghost."

Paal stood and stretched his legs. "We'd better return. I told Father I'd have the horses home before dark."

When she hugged him, Alexa whispered, "I have a plan to save all of us. Don't worry about the quest, Brother."

After they left, Zander slid down against the oak tree. Shadow climbed in his lap, and Zander scratched the pup's head.

He whispered to Shadow, "My name means defender of all, but it seems Alexa has taken on my responsibility."

CHAPTER THIRTY-SIX

Two Days until the Quest

Alexa

After a fitful night, Alexa woke on Sunday in twisted covers matching the feeling in her gut. She had a plan, but she wasn't sure she was brave enough to follow through with it. Then she thought of Zander alone in the forest with only a few tokens. She'd do almost anything if it helped him survive the quest.

"Alexa, hurry," her mother called from the stairs. "We can't be late for the blessing."

"Yes, Mother. Almost ready." She deftly braided moonstone beads for clear thinking and rose quartz beads for calm into her hair and dressed. She fed Fiona, who wasn't allowed in church, before she ran downstairs to the kitchen. Mother handed her a slice of apple bread, and Alexa ate tiny bites as they walked to the church.

"I don't understand why the quest is moved. Is Father Chance going to explain the reason today?" Mother chattered as they walked. "I'm glad it'll be over soon, and you have two days yet to earn tokens. Do you need more? Alexa?"

"What? Oh, sorry, no, I'll be fine. I have enough." Mother would panic if she knew about the black panther in Alexa's bag. Alexa couldn't earn a mountain lion, like Zander. She'd have to trust the cage would hold them.

Her plan would cause havoc. Mother wasn't going to be happy with her, but if it worked, the quest would be delayed and give Zander more time to collect tokens.

They followed Merindah's family into the church as the morning bells rang. After Alexa kissed her mother's cheek, she joined the other questers on the front bench. Although the fortune-teller rarely attended services, Melina Odella sat stone-faced with the priest facing the parishioners.

During the service, Alexa mulled her plan. More than once, she wiped her palms on her tunic. She couldn't stop her knee from bouncing. When Merindah whispered, "What's wrong with you?" Alexa shrugged. Merindah wouldn't have liked her answer.

The other questers seemed uneasy too. Odo fidgeted and Kaiya kept patting his knee. Paal twisted his hands in his lap. Cobie's foot tapped on the end of the bench until Alexa wanted to scream at him to stop. And making her even more uncomfortable, Dharien openly stared at her, ignoring the grimace she cast back at him. If he loved her, Dharien wouldn't be doing this to her brother.

Finally, the priest announced, "Fate has deemed the quest begin this week. As is our custom, we will bless the questers today in the hope they will fight their omens with intelligence and courage."

The fortune-teller motioned for the questers to come forward. Alexa's shaking legs nearly buckled as she followed the other teens to the front of the church. They stood to face the villagers. The elders with their families occupied the front rows. The Protectors sat in back. As she searched for her mother in the middle, a pang of remorse stabbed her at the embarrassment she was about to cause.

She reminded herself that she was doing this for Zander. Nothing else mattered.

Alexa sucked in a deep breath and stepped forward. Mother's confused expression almost stopped her. Across the rows, frowns greeted her, but she couldn't quit now.

In a clear voice, Alexa said, "There's something you need to know. Father Chanse and Melina Odella hide a secret." She paused for the whispers to die. "I saw them kiss." Alexa covered the snake omen with her foot.

Shouts erupted, and Elder Terrec yelled above the noise, "Is this true?"

The priest raised his hand demanding quiet, but his shocked eyes and the flushed cheeks of the fortune-teller belied his attempt at denial. As the villagers continued to demand the truth, he turned toward Alexa and scowled, "She lies! You can't believe her over me."

Elder Warrin called out, "You deny her accusations? Reply carefully, Father. The truth will reveal itself. Don't add deceit to your sins."

Father Chanse stepped back at the force of the angry parishioners. His face matched his red hair as he stumbled from the altar and disappeared through the side entrance. Melina Odella darted after him.

Alexa held up her hand. "There's more." She glanced nervously at Elder Warrin. "Dharien blackmailed Melina Odella into moving up the quest. She stole Zander's tokens for him."

Elder Warrin crossed his arms over his chest. "What proof do you have?"

"I heard them talking."

"So, no proof." He twisted in his seat to stare purposely at the other elders. "My son had nothing to do with this."

The others nodded and Elder Warrin turned back to Alexa. "The board will investigate the relationship between the priest and the fortune-teller. If we find you've lied, there will be consequences." He stood to leave.

Panic rose in Alexa's throat. This wasn't going as she expected. "What about the quest?"

"Moira has decreed that it begins this week."

"But . . ."

His eyes grew steely. "You question Fate?"

When Alexa shook her head, Elder Warrin strode to the back of the church and out the door with Dharien close behind. The others trailed down the aisle and lingered outside. Their outraged voices drifted into the church. Alexa had set off a maelstrom, but it didn't go as she'd hoped.

The bewildered questers milled around at the front of the church, unblessed.

Merindah whispered, "You could have waited until we were blessed. Your plan to save us had better work, Alexa. It better work."

The others murmured in agreement as they drifted out the front door to join their parents. A chill spread from Alexa's head to her toes, but she wasn't done. Now, she had to find the fortune-teller.

Once outside, Alexa spied her mother in tears and rushed to her side. "It'll be all right, Mother. Go home. I need to stay here and talk to Melina Odella."

Alexa's father appeared behind her mother. His voice cracked. "Where's Zander? Cobie said you know."

"He's in the forest. He'll return for the quest." It wasn't wise, but she added, "Father." When her mother clasped her hands to her heart, Alexa added. "Zander and I know we're twins."

Her father caught her mother as she collapsed.

"No, you cannot know."

Alexa reached out, and then dropped her hand. She should have waited. When she glimpsed Melina Odella leaving the side door of the church, Alexa whispered, "I'm sorry, Mother. I have to talk to the fortune-teller." Regret chased her as Alexa rushed to catch the one person who could help Zander.

Alexa waved to catch her attention and waited as Melina Odella strode to meet her.

She grabbed Alexa's arm. "What have you done?"

Pulling her arm free, Alexa straightened her shoulders. "I spoke the truth."

"You don't know the truth," the fortune-teller spat.

"I know enough of it."

Melina Odella slapped her.

Alexa's cheek stung, but she smiled. "Melina Odella?"

The fortune-teller glowered.

"Your secret is out. Dharien no longer controls you. Zander doesn't have to die in the quest." When Melina Odella paled, hope swelled in Alexa's chest. "Will you help him?"

"Why should I?"

"Because Zander didn't do anything wrong."

Confusion washed across the fortune-teller's face. She pulled Zander's heart necklace over her head from where it lay under her scarf. "This belongs to him. It's small, but holds strong magic."

Tucking the token into her bag, Alexa asked, "Dharien can't blackmail you now. Can the quest wait?"

Melina Odella shook her head. "Chanse and I both vowed Moira requested the change. The elders would imprison us for lying."

"And what of Moira? Are you not afraid of what she will do?"

The fortune-teller pursed her lips. "I know what the village will do. I'll take my chances with Moira." She turned to leave, and then stepped back to Alexa. She brushed the cheek she'd slapped and whispered, "I didn't want to steal his tokens. I'll do what I can. I don't want Zander to die."

CHAPTER THIRTY-SEVEN

Two Days until the Quest

Zander

Defender of all. Zander pondered those three words. If Tshilaba was right, and he had no reason to think she wasn't, he held a responsibility for the safety of the questers. Not just himself and Alexa. When Zander searched his heart, he knew it was true. He would sacrifice to save any of them. Even Dharien, as perplexing as that seemed. Did his parents realize when they named him they were giving him such responsibility?

What about Puck's ghost, whom no one else seemed to hear? Zander had listened to his whispers all of his life. Why him? How did Puck expect Zander to unite the tribes after two hundred years of division?

And then there was Moira. Her role in his life confused Zander. He'd once believed she had his best interests in mind, and he'd tried to do right, to please her. But after finding Alexa, he wasn't as sure. Was the curse of the twins because Moira hated them or because twins never followed the rule of questing alone? Either way, with the black panther omen in their bags, he and his twin were in trouble.

As he thought of her, Moira shimmered in front of him and then faded away. Zander was uncertain if she was real or if he'd imagined her, but a flat black and white stone the size of his palm appeared at his feet. He held it for a long while, unsure whether it was token or omen, turning it round and round before he added it to the others.

As night fell, he curled into a ball with Shadow next to him and slept next to the oak tree. In the morning, he would return to the village. He needed to see Father before the quest.

After a breakfast of wild strawberries and golden chanterelle mushrooms, Zander hiked out of the forest with a lighter heart than he'd had in a very long time. As the noon bells rang, Zander reached his house but found it empty. While he and Shadow waited inside the simple room he'd known as home, memories came unbidden.

Father hadn't always been a drunk, and when Zander was younger, he'd acted almost cheerful. It was as he grew older, Father spent more and more time slumped over a cup of mead.

Sitting at the table reminded him of when Father taught him his letters and numbers. He'd been pleased when Zander learned quickly. He recalled his father showing him how to pull a bow, and the first time they'd hunted. He was five, but he'd shot a rabbit on his second try. Father had told Zander he'd grow to be a great hunter, and Zander had worked hard to prove it true.

He never went to bed hungry like Odo and Kaiya. Zander remembered the good moments he'd buried beneath the images of his father's drinking and bad temper. He welcomed the memories into his being like a dry sponge draws water.

After an hour of waiting, Zander hiked to the market in search of Alexa. He stood outside the bakery windows, transfixed. Alexa sat next to their mother and their resemblance made him feel soft inside. Father sat across from them with his broad back to Zander. He'd cut his hair and combed it behind his ears. The family he'd dreamed of drew Zander closer to the window, and when his mother glanced up, her hands flew to her mouth.

Alexa's grin split her face. She darted out the door and tugged him inside.

Once inside, his mother folded him into a cautious hug. The scents of vanilla, sugar, and cinnamon surrounded Zander as they embraced. He'd ached for his mother's touch as long as he could remember.

As they sat together as a family for the first time in fourteen years, Zander listened to Alexa's animated stories as she laughed with their father and showed off an embroidery cloth. Father looked impressed as stitched doves circled an ash tree and the scene moved.

Questions rolled around in Zander's head. It might be his last chance to find the answers. He cleared his throat and when the other three looked up, he said, "I know about the curse of the twins, but why did you think separating us would work?"

His mother blanched, but set her lips as if determined. "After your second birthday, we decided you were still too young to re-member, so we made a plan to raise you apart. We pleaded with the other villagers to keep our secret, although Melina Odella warned us Moira would do as she pleased." Her eyes filled with tears. "It was the only thing we could think of. We had to try something. I couldn't bear the thought of losing one of you."

"So Zander and I lost fourteen years of our lives together?" Alexa glared. "And now we might still lose our future."

Father moved to put his arm around Alexa's shoulder. "We did what we believed was best. We didn't think you'd discover the secret. If you'd both survived the quest, we would have told you when you returned. We agreed the risk was worth the pain."

She leaned into his hug. "And if only one of us returned, we never would have known?"

Father shook his head, and Alexa burst into tears.

Zander blinked back his own tears. When Alexa's crying turned to sniffles, he asked another question. "Did Elder Warrin know when he paid my way out of jail that I might not live to repay him?"

"Of course not," his father said. "Unless it involves money, the elders are oblivious to what happens in the village—even Elder Warrin."

After they sat in silence for a few minutes, Father rubbed the back of his neck. "Any other questions?"

Alexa's eyes sparkled. "I have something I've wondered about since Zander and I found out we were twins." A small smile tugged at her lips. "Who's older? Me or Zander?"

Leave it to Alexa to ask that question.

Father laughed. "You came first. We didn't know there was a second baby, although I think the midwife suspected it. She didn't act surprised when Lark's contractions started again and a few minutes later, Zander came."

"I knew it! I knew I was the oldest."

Zander leaned across the table and patted Alexa's arm.

"I'm bigger."

"Sibling rivalry." Father turned to Mother. "See what we missed?"

They laughed together, but Zander couldn't help noticing Mother's worried glances at him. He smiled to reassure her, but unease ate at him. As much as he'd wanted a family, he longed for the silence of the forest, where his feelings were clear and not the jumbled mess that threatened his calm.

When it grew late, Zander stood. "I'm going home. It's an important day tomorrow."

Father clasped his shoulder. "This is our home now, Son. We'll sleep here."

His mother's voice cracked as she whispered, "I have a room for you." She kissed his cheek and searched his eyes. "Promise me, Zander, you'll follow the rules of the quest. You and Alexa need to stay away from each other."

Zander gulped to swallow his rising panic. How could he promise? Instead, he said, "I'll do what's right to see we both survive."

She accepted his answer and led him up the stairs to a small room at the end of the hall. A real bed, not a sleeping mat, sat in the middle with a clean comforter tucked over a fluffy pillow. After he changed into the nightclothes folded at the end of the bed, a knock startled him.

Father stood at the door fiddling with his hands. "Your mother and I never should have broken our family for the quest, but you need to understand. She was terrified of the curse. I couldn't reason with her; and finally, you and I moved to the mud hut. I knew we couldn't cheat Fate, and I was right. You were bound to find each other."

"Is the curse real?" Zander whispered. "We can't escape it?"

"I don't believe in any curse, but this I know. Your mother will be devastated if you don't both survive. You'll be fine. You have experience in being alone in the gulch, but your sister—Alexa has little knowledge of the dangers."

Father didn't know how wrong he was. Zander had experience, but almost no tokens.

"Son, whatever it takes, promise me you'll bring Alexa home."

That was a promise Zander could make.

"I will, Father. I promise."

But the hard question was—would Alexa be safer with his help or without it? And would he have to lose Shadow to save her?

CHAPTER THIRTY-EIGHT
Quest Day One

Alexa

Alexa woke as the sun peeked through the curtains and warmed her face. Fiona jumped across the bed and tumbled head over paws to the floor. Alexa slid out of her covers and cuddled her patron. One tear rolled down her cheek.

The quest began at noon.

"I'll try my best not to call for you." She sniffed in Fiona's neck. "I don't want to lose you." But it would be worse to lose Zander.

Her family risked being torn apart because of Moira's test. After she dressed, she pinned the embroidery under her tunic and slipped her bag of tokens and omens over her head. She fished out the black panther and brooded over the memory of how she had earned it.

Cheating.

Did she cheat with her plan to bring the questers together? That was the unanswered question. Didn't the priest and fortune-teller cheat when they changed the quest? And didn't Dharien cheat when he had Zander's tokens stolen? She needed answers, but none were forthcoming. Moira had better be prepared to explain when she came to Alexa after the quest.

She wandered into the kitchen, led by whiffs of apple bread and something spicy. She found Zander, hunched over the table as he talked with their mother. Across from him, Mother's plate of food remained untouched, although she pushed at the sausage links and poached egg with a slice of oat bread.

As Alexa entered, they stopped talking. Zander's forced smile didn't reach his eyes, but the worry on his wrinkled forehead did. Maybe he shared her dark thoughts of the panther omen.

She squeezed Zander's shoulder as she settled on the bench next to him. "Today's the day." Dread settled in a lump in her stomach.

Father placed a plate in front of her. "Eat. This will be your last hot breakfast before the quest ends."

As she picked up a sausage, she peeked at the father she didn't know. His strong arms triggered a hazy memory of laughter as he carried her upside down through the kitchen. She'd been cheated out of years of memories because of her parents' fears, and now she and Zander still might not survive.

"Father? The Raskan fortune-teller told Zander his name means defender of all, but she wouldn't tell me what mine means."

Father sat back and smiled at Mother. "Your names are a split of one name. Alexa plus Zander becomes Alexander. Together they're whole. Together they mean defender of all."

Stunned, Alexa felt for the embroidered cloth she wore hidden. It was the sign she needed. She would cheat Fate and save them all.

Mother touched her arm. "But you must stay apart during the quest. In the past, it has always been because one twin saves the other. If you quest alone, you'll be fine."

As she scanned Zander's face, Alexa lied. "Yes, that's what we'll do. Don't worry, Mother. We'll both return." Zander's face darkened when she covered the snake omen that materialized next to her plate.

She leaned forward to hear their father's quiet voice. "You know how to use your tokens? No omens you can't fight?"

Alexa snuck a glance at Shadow. He *could* fight a panther. She shook her head along with Zander and covered a second snake omen as Zander did the same. She was thankful their parents' eyes were on each other's and didn't notice.

Zander stood. "Alexa, it's time to go."

She kissed her mother's cheek and hesitated before running to her father. He crushed her to his chest. "Daughter of mine," he whispered. "Zander will keep you safe."

Father was wrong. She would save Zander. And apparently, based on her name, she'd save the others as well.

CHAPTER THIRTY-NINE

Zander

Zander grabbed Alexa's hand. "Ready?" he whispered. Her energy, strong and determined, filled him with hope. Mother wanted them to fight alone, but Father asked him to work with Alexa. He had a choice to make, and he wasn't sure of his decision. Would he help or hinder Alexa if he fought beside her?

What their parents didn't understand was that it was more than their name that bound them. Only together were he and Alexa whole. The day with the night. The curse was the bond that called them together like a lodestone pulled at iron. Whatever Mother and Father wanted, Zander wasn't at all sure it would be possible to stay away from Alexa in the quest.

As they approached the church, doubt squeezed Zander's heart. He clutched at his bag of tokens where it hung securely at his neck. If Alexa's plan of fighting together didn't work, how would he defeat his omens? He touched the heart token Alexa had returned to him from the fortune-teller. She'd offered help, but Melina Odella had betrayed him. Could he trust her?

Zander walked to the church for the first time since learning Melina Odella had stolen his tokens. His steps slowed the closer they came.

"I know you're nervous, but Melina Odella promised to help," Alexa said. She clenched her jaw as Dharien strode past them and disappeared through the church door. "Moira will surely punish him when he uses your tokens. I hope he dies."

"No, Alexa, don't say that." Zander stopped and pulled her to stand in front of him.

"Please? Forget about Dharien. He's questing alone."

Alexa nodded, but Zander could feel her hatred. "You need a clear head during the quest. Don't let anger cloud your judgment. I learned during my time in the forest that hate holds you down."

Together they walked into the church. Zander didn't want to hear Melina Odella's lies. They weren't ready for the quest. None of them. If they had been given the remaining six weeks before the quest, they could have learned from their mistakes and then earned more tokens than omens.

Zander pulled at Alexa's hand.

"Is this right? Should we work together?"

"It's the only way."

His shoulders relaxed. She was right. They had to fight in the quest as one. When they entered the classroom, Melina Odella stood with the students. The priest was missing.

Melina Odella recited their instructions. "After the noon meal, you will be led to your entry point into the forest. Today, you search for shelter, food, and water. At dawn, Moira will send the omens; and over the next three days, you'll fight to prove your worthiness. You'll have a respite from the omens once the sun sets, but you can call on your tokens at any time. Use them wisely. Above all else, remain calm." She glanced away. "What happens now is in the hands of Fate."

Zander cleared his throat. "Do we really have any control, or has Moira already decided who lives and who dies?"

He caught the doubt in Melina Odella's eyes as she replied, "Your choices determine your fate." She waved her hands toward the door. "You are dismissed for the communal meal at the Quinary. Good luck on your quest."

Frightened faces filed from the room. Merindah clutched her prayer beads. Kaiya looked over her shoulder with wide eyes as she followed Odo.

Alexa closed the door. Zander crossed his arms over his chest as the fortune-teller paced the room. "Where's the priest?"

"He's in seclusion. He won't have anything more to do with this quest."

"And what of you? What role will you play?"

Melina Odella stepped in front of him, her face twisted. "Zander, I'm sorry. I know it doesn't mean much to you now." He shook his head. "I've recalled the times you earned tokens, and I didn't give them. You had so many I didn't think you needed more."

"I didn't until you stole mine."

Melina Odella shoved a bag at him. "Here."

Alexa reached for the pouch and poured the tokens into her palm. She squinted, confused. "So few? You told me you'd help him."

"It's all I can do." Melina Odella bit her lip. "Is it true you both earned a black panther?"

"It's true. I have a mountain lion token that will help." Zander glanced at his twin. "We'll figure out something for Alexa's." Something that didn't involve Shadow.

Melina Odella gasped. "You can't work together in the quest. Remember the twin curse."

"You've given us no choice." Alexa glared at her. "Because of you, Zander doesn't have the tokens he needs."

"You can't break the rules without consequence."

"You didn't have any trouble changing the quest when it benefitted you."

Melina Odella flushed. "Dharien gave me no choice."

Zander stepped between Alexa and the fortune-teller. "There's always a choice. Alexa and I will deal with ours during the quest. How will you live with yours, Melina Odella?"

She backed away and covered her face. "It's the priest who suffers now."

The anguish in her words overwhelmed Zander. Knowing Father Chanse loved Melina Odella made him feel sorry for her. "Melina Odella?" He pulled his tunic down to reveal the red heart token hanging against his chest. "Thanks for returning it."

Taking Alexa's hand, Zander stepped out the door. They strolled to the Quinary, in no hurry to join their parents. This might be the last time they'd be alone.

Zander walked past the food tables, laden with dishes hastily prepared. Usually there was more time between the May Day Festival and the Questing Celebration. He and Alexa found their parents sitting with Merindah's family. Without the priest, the noon meal began unblessed.

Mother whispered to Father, "The questers weren't blessed by the priest and now the meal?"

He didn't care about the lack of blessing, but Zander picked at the smoked pork on his plate, unable to find his appetite. For the families without questers, it was an excuse to celebrate, and the noisy chatter under the pavilion grated at his nerves. The fear his mother couldn't hide made him feel guilty. What if Alexa's plan didn't work? If he returned without his twin, could Mother forgive him? And if he died, his last thought would be of her grief.

As the meal ended, thirteen villagers representing the guilds assembled in a line. Mother flinched, and Father lumbered to his feet. Zander followed Alexa as she hugged them.

Amid tears, his mother clasped him to her chest. "Come back to me, my Son."

His father held Zander's shoulders at arm's length. "Follow your heart, Zander." He leaned in to whisper, "Protect your sister."

Elder Warrin interrupted. "Zander? I want to wish you well in the quest. When you return, I hope you'll consider working for me. I'm sure Moira will reward your gift for hunting."

"Thank you, Sir. If I survive, perhaps Moira will allow it."

A chuckle rumbled low in Elder Warrin's throat. "You'll return. I have confidence in you."

The elder's arrogance didn't sit well with Zander. "Sir, did you know Alexa is my twin?"

The color drained from the man's face. "I . . . I didn't know."

"So, my return is not guaranteed." Zander felt a perverse satisfaction at the elder's discomfort.

He knelt and pressed his face into Shadow's fur. "Father? You'll take care of him while I'm gone?" When Father nodded, Zander continued, "If I don't return, Greydon agreed to take him." He held Shadow's face between his hands and whispered, "Stay, boy. I'll be back." He choked back a sob.

Zander turned to the metalsmith waiting to guide him to his entry place into the forest. "I'm ready." The metallic tang of copper intermingled with the sweat soaking the man's tunic as he shifted back and forth, unused to ceremony. The other questers looked anxious as they followed the flags of the other guilds toward the forest. Even Dharien's eyes had lost their defiance as he trudged behind the flag of the healers.

Alexa flew to Zander and grabbed him. "Find me," she whispered before she bolted back to follow the weavers guild flag.

Zander jerked back at the conviction in her eyes to save him, even at the cost of her own life. His stomach clenched. Once again, he questioned if finding her was best.

When he glanced to the heavens, Zander gasped as Moira stood at a wheel of fortune. Two words blazed in red across the wooden circle. Live. Die. He gawked as she spun the wheel, but the scene faded from his vision before the wheel stopped.

CHAPTER FORTY

Alexa

As soon as Alexa left the sight of her guide, she pulled the embroidery from under her tunic. As she studied the quester's positions, Paal's likeness headed toward her own. Merindah hesitated, as if unsure.

Zander had entered the gulch at the far end from her and moved quickly down the side and in the opposite direction. Dharien followed Zander. The rest of the questers moved uncertainly, one way and then turning in another direction.

She hiked toward Paal to close the gap between them. Together they could find Merindah. He stumbled through a tangle of bushes as birds startled and flew to the top of a hickory tree, loud in their protest at being disturbed.

"Hoy, Paal! I'm here!"

His easy smile boosted her spirits.

"Your plan's working. Eleven to go!"

She touched Merindah on the cloth. "She's next."

Paal pointed at Zander's figure with Dharien not far behind. "What's he doing?"

"I hope he knows. He's not heading for the tree."

When they reached Merindah, Cobie walked next to her. On the cloth, Odo and Kaiya moved together, but going the wrong way. The other five slowly headed toward the tree from different directions. Zander and Dharien still traveled away from the tree. What was her twin thinking?

"Let's find the tree and then see who needs help," Cobie said.

As they searched for the gathering place, they came across three bows and two of the knives Alexa had stitched on the cloth. Paal tested the bows. As he pulled on the strings each one snapped in half. Cobie threw a knife and gasped as the metal crumbled when it hit his target.

Alexa mumbled, "Forget them. Let's keep going."

They stopped at a pond with black and undrinkable water. Alexa sulked as she clutched the cloth. The stitched ponds darkened, one by one.

Merindah folded her arms over her chest. "I told you cheating was wrong. Something bad is going to happen because of your embroidery."

"We're still stronger if we work together."

"That's not how the quest is designed. It's supposed to test us. I'm completing the quest on my own." Merindah turned to leave.

Reaching for her arm, Alexa begged, "Please don't go. Come with us for tonight. Please, Merindah?"

"No. I won't risk my life by cheating."

"Melina Odella said only six returned the last time there were thirteen questers."

When Merindah hesitated, Alexa grabbed her hand. "Stay with us tonight. Decide in the morning if you want to leave the group."

"I'll stay tonight. But tomorrow I *will* go alone."

When they reached the tree, the yellow ribbons had turned brown and fluttered dejectedly from the branches. Bindi and Yarra sat solemnly at the base. Alexa spread out the embroidery next to them. Odo and Kaiya still wandered one direction and then another. Zander and Dharien headed deeper into the gulch away from the tree. Tarni, Jarl, and Waku had teamed up and slowly made their way to the group.

Alexa pointed at the cloth. "We need to go after Odo and Kaiya. They look lost."

Paal and Cobie stepped forward. Their voices rang out as one. "I'll go with you."

She scanned their faces, both earnest to help. "Paal? Come with me. Cobie, will you stay and help the others?"

Both the boys nodded, although Cobie's shoulders slumped.

The first step in getting all the questers together was proving more difficult than Alexa expected. Merindah's refusal felt like a slap in her face, although Alexa shouldn't have been surprised. Merindah could be stubborn about what she believed was right and wrong. More troubling was Zander heading away from the meeting tree with Dharien close behind.

Alexa remembered Dharien's hatred the day he threatened the fortune-teller. His terse words haunted her. He'd said, "I want Zander to die."

CHAPTER FORTY-ONE

Zander

Zander entered the forest, unsure if he would join Alexa. Dharien trailed twenty yards behind. The thief had his tokens, what more did he want? Without betraying he'd seen him, Zander hiked away from where the group planned to meet. Zander could lose Dharien if he wanted, but first he needed to know Dharien's intentions, and he didn't want to lead him to Alexa. Let him fight alone.

He had a sudden thought. This could be his chance to reclaim his tokens. He'd lead Dharien away from the others and then loop around behind him. They were evenly matched, but if he surprised Dharien, he could do it. He could get his tokens back, and then he wouldn't have to worry about being a danger to Alexa. He kept his pace steady and let Dharien shadow him. The diversion gave him time to think. To join Alexa or not. He had to decide soon. If the cage she'd stitched didn't hold the panthers—and Zander didn't think it would—Alexa couldn't fight one alone. His mountain lion token might kill one panther, but not two.

According to the curse, if they worked together, one of them would die. If he joined her, he couldn't be certain he would protect her. The determination he'd seen in her to save him made Zander afraid she'd do something stupid. It should be him, not Alexa, who paid for his mistake of losing his tokens. If he'd heeded Tshilaba's warning this never would have happened.

If they hadn't earned the panthers, the decision would be easy. Greydon had told Zander the omens started with the easier ones. Zander hoped he could wait one day before he made a decision.

He didn't trust the embroidery. He'd tried one of the bows she'd stitched. When he'd shot an arrow, it didn't fly true. And he'd passed a pond with brackish water that didn't belong. He headed toward the stitched panthers. No omens could appear until tomorrow. He'd be safe.

The panthers' low growls made him move cautiously before he spotted the cage. The bars held as the snarling animals threw themselves at the sides. What would happen tomorrow when the quest truly began? He hiked away from the panthers, away from the gathering tree while he considered his choices.

And still, Dharien shadowed him.

An hour later, Zander was no closer to a decision. Would it be best to join Alexa or fight on his own? If he chose to go alone, the outcome looked bleak unless he could get his tokens back. It was time to make his move.

He stopped abruptly. While lost in his thoughts, he hadn't noticed that Dharien was no longer following him.

By not paying attention, he'd blown any chance to survive the quest.

CHAPTER FORTY-TWO

Alexa

Frustration with the peasant cousins caused Alexa to snap. "Why don't they stay still? We'll never find them if they keep changing directions."

"Maybe they don't want us to find them."

She stopped so abruptly Paal bumped into her.

"You think they don't want to join us?"

Paal spread out his hands. "We don't know if your plan will work."

Alexa flattened the embroidery on the ground. She gasped as Zander stopped at the cage of panthers. Odo and Kaiya had stopped moving, and the rest of the questers gathered at the tree.

Disappointed that the bows, knives, and ponds she'd stitched had proven useless, she worried over her plan to control the quest. She hadn't needed to assume responsibility for the others. Zander was the one she cared about.

Standing with his back to her, Paal awaited her decision. Alexa glanced at the cloth and fear rose from her gut, sticking in a knot at her throat. Dharien knelt at the cage and the panthers raced free. Why would he release them? Did he know they were omens for Zander and her?

"Paal?"

He faced her.

"Did you tell Dharien about the panthers?"

"Uh, yes. I didn't know it was a secret."

She pointed to the cloth.

The blood drained from his face. "I'm sorry, Alexa. I'm so sorry!"

She recalled her father's words. *Fate can't be cheated.* It became clear what she had to do. "Let's find Odo and Kaiya. Then I have to go to Zander. I have to warn him."

They found the cousins arguing over which direction to go. Relief washed over their faces when they saw Alexa and Paal. As the shadows of dusk settled around their shoulders, the four joined the others at the tree. Their grim faces showed Alexa the fear the questers shared.

Merindah sat under the tree, hands folded in prayer. Her eyes accused Alexa. "This isn't right. We're supposed to be on our own."

"No one said we couldn't work together," Alexa said calmly. "If anyone wants to go it alone, I won't stop you."

Kaiya spoke, "I'm scared. I'm staying."

"I agree," Paal said. "Together we increase our chances. I think we need a leader."

Their eyes turned to Alexa. She lifted her chin. "I'm going after Zander."

"I'll go with you," Paal said.

"No, stay. I'll leave tonight and convince him to join us."

The others murmured their approval of Paal as their leader, but Cobie challenged her. "It's your plan to work together and yet you desert us?"

"I have to find Zander. We have the worst omen to defend against. We need each other."

"Dharien also has a black panther," Cobie said. "I caught him stuffing it in his pocket the last day in class."

Eyes flashing, Alexa retorted, "He must have earned it when he conspired with the fortune-teller to steal Zander's tokens."

Paal asked, "How did you earn yours, Alexa?"

She chose not to answer. She'd earned it by cheating with her favor, and now she planned to save them with her favor. She ignored their suspicious faces. Merindah wasn't the only one worried.

"I'll return tomorrow with Zander."

CHAPTER FORTY-THREE

Quest Day Two

Alexa

It was a cloudy night with not much of a moon as Alexa picked her way through an overgrown trail, trying to follow the embroidery's path to Zander. A tawny owl swooping overhead made her duck. She froze when a rabbit darted across her feet and waited for her heart to slow before she moved again. The forest even smelled different at night—earthy and thick. She regretted not taking Paal's offer to accompany her.

Alexa fished out the star token she'd received from the Raskan girl. "I call upon the star token for a night of light." The dark slid into dusk, bright enough to see her embroidery and guide her feet.

When she'd hiked for so long her legs ached and she stumbled in the near dark, Alexa found a spot under a willow tree. Curled next to the trunk with the branches floating in a veil around her, she felt safe. Dreamless sleep carried her until dew dripped on her face from the slender leaves. Confused at first that she was crying, Alexa wiped her cheeks. Why she was sleeping under a tree?

She slapped at a buzz near her head. A blaze of heat shot through her neck as a hornet sting welted, and real tears filled her eyes. The quest had begun. The hornet would be the least of her challenges.

She checked the embroidery. Zander wasn't far. Her stomach

growled as she trudged the path, but she didn't take time to find breakfast. It wasn't long before screeching peacocks, followed by Zander's swears, led her in the right direction. When he burst through a thicket of evergreen bushes, she couldn't help but giggle. Iridescent blue peacocks surrounded him, their fancy tails spread wide, pecking at his feet and pants. He glared over the birds as he hopped away from their sharp beaks.

His dark look faded. "Alexa, your neck!"

Before she could respond, Dharien crashed into the clearing, chased by his own cluster of peacocks. Jumping over a bird, he yelled, "What token do I use?"

Grimacing at the peacocks surrounding him, Zander kicked at the closest fowl. "If you share, I'll tell you. I know you have plenty."

When Dharien nodded, Zander said, "Throw out sparrows. One for each of the peacocks."

After struggling to open his pouch Dharien flung out the tokens. The tiny trinkets transformed into twittering sparrows that darted back and forth to peck at the large birds' heads. The peacocks ran in circles, ducking and squawking until the sparrows chased them into the woods.

Dharien's mouth dropped. "Huh, it worked. I should have paid more attention in class."

Zander searched among the nearby plants until he found a comfrey leaf. He crushed it in his hands, spat on it, and then pressed the paste to Alexa's neck. "Hold it there while I search for breakfast."

Surprised at his knowledge, Alexa sighed as the poultice pulled the fire from the sting. She wondered if he'd found the plants she'd stitched. Maybe her embroidery *would* help.

While she held the glob on her neck, she snuck a peek at Dharien. With so many things she wanted to say to him, Alexa found she couldn't speak. He seemed to have the same problem, opening and closing his mouth before giving up and glaring at her.

They spent several minutes in uneasy silence before Alexa found her voice.

"You have all of Zander's tokens. Would you please give them back to him?"

Dharien turned scarlet and stared at the ground. "I need them."

Anger flooded her, but she heard Zander returning.

She struggled to control her emotion before she spat, "At least give me Shadow's token. He won't help you."

Dharien dug the token out of his bag and held out his hand without looking at her.

Alexa snatched it and hid it in her pocket.

When he joined them, Zander glanced at Dharien and then Alexa before he held up shaggy ink cap mushrooms and tender green dandelion fronds. His water skin bulged.

While Dharien fiddled with his pouch, Zander threw a mushroom at him.

"I'll trade you breakfast for saving me from the peacocks."

Dharien dug out a bread token and held it in his palm. He frowned when it didn't do anything.

Alexa said, "I had to say something when I used my star token."

"Breakfast?" he asked the token, and almost dropped it when it turned into a real loaf of oat bread. He handed it to Zander, who pulled off ragged chunks and stuffed them with mushrooms and greens.

They ate in silence. Alexa had never eaten raw mushrooms, but with the bread and greens, she was surprised at how much she enjoyed them. Or maybe she was really hungry. She turned to Dharien and took a deep breath. She needed some answers. First, she spread out the embroidery cloth between them. Then, she pointed to the broken cage. "Why did you release the panthers?"

Zander glanced up in surprise.

Dharien flushed, but remained silent.

"Cobie said you have a black panther too. I don't know why you hate Zander or me, but we need to work together or none of us will live."

Instead of answering, Dharien asked, "Are you really twins?"

She said softly, "It's true. We only found out ourselves."

Dharien stared at his clasped hands. "I don't hate you, Alexa. I love you."

What would Dharien say if she told him of the potion? It wasn't fair for him to think he loved her. A confession felt past due. "No, you don't. At the Festival of Victoria, I put a love potion in the cider. Paal was supposed to drink it, not you. So you see, you don't really love me."

"You wanted Paal to fall in love with you?"

It was Alexa's turn to blush. "I thought I did. I was wrong to try to force anyone to love me."

"You tricked me?" Dharien stood and backed away as disbelief colored his face. His voice choked. "How could you, Alexa? I didn't release the panthers. I wanted to protect you. When I knelt to check the door, the bars fell apart and they escaped." His wild eyes searched her face. "And I do love you. I've loved you since the first day of class. Before the potion."

Her heart raced at his confession. She'd assumed the worst of him when she'd watched the panthers run free. He didn't truly love her, did he? She cringed at the grimace of betrayal flooding his face before he turned and bolted.

At least she had Shadow's token. It might save Zander's life.

Zander studied Alexa as he chewed his final piece of bread. "That went well." He snorted. "I was going to try to steal my tokens back."

"I should have waited until the quest ended, but I couldn't let him believe a lie any longer."

"You did the right thing."

Alexa stiffened. A pale gray snake with a black zig-zag along its body coiled next to Zander's feet ready to strike. A poisonous adder!

She whispered, "Don't move." Her heart rose to her throat. She couldn't lose Zander now. Saul had died last year from an adder bite. She dug through her bag and held out a mouse and a bird token. "Which one?"

He flicked his eyes toward the mouse, and blanched as she tossed it between him and the hissing snake. After the mouse came to life, it scampered to hide behind Zander. Alexa jumped back and the bird token fell from her hand. As she reached to the ground, the snake lunged.

"No!" Alexa screamed.

Zander jumped to the side, exposing the mouse. The adder struck and the rodent lay on its side. As the snake opened wide jaws to swallow its prey, Zander and Alexa backed away.

Zander lifted his eyebrows. "One down, three to go."

Grimacing, Alexa admitted,

"I have four too. Let's get out of here."

As they walked the trail together, Alexa asked, "Why didn't you come to the tree?"

Zander stopped. "I'm not sure it's a good idea to work together."

"Why? You agreed to the plan."

He searched her eyes. "If one of us has to die, it should be me. I'm the one who lost my tokens."

Alexa grabbed his arm. "No, neither of us has to die. Not if we fight as one."

"But what if there *is* a curse? What then?"

"I don't believe in curses. We'll work together, and we will survive."

By the time they reached the gathering tree, Alexa's cheek throbbed from her second hornet sting. Zander had stepped on a honey locust thorn so long it pierced through his sole and into his heel. He limped the final steps, cursing the priest for giving him so many thorn omens.

As they stepped into the clearing, Odo stood pressed against the tree eyeing an adder coiled at his feet. Paal tossed a bird token into the air and jumped back.

A sparrow hawk materialized and circled above the tree.

Distracted, the snake swayed back and forth eyeing the bird. The hawk folded its wings and dove. It snagged the snake and swooped up and out over the treetops.

Odo slumped to the ground. "That was close. Thanks Paal."

It appeared the questers had battled a few other omens as well. Several had welts from stings. Alexa prepared a comfrey poultice and passed it around.

"Where's Merindah?"

"She muttered prayers half the night." Paal sighed. "When we woke, she'd gone. She has plenty of tokens and not many omens. She'll be all right."

The sting of her best friend's distrust hurt worse than the welt on her cheek, but she nodded. "We talked with Dharien this morning. He's going it alone too."

"Zander!" Kaiya cried out, "On your shoulder!"

Zander's eyes flared as a yellow-tailed scorpion inched toward his neck. The pinchers snapped, and the tail flipped over its back.

This was too much, too soon. Alexa froze. Her tokens fell from her trembling hands as she ripped open her bag.

Kaiya plucked a token from her pouch and tossed it at Zander's chest. The rest of the questers stared in horror as the dove dived toward Zander and snatched the scorpion off his neck. The poisonous stinger whipped out and missed him by a hair.

Kaiya rushed to Zander. "Did it sting you?"

Zander rubbed his neck.

"No, you threw out the token in time. Thanks."

"This is why we need to work together," Alexa choked out. "Zander would have been stung without Kaiya."

Cobie asked, "But what happens when we run out of the tokens we need?"

"Let's play the game as we did in class. We'll make sure we're each prepared for our omens, and then we'll know what we can share." Alexa slid her journal from her bag.

They spent the afternoon strategizing, interrupted by hornets and one snake, easily taken care of with a hawk token. Deep in thought, Alexa ignored the grunt behind her.

"Look out!" Paal called from across the circle.

When she whipped around, she stared into the crazed eyes of a razorback pig, hackles raised, five feet away. It pawed the ground and lowered its snout to charge.

"Use a butterfly," Zander yelled.

Her fingers trembled as she fumbled with her pouch. She held out a butterfly token, wondering how it could possibly vanquish a pig.

"Throw it, Alexa!" Kaiya yelled.

She tossed the token into the air. It fell like dead weight, but before it hit the ground a two-foot body appeared with giant black wings that swooped up and over Alexa's head. It hovered above her until the pig charged. Alexa fell back on her butt. The pig's breath gagged her and she waited for the tusk to tear into her.

In a blur, the butterfly landed on the pig's back and latched on while the pig bucked and squealed. Then it wrapped its wings around the pig and squeezed until the pig lay dead.

"Bravo," Zander said. "That was awesome."

Alexa gaped as the butterfly flew off and disappeared over the treeline. She shook her head in disbelief. "I didn't think it would work." She glanced at the questers encircling her. "How many pig omens and butterfly tokens do we share?" It was time to get to work before any more surprises.

The questers dumped their bags onto the ground and separated them into piles. Odo counted. "Two more pigs than butterflies."

Paal frowned. "What else could we do?"

Scrunching her forehead, Alexa chewed on her thumb. "Could we turn a snake omen against a pig omen?"

"Call for an omen? Instead of waiting for it to appear?" Zander's eyes lit. "It might work."

"We take the risk of both turning on us, but if someone is prepared for the snake omen, we can reduce the danger." Alexa rested her elbows on her knees and steepled her fingers in front of her face. "Let's try it."

Jarl planted his feet and crossed his arms over his muscled chest. "It sounds risky."

Even though her heart thumped, Alexa met his glare. "Anyone else have a better plan?"

No one else did.

CHAPTER FORTY-FOUR

Zander

Zander hid a smile as Alexa took charge. He admired her determination to keep them safe. And she was smart. He never would have considered using an omen against an omen or calling for an omen so they'd be ready.

"Who has a pig?" Alexa called out.

All but Kaiya raised their hand.

"Let's see if this works. Paal, throw yours out. If a pig appears, then Cobie, you throw out a snake omen. Odo, you be ready with a butterfly." She handed Zander a bird token. "Here's a hawk."

He'd be ready to do more if her scheme didn't work. The vibration from the red stone in his pouch confirmed his feelings. He'd protect them.

Alexa motioned to the others. "The rest of you stand behind the tree." She hesitated. "But watch for your omens."

Paal took a deep breath. He tossed the pig omen to the ground and it came to life. Coarse hair bristled along the back and sharp tusks extended from the flat nose. It swung its head from side to side, ready to charge.

"Cobie, now!"

Cobie flung the omen, but he threw too hard. It landed closer to Zander than to the pig, and an adder coiled in front of him ready to strike. Zander stilled, and silence fell over the group. Blood pounded in his head and sweat dripped down his temples.

Unmoving, he waited.

The pig lunged toward Paal and caught the snake's attention. It struck the pig again and again until the boar fell to the ground twitching. Zander threw the bird omen into the air. He fell to his knees in relief as a hawk swooped in and snatched the snake. That was too close.

The questers gaped at the dead pig, a reminder it could have been any one of them. They each had earned at least one snake omen.

Zander struggled to speak. "Well done. We know it works. Now let's revise our strategy."

Together, they examined omens, discussed scenarios, and challenged each other's ideas. Zander was proud of how they worked together. Occasionally, someone's temper flared, but Kaiya skillfully negotiated them to a peaceful solution.

By nightfall, they had an organized plan they agreed on. At Alexa's suggestion they were going to specialize. She would carry the butterfly tokens, and Paal would carry the bird tokens. Each quester knew exactly how to use the tokens they carried. The system made them dependant on each other.

No one spoke of the panthers. Zander hoped his mountain lion token would handle one of them, but he didn't yet have a plan for the second. He still had no idea how to use the two stones in his pouch, the horse, or the heart he wore around his neck. He had to trust he'd know how to use them when the moment arrived.

Mentally exhausted but happy to have survived the first day of the quest, the goup shared a meal of mushrooms, fiddlehead ferns, and peppermint-infused water. Zander wished he could have found a way to roast the pig, but without a knife or a fire, it proved impossible. He and Cobie dragged the carcass far from the tree in case it attracted predators.

When they returned, Zander studied the scared faces of the other questers. Nightfall brought a reprieve from the challenges, but there were other dangers in the forest besides their omens. A coyote or mountain lion could appear and no token would vanquish a non-omen. He examined the oak towering over him. Thick branches spread out horizontally. He'd slept in a tree once when he was thirteen and run away from one of his father's drunken tirades. They'd be safe there.

"Let's sleep in the tree."

Bewilderment, astonishment, and undisguised disgust swept across the faces of the questers. Zander almost laughed.

Kaiya broke the tension. "The quest is about testing us. I've never slept in a tree. It might be fun." She smiled at Zander. "Give me a hand?"

First Kaiya and then Alexa climbed into the tree and found wide limbs.

"Don't go too high, in case, you know, you fall?" Zander said when Cobie scampered above Alexa.

The rest followed as Paal helped Zander boost them to the first branch. A bolt of lightning flashed across the sky and thunder rumbled above them. Eleven teens in a tall tree might be a mistake. As a light rain began falling, the lightning moved on to the east. They'd be uncomfortable, but safe from a strike.

"I'm too big to sleep in a tree," Jarl grumbled.

Zander shrugged. "You don't have to, if you'd rather stay here by yourself."

Jarl shook his head and settled on the bottom branch. Paal climbed up next and found a spot near Alexa.

Rain filtered through the leaves as Zander grasped a lower limb. His foot slipped on the wet bark, and his head slammed against the trunk. He half-fell, half-climbed back down and parked at the base of the tree.

"Zander?" Alexa called to him. "Are you hurt?"

"I'll be all right." Dizzy and feeling vulnerable, he decided to keep watch. In the dark, the meaning of his name weighed on him. Defender of all.

As Zander settled against the tree, an eerie moan drifted across the lower gulch, following tendrils of swirling fog. Puck whispered the names of the questers, one by one.

Branches groaned as the young people struggled to sit.

"Is that you, Zander?" Paal called down.

Zander laughed. At last, someone else heard Puck. "Not me. It's our ghost of the gulch."

"Questers, unite the tribes."

Alexa whispered, "What does he mean?"

"Save the village."

"Is he crazed?" Cobie asked.

"Complete my task." The voice faded off as if content he'd made contact.

"That was creepy," Kaiya said. "How do you stand hearing him, Zander?"

"I usually ignore him. He's just a ghost."

A few leaves drifted down on Zander as the others got comfortable again. Zander had a feeling that sleep would come slowly to his spooked companions. As he sat, rain trickled down the trunk and soaked his tunic. Sleep pulled at him, and he was helpless to fight it. He woke on his side with his cheek pressed into the wet grass. His head throbbed, as did his right leg. In the early pink of dawn, he spied a snake coiled around his thigh, its narrow eyes gleaming.

At first, he was too fuzzy to recall who carried the bird tokens and then it hit him. He whispered, "Paal? I need a bird."

Quiet snores replied. Zander would have to wake them all before Paal heard him and by then, the noise would likely make the snake strike.

The fox token might be his only defense. He inched his hand to the pouch at his neck, found the token, and flicked it to the ground. A red fox appeared. The hair on its back bristled as it crouched at Zander's side. When the snake recoiled to strike, the fox snapped at the head and clenched it between sharp teeth. Zander uncoiled the limp body from his leg as the fox tugged it free and then disappeared.

Leaning into the tree, Zander fingered the red heart token. Calm spread through his body even as dizziness washed over him. He wasn't sure if it came from his near miss with the snake or the bump on his head from the night before. He slapped at a buzz near his ear as a hornet stung his cheek.

Before the others woke, Zander left to find comfrey. He returned an hour later with a poultice on his cheek and enough wild strawberries to share for breakfast. Frantic faces greeted him.

Kaiya clasped her hand to her heart. "Where were you?"

"I thought you left." Alexa's red eyes stared at him.

Guilt stabbed at his gut. He hadn't thought they would worry. His head still pounded, but he forced a smile to reassure them. "Hungry?"

Zander wasn't the only one with a sting. He shared the comfrey he'd collected. Pale faces with dark circles under their eyes told him the wet questers did not feel prepared for the second day of challenges.

Neither did he.

CHAPTER FORTY-FIVE

Quest Day Three

Alexa

With the sun struggling to break through leftover storm clouds, the questers huddled in a damp circle. They had bread to go with the strawberries, but Alexa longed for the warm kitchen in the bakery she never thought she'd miss. Fresh mint leaves stuffed in her water skin helped push the sleep-deprived fog from her mind. After Puck's visit, she'd had a hard time falling asleep.

As she chewed the last bite of bread, a thorn pushed into the hand she leaned against. "Ouch." She pulled the thorn out of her palm and rubbed the puncture to stop the bleeding. Annoying, but she had more dangerous omens to worry over. She scanned each tired face surrounding her. "Let's fight all the pig omens today."

Shocked faces stared at her. Odo's swollen eye and Kaiya's bleeding thumb reminded Alexa of the omens they'd already battled. They would recover from those, but an unexpected pig or snake could kill.

Her determination hardened. They *would* survive. All of them. She ignored her gut's reminder of the panthers, hoping they wouldn't show until she and Zander left the others.

Zander draped his arm over her shoulder. "She's right. Let's fight the dangerous omens today."

"What about the panthers?" Cobie asked.

Shrugging, Zander stared at his friend. "I think Alexa and I will be fighting those on our own. For now, let's work together."

A beam of sunlight broke through the clouds, and the warmth that spread across her face matched the pride that filled her. Alexa stood tall under Zander's arm. "We can do this."

"I'm tired of getting stung." Kaiya rubbed at a welt on her wrist. "Let's throw out all the turtle tokens."

The questers searched their bags, and soon, ten turtles milled around the tree. They tossed their hornet omens to the ground where turtles twirled in circles as they snapped them up and then wandered off.

Without the buzzing hornets, they could focus on the remaining eight pigs.

"I have an idea." Alexa held up her hands. "Why don't we climb the tree and throw out the omens? Then we'll be safe if we make mistakes."

Zander grinned and warmth flooded her. They would do this together. The quest wasn't so hard after all. Her happiness overrode the prickle in her gut.

"Yes! That's a brilliant idea." Paal headed for the tree. "Let's get up there before any pigs show up."

Jarl and Zander boosted the others into the tree where they scrambled for places along the branches. When they were all in place, Zander pulled himself up to sit next to Alexa. "What's next?"

"Pull out your pig omens. We'll . . ." The sound of raindrops plopping on the leaves interrupted Alexa, but it wasn't raining. Something soft fell on her head and began crawling through her hair.

"Ugh, a spider fell on my arm," Cobie hollered.

Kaiya screamed. "They're all over me!"

Spiders covered Alexa's arms. "Get out of the tree! They're everywhere." She scooted for the trunk while brushing off the creatures.

Thorns sprouted from the wood and stabbed her palms. Blood oozed from the punctures.

"Stars! Moira's punishing us for cheating," Paal yelled. "Throw out all the sparrow tokens."

Alexa opened her pouch and screamed when a spider scuttled out. She knocked it away and grabbed the tokens. As scores of tiny tokens became birds, the sparrows darted between the branches snatching spiders.

Jarl dropped to the ground with a thud. "Jump," he shouted to Bindi and Tarni. "I'll catch you." He yanked a thorn from his hand just before Bindi dropped. He caught her and quickly set her down as Tarni and then Yarra fell one after the other.

Zander jumped down next to him and together they helped the others out of the tree. Odo thrashed about as he brushed spiders off his head and tried to avoid the diving sparrows. Cobie and Waku calmly picked spiders off the others as they descended from the tree. Sticky blobs of white bird poop peppered their hair and clothes.

"I hate spiders," Paal grumbled. "They're even up my pants legs."

Alexa was the last to drop from the tree. She shuddered at the thorns thrusting out all over the tree. There were still enough crawling spiders to make the branches look alive. The others would never trust her again.

"Move out from under the tree." Zander led them to the clearing. He wiped bird poop off his forehead before he put his hands on his knees and bent over shaking.

Alexa rushed to him. "Are you hurt?"

He shook his head and then burst out laughing.

Alexa stepped back. "This isn't funny."

Cobie snorted and Kaiya giggled. Soon everyone but Alexa and Paal were rolling with laughter.

"I don't see what's funny. I hate spiders." Paal stomped off.

Zander reached out to wipe a white speck off Alexa's cheek. "It's pretty funny."

She struggled not to smile. "I guess hiding in the tree is out."

A grunt from behind the tree sobered their mood. They turned as a razorback focused in on Odo. As it charged, Odo tossed a token in the air above it. An iridescent green butterfly floated down to drape its wings over the pig, inches from Odo.

The questers watched in fascination as the pig squealed and then went limp. A cheer erupted. Another omen defeated.

After two scorpions, a pride of peacocks, and a lengthy discussion, the questers agreed to Alexa's plan. They'd take control and summon the omens, but from the ground this time.

The first time worked like they hoped. The knot in Alexa's stomach released. They could still do this.

When Paal threw the next pig omen to the ground, it startled Cobie and he dropped the snake omen at his side. The snake locked its gaze on Kaiya instead of the pig and couldn't be deterred. Zander threw out a bird token. An owl flapped silently toward the snake until the pig squealed and startled it. The owl changed course and landed in the tree, wide eyes blinking at the scene below.

"Run, Kaiya!" Odo screamed at his cousin.

Kaiya scrambled to get away as the other questers scattered. The snake slithered after Kaiya.

"Throw out another bird," Odo yelled to Zander. He glared at Alexa, "Get rid of the pig."

She tossed a butterfly token at the pig as Zander ran after the snake and dropped a bird token in front of it. Alexa sighed in relief as the hawk snatched the snake, and the butterfly killed the pig.

Odo whipped around to confront Alexa. "This isn't working. Your plan almost killed Kaiya." Jarl and Waku lined up next to Odo.

Zander moved to Alexa and draped his arm over her shoulder. He whispered, "We stand as one."

Bindi, Yarra, and Tarni joined Odo.

Paal rubbed his hands together. "Odo might be right. Kaiya had all the correct tokens until you had us share them."

Betrayal stabbed her gut as Paal moved next to Odo's group and Cobie followed. Doubt filled her, but she held firm to her plan. She turned to Kaiya, who stood alone between the two groups. "I'm sorry. We might need to make some adjustments, but I think this will still work."

"Not for me." Odo shook his head. "And not for my cousin. We'll finish the quest alone."

"You can't. It won't work." Alexa dreaded the reaction to her next words. "The tokens and omens are all mixed up. We don't know which ones belong to which quester."

The others' voices rose in anger as they cried out their displeasure.

"Wait." Kaiya held out her hands.

"I'm the one who almost died."

One by one the questers stopped shouting and turned toward Kaiya.

"We've made mistakes and we've learned from them. I had a close call, but I'm all right because we worked together." She stepped over to stand next to Alexa. "I trust the plan."

Still angry, Odo pointed at Alexa. "If anyone dies, it's your fault."

"That's not fair." Zander looked at the others stone-faced. "We don't know what would have happened if we'd each quested alone. We're the unlucky thirteen. Remember what Melina Odella said about the last group of thirteen?"

Grateful for his support, Alexa took hold of Zander's arm to steady her. "Kaiya's right. I made some mistakes, but I know we can do this if we stick together." She reached out for Kaiya's hand and pulled her close. "If Kaiya can forgive me, can the rest of you?"

"What choice do we have?" Odo grumbled.

Paal broke from the group. "Let's get rid of these pigs."

The others nodded reluctantly and followed Paal to a cluster of bushes.

Alexa pulled her sweaty hair into a ponytail and tied it with a red silk thread. "Let's do it."

Kaiya tossed a pig omen to the ground, but with his back to her, Odo didn't see her and threw out one at the same time. The boars turned to each other, hackles raised.

Before Alexa could toss the butterfly token, a pig charged her. Backing away, she tripped over a turtle. She thudded to the ground and blood flooded her mouth where she bit her lip. The pig grunted over her as if defending its prize from the other boar. With a pig on either side of her and the butterfly tokens in her bag, Alexa curled into a ball.

The stink of pig filled her nose as shrill squeals surrounded her. She cupped her hands over her ears. Zander shouted, but he sounded far away, filtered through the stamping hooves next to her head.

Cobie's voice drifted through her dizziness. "There's a butterfly token on your left side."

As her fingers curled around the token, a pig stomped her hand. Fire radiated up her arm. Wincing, she flung the token over her head.

She heard the swoosh of the wings and squeals from the pig. Paal reached in and dragged her away from the other pig as Cobie slung a snake omen in the air above it. Alexa shuddered as the snake repeatedly struck the pig. As the pig fell, a hawk swooped in and grabbed the writhing snake.

Zander and Paal knelt on each side of her, while Cobie hovered at her feet. Her twin touched her cheek, and she winced.

"Ouch." She licked her swollen lip and tenderly felt her swelling eyelid.

He grimaced. "You'll have a black eye. Let me see your hand."

Trembling, Alexa held out her hand. Angry welts scraped across the top. She flexed her fingers. Nothing felt broken.

"Here, rinse your mouth." Kaiya held out a water skin.

Cobie spread a comfrey and lavender poultice across Alexa's hand and used a strip torn from his tunic to wrap it.

"Do you think you can stand?" Zander's eyes tightened with fear.

Paal and Cobie each took an arm and eased Alexa up. When she put weight on her right leg, she buckled and cried out. "My knee."

Zander helped lower her to the ground and Kaiya lifted her pant leg. The needle Alexa carried in her tunic hem was buried to the eye in the side of her knee.

Nerves made Alexa laugh. "Mother warned me about carrying a needle in my hem."

Zander muttered, "Not so good at listening, are you, big sister?"

CHAPTER FORTY-SIX

Zander

Zander couldn't grasp enough of the needle to pull it out. His fingers would slip off, and each time he felt her pain as if it were his own.

"Odo? Bring me a couple of the longest hairs you can find from the dead pig."

When Odo returned with three coarse hairs, Zander threaded them through the eye of the needle. He touched Alexa's arm. "Close your eyes and take some deep breaths."

He nodded at Paal who sat at Alexa's side. "Grip Paal's hand."

"It's all right if you cry," Paal said as she grabbed for him. "I can tell it hurts."

Alexa shook her head, but tears slid out the corners of her shut eyes.

Zander took a moment to center his own energy. "On three, Alexa. One, two." He pulled on the hairs and to his relief the needle slid out on the first try.

Cobie spread lavender over the hole, but the deep puncture risked infection. She'd been brave—braver than he would have been. With her left hand swollen to twice its normal size and her right eye bloodshot and puffy, Zander worried if she'd be able to travel later. They needed to fight their panther omens away from the group.

After tending his sister's injuries, Zander sent Cobie and Kaiya to search the woods for more herbs while Odo foraged for lunch. Paal hovered over Alexa as she rested against the tree.

Zander couldn't shake the fear he'd felt while Alexa cowered between the pigs. He needed time alone, but he couldn't go far in case an omen appeared. He wound down to the spring and filled their water skins. As he stood underneath a white willow sprouting new leaves, he imagined roots growing from his feet and joining the tree's as it searched for water. Tension flowed from his body into the earth, and calm filled him.

When he opened his eyes, he was refreshed and ready to resume fighting. It only took a minute to rejoin the group.

Cobie and Kaiya had found a few twigs of lavender and mint, and Zander added them to the water. Paal laid two loaves next to the golden chanterelle mushrooms and cow parsley greens Odo had gathered.

As they ate, Alexa reminded them, "Four more pigs."

Paal scowled. "Give me your butterfly tokens. You're done fighting."

Reluctantly, Alexa handed him the bag. Zander held his grin. She was a fighter, his sister.

The first two went as planned, but then an unexpected pig charged Zander, and Cobie wasn't ready with the snake. The tusk gored Zander in the thigh, tearing through his pants and ripping into his flesh. Fire burned through his leg as he fell to the ground and rolled into a ball as the pig butted him. Grunting filled his ears. First Alexa and now himself—was this the curse? Another thrust knocked Zander against the tree, scraping his back and jarring his spine.

Distracted by Paal waving a stick, the pig stilled long enough for Cobie to throw out the snake. It struck three times before the pig collapsed.

Zander huddled next to the tree as he struggled to catch his breath. He glanced up and spied the hissing snake a foot away. The snake sidled closer. Zander had the bird tokens in his bag. It was a definite disadvantage to one person carrying all the tokens.

The snake lunged. Zander dove to the side too late. The fangs struck his chest. As it recoiled to strike again, Zander closed his eyes waiting for the poison to spread through his body. It would kill him as surely as it had killed the pig.

The second blow never came. After a heavy thud, Paal exclaimed, "Got him!" Paal's flushed face glowered. "I hate snakes." The adder lay mangled under a gray rock.

After scrambling to Zander, Alexa pulled at his tunic. "Where did the snake strike?"

He rubbed his chest and started to laugh. As the questers stood in a circle around him, he pulled the heart token from his tunic. Two fang marks dented the wood. "I guess Melina Odella saved me today." He moaned as he tried to stand. "Not so lucky with the pig though."

Kaiya's face crumpled, and Zander hated seeing her upset. He took her hand and pulled her in to sit next to him while Cobie pressed a poultice of lavender and comfrey onto his wound. He tried not to flinch when Odo tied a strip of hemp around his thigh. Odo had torn it from his tunic and after three days in the woods, it wasn't the cleanest. But it was all they had.

"You're going to scar," Kaiya whispered.

He didn't like seeing her worry. "But I'm alive."

"You still have the panther to fight." Her eyes filled with tears.

Zander took her hand to reassure her or maybe to reassure himself. She leaned against him as the others finished with the pig omens.

Odo tossed out a pig. Cobie threw out the snake. After the adder killed the pig it slithered over to Paal, who had his eyes closed as he leaned against a tree.

"Paal," Zander yelled. "Pay attention. Throw out a bird."

Paal grabbed a token and tossed it in the air, but no bird appeared. When it hit the ground, a brown and white retriever came to life and snatched the snake. It took a few seconds before Paal realized what had happened. "No," he shouted. "Not Silk. I didn't mean to use that one." He ran a few steps before he dropped to his knees. "Come back, Silk!"

Each of the questers looked on in shock as the dog and snake disappeared into the woods. It was the first patron used. They all knew it would not return.

"Not Silk. I loved him." Paal banged his fist against the ground. "How could I have been so stupid."

Zander's gut clenched. Dharien had Shadow's token, but he knew the coyote wouldn't help Dharien. Unlike Silk, Shadow was safe. No matter what happened, Zander wouldn't be tempted to use him if he didn't have the token.

There was no time to grieve. A pig materialized next to Odo. Kaiya jumped up and ran over to release a butterfly. They disappeared as another adder showed. Hissing at Yarra, the snake coiled to strike. The only token she carried was her patron's. Her eyes wild, Yarra threw it to the ground. The tiny piglet took the strike intended for Yarra and then vanished with the adder.

Another patron used.

Another quester devastated.

Another punch to Zander's gut.

Kaiya and Waku sat next to a slumped Yarra.

"She was just a baby," Yarra cried out with her head in her hands. "She was so brave. She saved my life."

A final pig charged from the woods. Cobie tossed a snake to the ground. This time Paal was ready with a bird token. They sighed in relief as the hawk carried away the snake.

The questers sagged to the ground surrounding Zander who sat with Kaiya on one side and Alexa on the other.

Paal wiped his eyes and held out the remaining butterfly tokens. "We did it with two left. Alexa was right. Working together was the right thing to do."

Alexa blushed. "Everyone worked hard." She patted Paal's arm.

"We still have a few snakes and scorpions, but we're almost done." Paal stared at Alexa and Zander. "Let us help you with the panthers."

His twin shook her head. "What can you do? We don't know how to fight them. We need to find Dharien. He has a black panther too." She glanced at Zander, but wouldn't meet his eyes.

He didn't want to worry Alexa, but Zander wasn't sure how well either of them could travel. Pig tusks carried their own poisons, and he could feel heat throbbing through his leg. As he tried to stand, he collapsed. Seeing Kaiya's look of panic, he said, "Give me a few minutes."

She crushed lavender and mint into Zander's water skin. "This will help."

As Zander waited for the tea to infuse, he slapped at his cheek. He killed the hornet, but not before it stung his cheek. Where was that turtle?

While she pressed a wet comfrey leaf over the swelling, Kaiya said, "It's not fair. You had all those tokens. You shouldn't be injured. I hate Dharien for stealing yours."

Zander caught her hand. "Don't hate him, Kaiya. It harms you, not him, when you hate."

She blushed, but nodded. "You're right, but it's still not fair."

"Father taught me a long time ago that life's not fair. You know that, Kaiya, or we wouldn't have so many kids in our village who go to bed hungry at night."

"That's why I want to hunt. Before you brought us food, I never thought we had any choices. Now, I know how to help."

"After the quest, I'll show you where it's safe. You can't let the elders catch you." He grinned and out of habit, ran his tongue over his chipped tooth. "I'd like to see the look on the elder's face who catches a girl hunting illegally."

"Drink your tea." Kaiya fluttered her lashes at him. "And who says they'd catch me?"

Zander noticed the smile she tried to hide. He drank the cold tea, spitting out leaves and stems. "Needs honey."

As she touched the sting on his cheek, Kaiya teased him. "I think we'll stay away from bees today."

Together, they watched the others toss out omens and tokens. It was dangerous, but he couldn't help laughing when Paal jumped into a wild rose bush running from a snake and came out with enough thorns stuck in his arm to take care of the rest of his thorn omens. Cobie concocted comfrey poultices for the injuries and rosemary tea for clear thinking.

Caught away from the group, Tarni used her patron canary to defeat a scorpion. She turned a brave face to the group. "I thought she was only good for singing." She collapsed to her knees in tears. Odo comforted her with a hug.

By late afternoon, they'd rid the group of the most dangerous omens. The questers slumped to the ground, retelling the stories of their heroism. Tired, but proud, they mocked their earlier fears. Now, they had a full day to deal with their minor omens and rest. Zander tried to ignore the not-so-subtle glances sent his way. They were all trying to avoid one fact. Alexa and Zander still had the panthers.

When Kaiya changed the bandage on Zander's leg, Alexa's eyes narrowed. "I think it's infected."

Spasms raced from his thigh to his ankle when Zander stood. He grimaced. "Can you travel? We need to leave soon. I don't want those panthers anywhere near here."

She nodded. "Kaiya? Would you make us a tea of rosemary and lavender?" To Zander she muttered, "It's going to be a long night."

CHAPTER FORTY-SEVEN

Zander

Zander leaned against the tree, drawing what strength he could while Alexa checked her embroidery for Merindah. Alexa was obsessed with confirming the safety of her friend.

"Are you sure you need to leave?" Paal paced around the questers. "You don't have to fight the panthers alone."

Ignoring the fire shooting through his thigh, Zander shook his head. "There's nothing you can do. You've fought your omens. These are ours."

Cobie picked at a red sting on his hand. "We have a few tokens left. Maybe they'd help."

Meeting Alexa's eyes, Zander shrugged. "I don't think so. None of the tokens are strong enough."

They left as dusk closed in on the gulch. It would take an hour to hike to Merindah, and then Zander wanted them far from her before they stopped for the night. He hoped the panthers wouldn't appear at dawn. They'd disappeared from the embroidery, so there was no way of knowing where they were.

Zander moved slower than Alexa. It hurt him to look at her black eye even though it was no longer swollen shut. She held her injured hand at her waist. She said it throbbed too much if she didn't.

The moon filtered through the trees throwing shadows across their path. Alexa startled when an owl hooted above them.

"With my injured leg, I'm not much protection, am I?"

"That's why we're in this together, Zander."

Grinning through his pain, Zander flung his arm over her shoulder. "I'm still not used to having a sister. Having a family."

Her smile told him she felt the same.

When they stopped for their third rest, Alexa checked the embroidery. "She's close. Merindah?"

A startled voice replied, "Alexa? I'm here."

Alexa found Merindah resting against an elm tree, arms wrapped around her knees. A long scratch, almost healed, curled across her cheek.

"Merindah? Are you all right?"

"I've fought my omens. I'm fine." Merindah's mouth dropped open. "What happened to you?"

Sliding down to sit next to her friend, Alexa told the story. When she finished, Merindah shook her head. "I told you not to carry your needle in your hem."

"Maybe I'll listen next time." Alexa sought Merindah's eyes. "The rest of the questers have fought their omens. Will you go to them tomorrow? There are dangers in the forest besides our omens."

"What about you and Zander?"

"We still have the panthers."

"Could you believe those butterflies?" Merindah giggled. "I was scared they wouldn't work against a pig."

"I'm proud of you for fighting your omens alone. You're braver than me."

Merindah sobered. "It's the way we're supposed to do it."

Alexa shrugged. "I think once the quest begins we can do it however we want. It worked for the others to fight together."

Noticing Zander's wrapped leg, Merindah asked,

"You're hurt too?"

"Wayward pig gored me."

Digging through her pouch Merindah handed him a jar of ointment. "This should help both of you."

"How did you earn it?" Zander held it up and sniffed as he tried to identify the herbs.

"I helped nurse a friend of my mother's who suffered a bad flu. When I returned home, I found the token on my bed." She pointed to her cheek. "I used it on this thorn scratch, but I don't need it now."

Relief flowed through Zander as he spread the oily cream on his wound. The stabbing fire subsided to a dull ache. He patted the ointment on Alexa's face, hand, and knee.

As the girls exchanged stories, Zander rested with his leg propped up against the tree. He smiled as Merindah giggled at Alexa's account of how they got rid of the pigs.

Merindah turned serious. "You're both injured. How will you fight the panthers?"

That was the question with no answer. Silence stretched between them until Zander stood. "Alexa? We need to leave."

She glanced up and brushed away tears. "We'll figure out a way. We have to."

After hugging them, Merindah said, "I'll see you both on Saturday at the village?"

Alexa's voice shook. "I hope so."

"I'll pray for you."

After Zander finished tying a new bandage on his leg, he said, "You'll make a good nun if Moira allows it."

She blushed. "I don't know what I'll do if she doesn't."

"You'll be all right." He stood and tested his leg.

"See you Saturday."

The ointment had made him stronger already, but his thoughts were far from strong. Would Moira choose the nunnery for

Merindah? What would Fate choose for him if she allowed him to live? Would she allow him to live?

Zander was afraid he'd have to beg Dharien for Shadow's token. That thought worried him the most.

CHAPTER FORTY-EIGHT

Alexa

The quiet of the forest seeped into Alexa's bones. Seeing Merindah had brought out conflicting emotions: happiness that she was safe, and self doubt because her friend had chosen to quest alone. Merindah might have been right when she said they were supposed to complete the quest on their own. Had Alexa wrongly insisted the others follow her plan? Her heart had broken with Paal, Yarra, and Tarni when they lost their patrons. If she hadn't insisted they work together, they might not have had to use them.

She'd had Shadow's token in her hand when the pig gored Zander, and again when the snake struck him. Thankfully, she hadn't needed it.

Zander would never forgive her, but if his life was in danger, she'd use the token. The priest and the fortune-teller had changed the rules and forced them into the quest unprepared. What worried her was why they did it. It was because of Dharien, and that brought her to thoughts she'd tried to ignore.

Zander reached for her. "You're quiet. Are you scared?"

Grateful for his interruption, she answered, "Just thinking."

Squeezing her hand, he said, "I think the purpose of the quest is to make us think. We're tested by the omens, but the real challenge is to our beliefs over who we are and what we want in our life."

She peered at his earnest face, shadowed in the moonlight. "You did that when you went into the gulch alone?"

He nodded. "I realized how my anger clouded my thinking. I wanted to be a Protector, but now I'm not sure. I wanted to leave Father and do something that made me important. Now I have you. I have a family."

Remembering how she'd schemed to make Paal fall in love with her, Alexa closed her eyes. Her dream had also changed since she'd found Zander.

Zander continued. "Those days by myself, I felt the anger I'd pushed away for so many years. I'd blamed it on Father and Dharien. I even blamed Moira. My anger led me to cheat in the tournament because I believed it would solve my problems." His voice softened. "But it made everything worse. I earned the most dangerous omen to fight in the quest, and I worried over the prize money until I couldn't sleep." Several minutes passed before he asked, "Alexa? Why did you cheat for me in the tournament?"

She jerked her hand away. "You had to win. You had to teach Dharien a lesson."

"You didn't trust me to win on my own."

Stumbling on a root, Alexa fell to her knees. Was that why she'd stitched the embroidery and tried to control their fate? Because she didn't trust her brother or herself to survive on their own? Or any of the others? Suddenly she couldn't ignore the awful feeling in her gut that doubled her over.

She whispered, "This is my fault."

Kneeling next to her Zander asked, "Why do you say that?"

"If Dharien hadn't drunk the potion, he wouldn't have been jealous of you. He wouldn't have blackmailed Melina Odella into stealing your tokens and changing the quest."

He rocked back on his heels. "We would still be twins."

"But if I hadn't stitched the embroidery, I wouldn't have gone to your house. I wouldn't have found out until after the quest."

"I would have known. I learned the secret in Father's eyes. I still would have followed him to the bakery that night."

She tried to stop her tears, but when Zander touched her shoulder, they spilled down her cheeks and fell like raindrops into the earth.

"Alexa?" He spoke softly. "Fate gave us our favors early for a reason. It was right we used them, but not to cheat in the wrestling tournament. That was wrong. We deserved the omens. But we don't deserve to die because of it."

"What are we going to do?"

Zander searched her eyes and they answered as one.

"Find Dharien."

CHAPTER FORTY-NINE

Quest Day Four

Zander

They traveled through a dense group of cedar trees, and Zander appreciated the extra light from Alexa's second star token. Around midnight, exhaustion made them stumble. When it was clear they could go no farther, Zander slid to the ground. "We need to rest. Let's sleep for a few hours."

"How's your leg?"

Although he wanted to lie, Alexa needed to know he wasn't at full-strength. "It's starting to throb again. How's your knee?"

"It hurts." She shrugged. "Should we take turns watching?"

"I think we need the sleep." Zander smoothed Merindah's salve on his leg and passed the jar to Alexa.

After she treated her own injuries, Alexa folded the embroidery for a pillow. Her breath evened out and joined the soothing gurgles of the stream behind them.

His twin's words nagged him. Had Alexa set this in motion when she used the potion? He rolled to his back on the cool ground and stretched his injured leg. As he stared at the stars, he thought of Moira. A shooting star streaked across the sky. Good luck? Or was there any such thing as luck? He rubbed the black and white stone between his palms.

He wanted to believe he had control over his life. The quest taught that his actions affected the outcome. He controlled the number of tokens and omens he earned by his behavior, but he'd had no control over Melina Odella stealing them. Tshilaba had warned he had *chosen* to fly toward the blackness. Could he have chosen differently? Or did Moira make him choose the way he did?

Lulled by exhaustion and the stone is his hand, he drifted into sleep.

He and Alexa were wading into a river. She struggled to swim upstream, fighting with the current. He floated away from her, content to let the water take him.

Zander jerked. Dawn filtered through the trees. They'd slept too long. He tried to rise, but the spasm in his leg pulled him to the ground. "Alexa?"

Her eyes fluttered and then opened to gape at him. Wincing, she pushed back her hair with a purple hand. She spread the embroidery on the ground and pointed at Dharien's figure and then their own.

Confused, Zander swore. "We went the wrong way last night. We'll never reach him in time."

"The three of us have to fight the panthers together." Alexa's sleepy eyes widened. "I dreamed it. It's our only chance."

Fumbling with his pouch, Zander held out the tiny black horse. Token or omen? It was time to find out. He tossed it to the ground and shuddered as it formed into a horse the size of Helios.

They would only get to Dharien in time if they rode.

Zander's heartbeat thrashed in his ears. Clutching the wooden heart, he closed his eyes, but the calm eluded him. The green stone Moira had given him for his anger on the first day of magic pulled him deeper into his fear.

He gasped, trying to suck in air as stars flashed in the dark closing around him. Alexa's mouth moved, but the roar in his ears left him deaf to her cries. He couldn't fight his fear.

A beam of sunlight pierced through the trees, and Zander understood. He wasn't meant to fight it.

He had to face it. Everything in his life had brought him to this point. His survival and that of his twin's depended upon him conquering the fear that paralyzed him.

He flinched when the horse approached. Forcing himself to still, Zander drew energy from the earth and pulled it up into his gut where it formed a ball of light. It seeped into his body and filled him with the energy he needed.

The blackness cleared. He nodded at Alexa to reassure her. Facing the horse, Zander gathered his fear. It surged from his belly through his chest and rolled into his outstretched fingers. He shook his hands once to release it.

The horse pawed the ground, impatient.

Zander touched the stallion's flank and then his neck, whispering, murmuring reassurances. A vision of being thrown when he was seven rose unbidden. Zander dismissed it with a flick of his hand.

His fear was that of a child, and he was no longer a child. His tight shoulders relaxed and the knot in his stomach dissolved.

As if the horse understood, he lowered his head and nuzzled Zander's face. Tears broke through the dam Zander had built to hold in his emotions, but he didn't feel weak, and he was not ashamed. A weight flew from his shoulders. He was free.

For a few minutes he stood with the horse. Then he turned to his twin and held out his hand. When she clasped it, her strength flowed into him.

Day and night. Both fortune-tellers had recognized it in them. Opposites, and yet one could not exist without the other.

Their fates were the same. They would live, or die, together. He accepted what Moira would bring, but could Alexa?

He gave Alexa a boost as she pulled herself onto the horse and then settled behind her. They would find Dharien. They would fight together.

CHAPTER FIFTY

Alexa

As Alexa rode in front of Zander, their energy flowed between them. His tender grip belied the power she felt. Together they were whole.

During the night, jumbled images of finding Dharien and fighting black panthers had tormented her dreams. They were attacked and they fell, but the end always faded. She couldn't see the outcome. The other questers would survive. Would Dharien, Zander, and she slake Moira's taste for death?

Two things she knew: she could not survive without her twin at her side and somehow, Dharien would be involved. It had been the three of them from the beginning. Even before the potion, Dharien had hated Zander and liked her. Had Fate arranged to bring the three of them together at the end?

Tshilaba's conflicting advice rolled through her head. Alexa could try to control her destiny or trust Fate. The final card had predicted she was the master of her destiny, but not in the way she was doing it. Tshilaba's words haunted her.

She glanced back at Zander. His brow furrowed, and she sensed his concentration. Was he thinking of his own prediction? They would know soon enough. It was the final day of omens. The panthers would come, and if she survived, she had some questions for Moira. And she wanted answers.

They rode into a clearing. Twenty yards away, Dharien slept propped against a tree. Hornet stings peppered his face and neck. A bandage wrapped one hand, and blood seeped through a pant leg. He groaned in his sleep.

Zander slid from the horse and stumbled when his sore leg hit the ground. He held out his hand for Alexa. When her knee gave way, he caught her. They were in no shape to fight the panthers.

As the horse faded into the trees, Alexa pointed at Dharien. "He looks bad." Her hopes fell. Dharien wouldn't be any help against the panthers. As she stared, a pig materialized in front of him.

"No!" Zander sprinted toward Dharien. "Hoy!" he yelled. "Wake up!"

Dharien opened pain-glazed eyes and his swollen fingers fumbled with his pouch.

The pig lowered its head and charged. Zander leaped to shield Dharien. He landed hard between them.

No, no, no. It wasn't the time for Zander to be a hero. Not for Dharien.

The pig lifted Zander and tossed him aside, but it gave Dharien the time he needed to throw out a butterfly. When the danger was gone, Dharien glared at Zander.

While breathing hard, Zander crawled to the tree and propped himself up next to Dharien. "You owe me."

Dharien scrambled away from him. "I don't owe you anything." His breath became ragged and he wiped at his eyes. "Why would you do that? Why would you risk your life to help me? I hate you." He slapped his hand against the ground. "I hate you!"

Zander shrugged, and Alexa moved in. She handed Zander the jar of salve. "You have a cut on your cheek."

Kneeling next to Dharien, Alexa opened her water skin. "Drink." He gulped until she pulled it away. "Not too much, you'll get sick."

Her warning came too late. Dharien rolled to his hands and

knees and vomited until dry heaves racked him. He wiped his mouth on his sleeve and stared vacantly at Alexa.

"Leave me to die. Moira must want it."

She motioned for Zander to help her lift Dharien to sit against the tree.

"We'll help you," she said softly. "No one has to die."

Zander tried to smear ointment on Dharien's stings, but he slapped his hand away. Zander flipped the salve to Alexa. "You do it."

Alexa removed the bandage on Dharien's hand. She gasped at the pus-filled lesion across his palm.

"What happened?"

"The first day a snake got me before I could throw a bird token. I had to use my patron to save my life." Shame colored his face. "He was brave for a mouse. He stood there and let the snake swallow him whole." Dharien shuddered and turned away, but Alexa saw his tears.

"I deserve to die. I can't go back to the village. Everyone knows how I got Zander's tokens. Father pretended he didn't believe you in church, but he did." He sobbed. "Even Greydon hates me. I'll never live down the shame."

Dharien would never be able to fight his panther in the shape he was in. Alexa had to do something to help him past his despair. She placed her hand on his cheek. "I need you, Dharien." At the look of hope in his eyes, she said, "I had a dream. We have to fight together or none of us will survive." It was only a small lie.

Dharien stared at Alexa as if for the first time and paled when he noticed her face. "You're hurt?"

"No worse than you." She searched his eyes. "Will you help me? If Moira wants us to die, we will, but please, Dharien, I beg you not to give up. Please?"

He looked down and then reached for her hand. When he brought himself to look at her, he seemed to draw from her energy.

"I'd give my life to save you, Alexa. I'll do everything I can to keep you and Zander alive."

She leaned in and kissed his cheek. "Thank you. I'll find some comfrey for your palm." She nodded toward Zander. "You two need to talk."

As Alexa hunted for the herb, she grimaced at the blackened plants she found first. Her embroidery hadn't helped like she expected. She found healthy plants and some berries and hurried back. She spied Zander's head bent toward Dharien, both nodding. Tokens lay on the ground. When a bird cried out behind her, they turned somber eyes her way. She'd wanted them to talk, but this looked more like scheming than a reconciliation.

"What's going on?" she demanded.

Her twin's cheeks flushed, but he met her stare. "We have a plan."

Alexa's gut clenched. She was sure she wasn't going to like it.

CHAPTER FIFTY-ONE

Zander

After Alexa had disappeared into the woods, Zander turned to Dharien. He looked stronger than when they first found him. Whatever Alexa had said to him had helped. "Look. You can hate me all you want, but we need to work together." When Dharien glared at him, Zander asked, "Have you fought your panther?"

Dharien tightened his lips and shook his head.

"You say you love my sister. We need to protect her. Together we have a chance."

After a moment, Dharien's face softened. "Do you think she could ever love me?"

Not in a hundred years, Zander thought, but he said, "Let's keep her alive and worry about love later, huh?"

His face hardened, but Dharien nodded. He opened his pouch and dumped the tokens to the ground. There weren't many left.

Alexa's voice rang out from across the clearing,

"What's going on?"

Zander gritted his teeth. He knew his sister, and she wasn't going to like their plan. "We've agreed to fight your panther first."

"We?" She crossed her arms. "I didn't agree."

Dharien leaned against the tree. "I said I'd help you. We'll protect you."

"Protect me?" She jabbed her finger in Zander's chest. "We've fought our omens together. Together."

Stepping back, Zander tried to reason with her. "And we still will, but yours first."

"No."

"It's yours or Dharien's." Zander rubbed his neck. "I can't control when mine shows."

He hid a smile as Alexa slumped next to the tokens and took out her bag. "What's the plan?"

As they munched on bread and berries, they surveyed the pooled tokens. Zander asked Dharien, "Where's my token for Shadow?" When Dharien looked confused, Zander added, "I don't want it. Keep it hidden." He caught Dharien's glance at Alexa.

Pointing to the golden mountain lion token, Zander said, "We'll use this first. It should take care of Alexa's panther."

She frowned. "We have bird tokens left. If we use two or three for the second panther, they might distract it while we fight."

They explained to Dharien how they'd fought omens with omens, and after he sat quiet for awhile, Dharien said, "We could use my final pig omen and hope it fights the panther. Even if it isn't killed, it would be weakened." He showed them a spear he'd made from a broken limb. "We could make another."

"Two more," Alexa added.

Zander blanched. "You're already injured, and you've never fought. We have."

"You're both injured too. It's going to take three of us." Alexa tilted her head, daring him to disagree.

Glancing sideways at Alexa, Dharien countered. "You could use the rabbit tokens. I have a lot of them and maybe they'd divert the panther." He studied Zander and blushed. "Your tokens."

"We're in this together now." Zander pulled out his stones. "I have these, but no idea how to use them. I called upon the red one when I meditated. Its power may be done. I don't know if the black and white one is a token or an omen. It was given to me as I pondered Moira."

Shaking off his uncertainty, Zander touched Alexa's shoulder. "I promise I'll do everything I can to help us through this. We'll be ready to face the panthers."

"You won't do it alone. Dharien and I will fight beside you." She glanced at Dharien. "Won't we?"

Dharien's shy smile at Alexa flustered Zander, but he gave a quick nod. "Together. Let's prepare." He broke a branch off a dead hawthorn tree. On the splintered side, he used a jagged stone to sharpen the ends for a second spear.

As he finished, Alexa gripped his arm. She pointed across the clearing. Three black panthers stood under the canopy of trees.

"No, no, not this way." Zander stepped in front of Alexa. "Don't be foolish. Let me protect you." He turned to Dharien. "Throw out the pig omen."

The pig faced the panthers and then turned tail to scramble for the woods away from danger.

The panthers held their positions.

Eyes intent on the panthers, Zander whispered, "The pig's not going to help. Get rid of it."

Alexa threw out a butterfly, and it swooped after the pig. She stepped next to Zander.

The panthers paced toward their prey.

Zander and Dharien stood shoulder to shoulder in front of Alexa. The boys brandished their spears as the panthers crept forward. Zander flicked the mountain lion token to his side. The power of the animal took shape beside him, and a low growl erupted from its throat.

"Throw out every token you carry, Alexa."

She stepped next to Dharien and tossed the tokens into the air.

Birds flew at the panthers, and rabbits scurried around their feet. Undeterred, the panthers advanced. The mountain lion met their snarls with its own.

Forcing his shaking body to still, Zander drew deep within the earth for courage. He touched the wooden heart under his tunic that had saved him from the bite of the snake. The familiar calm flooded his body and warred with the adrenaline triggered from the panthers.

Dharien leaned forward with both hands tight around the spear. "Let me protect you, Alexa. Get behind me."

The middle panther crouched to attack. Its hind legs pushed against the ground. It flew into the air. The sleek body soared toward Dharien.

Zander heaved his spear. It sailed into the chest of the panther. The cat crumpled, but momentum carried it on. A giant paw slashed out at Dharien's cheek before the panther slammed him to the ground. Blood oozed from Dharien's face as he struggled to free himself from the weight of the dead animal crushing him.

Alexa screamed as the remaining panthers sprung. The mountain lion lunged, and wrestled one of the panthers to the ground.

The third panther leaped at Zander. The heart tied at his chest wouldn't protect him from those fangs. Zander closed his eyes and accepted his fate, grateful it was him and not Alexa. The curse of the twins would win again.

Alexa's hand flew in front of him and tossed a token to the ground.

"No!" he screamed. Betrayal flooded through him as a flash of gold turned into Shadow.

CHAPTER FIFTY-TWO

Alexa

Alexa tossed Shadow's token to the ground and threw herself in front of Zander. The panther knocked her to the ground, and razor teeth tore into her throat. A blur of gold streaked behind the black body as Shadow slammed into the panther standing over her. Fire exploded through her as the coyote ripped the panther from her body. It seemed she'd used Shadow for nothing.

A heavy lethargy settled over her and the sounds around her grew distant and hollow. The smell of metal, like the coppersmiths, drifted from her chest as a blood oozed across her shoulders. Moira had won. Tears spilled down her temples and soaked her hair. She would have liked more time with Zander, but she didn't regret dying for her twin. She couldn't have lived without him.

"Alexa? Alexa?"

She struggled to respond as peace overtook her. Zander and Dharien knelt over her. Her twin pressed the red stone below the wound. The blood stopped flowing, but it was too late. She closed her eyes against the fear in their faces.

"It's all right, Brother." She tried to smile.

"We used all the tokens." Dharien sobbed as he held her hand. "I'm the one who should die, not you. I promised I'd save you and I can't."

She reached for his bleeding cheek. "Dharien . . . you're hurt."

He bent to hear her broken words. "I'm sorry . . . I tricked you . . . I was wrong . . . to try to control . . ." Coughs racked her. "This is my punishment . . . can you . . . forgive me?"

Broken, Dharien whispered, "I loved you even before the potion. I'll always love you, Alexa."

Turning to Zander, Alexa rasped, "I'm sorry about Shadow. I'm sorry it didn't work." She coughed and blood spurted onto her lips. "Tell our parents I love them, and remember—our hearts are always one, my Brother."

CHAPTER FIFTY-THREE

Zander

What did Alexa say? Their hearts were one? How could he have forgotten? Zander grabbed at the heart token hidden under his tunic and yanked it from the woven reed. As he pressed it to Alexa's heart, her hand gripped his. Dharien laid his hand on top.

Three hands clasped in love.

For one long, terrible moment, nothing happened.

Slowly, the color returned to Alexa's cheeks. Her ragged breathing evened. Zander stared as the wound in her neck closed, leaving a jagged red scar.

She would live. His sister would live! They had survived the quest.

Sitting back on his heels, Zander bowed his head. He had his sister, but he'd lost his best friend. Shadow was more than a patron. Moira had gifted him with a loyal companion. His throat tightened. How could he live without him?

A movement at his side caught his attention.

No!

An adder faced him, ready to strike. Zander sought Alexa's wide eyes and braced for the attack. The force of the blow knocked him flat. Shadow jumped in front of him and snatched the snake before it could strike again.

Zander clutched his chest where the heart token had protected him earlier. Venom surged through his body. He shook his head at Alexa's horrified face. "Moira won't be cheated after all."

"The black and white stone. Zander? Where is it?" She grabbed for his pouch.

In the fog of pain, what was once hidden now became clear. "The stone ties our fates together. Mine and yours. If we use it, we will live or die together."

Alexa dug it from his bag. "It came from Moira?"

He nodded.

Alexa held the stone over his body. "Tshilaba said I could control my life or trust Fate. I haven't done such a good job on my own. Maybe it's time to trust."

"I don't think Moira can be trusted." Zander struggled to push it away.

He closed his eyes and drifted down the river in his dream. Alexa floated next to him, holding tight to his hand.

He felt the peace.

Had she used the stone?

Was this their death? Their destiny to die as one?

In the haze of the vision, Zander glimpsed Moira standing next to him. She whispered, "Come back Zander. Death is not for you this day."

Zander opened his eyes.

Leaning over his chest, Alexa clutched his hand. She jerked up, eyes swollen, blood on her tunic. Dharien knelt behind her, one hand on her shoulder, his own tears falling.

When she opened their hands to reveal the black and white stone, a white circle scorched their palms. Her voice trembled. "Together we live."

Just then, the rest of the questers stumbled from the woods and formed a circle around the three. Paal raised his fist in victory. "Together we survived. We all survived the quest."

Zander rubbed at the numbness in his chest. Two punctures marked where the adder struck him. He'd have another scar. "Did you see Shadow?"

Cobie said, "He carried the snake into the woods and disappeared."

"We have to go after him. He saved me." Zander tried to stand, but fell back.

Kaiya's eyes filled with tears as she crouched next to Zander. "He's gone, Zander. His destiny was to save you." She touched his chest where the fangs hit. "I thought you died."

The teens slumped on the ground. Their faces reflected a multitude of feelings, and Zander shared each one. Relief, grief, pride, and shame warred in his mind. They ate a final meal of funnel cap mushrooms, strawberries, and the last of the bread tokens. They limped, they scratched at welts. Most of all, they held their heads high. They had survived.

Despite their weariness, they began to joke with each other. With each story told came more laughter. The camaraderie of the quest bound them. Zander shared their relief, but he couldn't stop watching for Shadow. He couldn't believe his patron was dead.

Dharien remained quiet amid the celebration. When he slipped from the circle, Zander followed.

"Dharien?"

He scowled. "Leave me alone."

"Come back to the group."

"I'm not part of the group," Dharien snorted. "I was meant to die. Everyone probably hoped I would."

"If Moira had wanted you to die, you would have."

"I'm a cheater."

"So am I." Zander met his eyes. "It's why we both had to fight the panthers.

"Alexa had one too."

"She cheated as well."

After confessing how he and Alexa used their favors to win the tournament, Zander said, "So you see. We're not so different, you and me." He stared past Dharien while he thought through his next words. "I think what's important is how we worked together to fight the panthers. And our actions, now the quest is over."

"You saved my life and put yourself in danger. Why?"

"It seemed like the right thing to do." Zander shrugged. "You risked your life for Alexa, even after her confession about the potion."

As they stood in silence, the energy of the trees renewed Zander's strength. "Dharien? How did Alexa get Shadow's token?"

"On the second day of the quest she asked for it before she told me about the potion."

"She had it all that time? And didn't tell me?" The wound of betrayal broke open. "Why didn't she tell me? Or give it to me? It was my choice, not hers."

Dharien stared at him. "She knew you wouldn't use it. She saved your life, Zander. Can't you see that?"

"But it wasn't her decision." Zander ran his hands through his hair.

"She betrayed us both." Dharien looked glum. "I promised to fight her panther, and I didn't even do that right. She'll never forgive me for stealing your tokens and getting the quest moved up." He rubbed the jagged cut on his cheek. "And how could she love me with this?"

Zander placed his hand on Dharien's shoulder. "We all have a lot to forgive. I cheated you in the tourney." He grimaced. "Forgive me?"

Dharien nodded. "Can you forgive me? I'll spend the rest of my life making it up to you."

He clasped Dharien's outstretched hand. "I forgive you. Today we begin anew."

"What about the potion? Do you think I'm under its spell?"

"I doubt the effects of Melina Odella's potion would last three months. Do you still love Alexa?"

Dharien stared at the ground. "Yes."

"Then, I think it's real." Zander shook his head. "It'll sort itself out soon enough. Let's join the others."

"Everyone hates me, and I don't blame them. I'd hate me too."

"You have to prove yourself to them. Show them you've changed."

As they stepped into the circle, the questers became silent. Alexa raised her eyebrows at her twin, and he tried to reassure her with his smile.

Standing with his hand on Dharien's shoulder, Zander cleared his throat. "Dharien wants to speak."

Dharien pulled back his shoulders. "I'm sorry for stealing Zander's tokens and getting the quest moved up before we were ready." He let his tears fall. "We survived because of Alexa and Zander. I hope you can forgive me."

One by one the questers rose and clasped his hand. Alexa approached last. She searched Zander's face before she turned to Dharien.

"Can you forgive me? I meant it, Alexa. I'll be there to help you anytime. For anything. All you have to do is ask."

"Yes. If my brother can forgive you, I can." Alexa hesitated. "We each did things that were wrong. Today we start new." She leaned in and kissed his cheek before darting back to the group.

Zander whispered to Dharien, "Who knows what my sister will decide in this new day, huh? She has her own scars." He pushed playfully at his shoulder. "Let's eat." As tired as he was, Zander felt euphoric at ending the quest.

More than a few of the questers stuttered when they wondered aloud what Fate would say in their dreams. Slowly they drifted off to lie in a soft patch of grass or lean against a tree, safe from the threat of an omen. They'd fought them all. Tomorrow, they would know their fates and see their families.

When Zander found his own spot, away from the others, emptiness swallowed him. He missed Shadow. He fell to his knees and bowed his head into his hands. A gentle touch on his shoulder made him scramble to his feet.

"Kaiya?"

"I'm scared. What if Moira gives me an apprenticeship as a servant? I used to think it would be all right to do what Mother does, but now . . . now, I want more." She burst into tears.

He pulled her into his arms and let her cry. When her sobs ended, she looked up at him. Stars! she looked so beautiful. He leaned down and kissed her.

CHAPTER FIFTY-FOUR

Quest Day Five

Zander

Moira appeared as a young woman in Zander's dream. "Walk with me," she whispered. Her silver hair flowed as she escorted him to the oak tree where he had meditated. They stood under the eaves of the giant tree, and the branches seemed to embrace their words and hold them secret.

"Well done, Zander. You survived the quest, and to you alone, I give a choice."

He searched her emerald eyes for clues. "Why me?"

"Zander," she spoke so he had to lean in to hear. "Because you bear the name—defender of all."

"What?" he whispered. "I don't understand."

"No, you don't." She smiled, and the warmth of it spread through his body and healed his hurts.

"I didn't defend them all in the quest. Alexa did more to keep them alive than I did."

"Your destiny calls upon your name. You have yet to fulfill it."

"My destiny?"

"You have a dream."

Zander's heartbeat pounded in his ears. He could choose to be a Protector.

"You saved Elder Warrin's son. He will take you as his own, and if you like, you may train with the Protectors." She pulled him close, lowering her voice, "But first there is something you need to know."

When she finished, Zander stepped back stunned.

"Choose carefully, defender of all, for you will speak first. One choice binds the others to your path. The other allows them to apprentice with the guilds. Only your sister is unaffected by your choice."

He had a choice, but what Moira had whispered to him would not be easy. "If I give up my dream, I have two requests."

"Go on."

Zander blurted, "I don't want to see secrets anymore."

"And the second?"

"I want Shadow back."

Moira's eyes narrowed. "Magic requires a price. Shadow saved your life. The price is his death. I can't alter that without another payment."

Zander's heart broke.

"My tokens are gone. I have nothing to give."

"About your favor. If you choose to become a Protector, I can change your gift to insight instead of knowledge. But if you choose the second, it will be needed. It is your choice."

"Is it?"

"You always have a choice." Moira stared past him. "You will do what's right." She looked back and studied him. "It is the nature of your name."

Zander woke, miserable and unsure of his decision.

CHAPTER FIFTY-FIVE

Alexa

Moira came as an old woman in Alexa's dream. "Take my arm," she instructed. They ambled to a wooden bench carved with runes, hidden beneath the branches of a gnarled old willow. A stream babbled behind them.

Moira held Alexa's chin in her bony hand. "I will not reveal your path, but I will tell you that it lies not with the traditional apprenticeships. You must honor your heart."

Alexa stiffened. "Then I will have my desire?"

"Yes, but it may be other than you have believed."

Dharien? Paal? Alexa wasn't sure what she wanted, but for now it didn't include either of them.

The old woman smiled, and Alexa's pain melted away. "You will choose last." She lifted the wooden heart hanging at Alexa's neck. "Feel with your heart as the others declare their future. Then, you will know."

It wasn't the answer she'd expected, but she had other questions for Fate. "Moira? Why did you allow Zander and me both to live?"

"It was chosen before you were born."

"Then it was for naught? The sacrifice our parents made? The quest?"

"Nothing is ever for naught."

While Alexa puzzled over her words, Moira continued. "Your

life has meaning. Your struggles have meaning. You cannot always control what happens *to* you, but you can *always* control how you respond. It has always been this way, and it always will be this way."

"I don't understand."

"You will, child, you will."

"Moira? Zander will never forgive me for using Shadow. Is there anything I can do to bring him back?"

"There is a price that can be paid." Moira whispered in Alexa's ear.

"I'll do it." Alexa's eyes filled with tears. "For Zander, I'll do it."

"Then, it is done."

Alexa woke, feeling unsettled. She had expected to know her future and she didn't.

CHAPTER FIFTY-SIX

Zander

In contrast to the last night's frivolity, somber faces greeted Zander as the other questers arose in the morning. They gathered for the last time as questers. Their instructions were to keep private their visit from Moira until the time of choosing. None seemed inclined to break that rule, although they each stole furtive glances at Zander. Only Kaiya smiled.

The responsibility of his decision weighed on him. Moira warned it would affect each of them except for Alexa. He mulled over the two choices. The only thing he'd ever wanted was to become a Protector. He'd belong with them. He was an excellent marksman and he could get rid of the favor of seeing secrets. But, he wasn't sure he could be content with that after what Moira had revealed.

Zander stood. "The quest is over. It's time to return."

As the questers gathered their journals, their patrons joined them. Jarl's shepherd loped to his side. A yellow cat curled around Odo's feet while Bindi's calico jumped in her arms. A green and blue chameleon appeared on Cobie's journal. A cardinal, sparrow, and crow flew from the trees and landed on their owner's shoulders.

The faces of Dharien, Paal, Tarni, and Yarra reflected the pain Zander felt. He glanced at Alexa. She was holding back tears. He didn't see Fiona.

Then a golden blur caught his eye. Shadow raced from the trees and barreled into Zander's knees, knocking him over. Shock coursed through Zander. He stared at his twin. Her tentative smile confirmed his suspicion.

Alexa had paid the price to bring Shadow back.

He motioned for her to join him. Alexa slumped next to Shadow and cried in his neck.

"Why?" Zander whispered.

"It was my fault. I had to."

Zander pulled her in for a hug. His other half. Day and night. Together they were whole.

The questers trailed in a single line behind Zander and Alexa in silence. Dharien brought up the rear. They entered the village and soon reached the Quinary.

Zander spied the fortune-teller as she paced, skirt swishing. Her hand flew to her mouth, and her eyes trailed from Zander to Dharien. Then her knees buckled, and she clutched the corner post to stay upright.

A roar erupted from the villagers as families raced to hug the questers, children no longer, but young men and women ready to take their places in society. Tears flowed when they realized all had returned. There would be no sorrow this year. No search parties for those who had not returned, and no funerals. No guilt for the parents whose children survived.

Zander's father hugged him until Zander couldn't breathe. His mother's tears looked at odds with her smile. She pulled him close and whispered, "We can be a family again."

The joy on Alexa's face was marred only by the purple bruise surrounding her eye. Zander wondered what she would choose as her apprenticeship. He'd made his decision, so he knew what the others must choose.

Together they celebrated. Venison supplied by the elders; wedges of cheese; all manner of breads, pastries, and savory dishes loaded the tables for the communal feast. Laughter rose like a sweet perfume.

Melina Odella recovered from the shock of all thirteen returning, although her cheeks remained flushed and she ate little. When the meal finished, she stood. At her signal, the guilds lined up around the Quinary, each holding their flags. Mother left to stand with the flag of the bakers.

"It is the time of choosing," the fortune-teller announced. "The guild you apprentice to becomes your family and guides you into adulthood. Moira appeared in your dreams. You will follow her guidance, for she knows what is best for you and for the village." She studied Zander. "Zander will choose first."

All eyes followed Zander as he strode forward with Shadow at his side. Zander faced the questers, hoping they would approve of his decision. "What I choose affects each of you, save Alexa." He gazed across the people gathered. His people. His voice sounded strong despite his trembling. "Moira has given me a choice, but warned me the safety of the village depends upon my decision."

The villagers murmured among themselves. Zander grinned at their whispers. "I am not deluded. The others can confirm the burden Fate has laid upon me." The questers solemnly nodded. His eyes swept the guilds. "My fate lies not with tradition."

The other questers' heads snapped up, and they gazed expectantly, waiting on his words.

Emboldened at their approval, Zander faced Melina Odella. "I am a warrior."

Not a respected Protector, but a down-and-dirty fighter with a favor he didn't want but would need. Not a pawn to the elders, but life-sworn to his village.

Cries rang out from the villagers.

"A warrior?" called a man from the metalsmith's guild.

"What does this mean?" cried a woman at the front of the crowd.

"What has Moira planned for our village?" asked a burly man with crossed arms.

Zander held up his hand. "We need to prepare for an attack on our village. Thanks to Moira, we'll be ready."

The villagers grew silent.

"There's more." He took a deep breath. "Puck's ghost has often spoken to me. He won't rest until we unite the tribes as equals."

"You're a liar and a fool." Elder Terrec strode forward and pushed Zander. "We won't stand for a boy telling us what to do."

Again, the crowd broke out in a frenzy of talk. Elder Warrin raised his hand for quiet. "I've heard Puck too. Zander, you may train at my estate." He glared at Terrec. "We've failed the vision for too long."

Rage flooded Elder Terrec's face. He leaned in to Zander and grabbed his tunic. Whispering low enough that only Zander heard, the elder said, "Not everyone believes Puck's death was an accident."

Stunned, Zander watched Terrec push his way through the crowd.

Melina Odella's voice rang out over the shouts of the villagers. "Moira has spoken. We do well to heed her counsels." She gestured to Paal. "What say you?"

Paal joined Zander and declared, "I am also a warrior."

Odo came next to stand with them. "I'm a warrior too."

Cobie gazed at the three before he took a deep breath. Nodding at Zander, he declared with quiet conviction, "I am to be a healer." He stood next to Eva, the lone healer in the village. Waku followed Cobie and Jarl joined Zander.

Dharien came last. Zander leaned in to whisper, "There's no glory in this, my friend."

His eyes met Zander's in fierce pride. "There's no other place I'd rather serve. I too am a warrior."

They clasped hands.

Once enemies, now they would fight together.

CHAPTER FIFTY-SEVEN

Alexa

As the boys declared Moira's choices, Alexa's heart thumped in her throat. Warriors and healers. What could this mean?

Struggling to speak above the crowd, Melina Odella's voice rose. "Moira has spoken." She turned to the girls. "Merindah? What choose you?"

Merindah lifted her chin and squared her shoulders. She joined the nuns. "I choose the nunnery." She raised her eyes to the heavens. "It has been too long since the church has held an anchoress. I declare my intention as such for when the priest declares me ready." The two nuns dropped to their knees in prayer.

Silence descended upon the crowd, shocked at the sacrifice from one so young to enter into seclusion. They turned to the remaining questers.

Gazing at Zander as she strode forward, Kaiya looked determined. "I am called to be a warrior."

Cries from the village rose as they understood her intention. Moira had called a female to fight?

Bindi and Yarra joined Kaiya. Tarni stood with Cobie next to Eva.

Alexa stood alone. Even in that moment, she knew not her path. She glanced at her mother's hopeful face and rubbed the heart token Zander had used to save her life and given her to keep. Calm seeped into her being. Her choice became clear. She almost laughed aloud as she stepped forward. "My path also breaks from tradition." She stepped toward Melina Odella. "It is the fortune-teller I apprentice with."

Her mother burst into tears and Father gasped. She would try to explain later her destiny had never been with the bakery.

As Alexa stood next to Melina Odella, a red-haired boy appeared next to her. His smile eased her nerves.

He whispered, "You don't smell like bread anymore."

"What do I smell like now, Zeph?"

Zeph wrinkled his nose. "Lavender. You smell like lavender."

She laughed. That would do. She touched her still-tender cheek. Her bruises would fade, but she'd live with the jagged scar at her neck. Her neck, Dharien's cheek, Zander's chest. They each had reminders of the bond that bound them.

Alexa rubbed the round scar remaining on her palm from the stone she'd used to save Zander. She glanced at the worried faces of the villagers. The quest had ended not as they expected. Warriors, healers, and an anchoress.

They would need a second fortune-teller.

CHAPTER FIFTY-EIGHT

Zander

Smiling, Zander touched his own scar as Alexa rubbed the matching one on her palm. He'd wondered what she would choose, but he never expected it would be a fortune-teller. What a strange turn that the one who betrayed them would now be her mentor.

He didn't know yet what it meant to be a warrior. His mind whirled. He'd been shocked when Elder Warrin offered his estate for training. Greydon had already approached him to volunteer. He hoped the fighters would not be needed, but his heart told him Moira would not be wrong in her choosing. And the girls as warriors? He wouldn't forgive himself if Kaiya came to harm.

The villagers glanced timidly at him. He would not view their secrets lightly. Even without his favor, he felt their fear. He would train hard to protect these people. His people.

Moira stood smiling behind the villagers. Puck wavered next to her. As much as Zander wished otherwise, they weren't done with him. Train warriors, unite the tribes, and save the village. Only then would they leave him in peace.

The calm power of the red stone in the pouch at his waist flowed into Zander. It had stayed Alexa's blood, and he might need it again. Whatever the future brought, he would do his best to deserve his name.

Defender of all.

EPILOGUE

Moira

The questers survived because their people need them. It will be less than a year before the warriors defend the village from invasion. If Zander can unite the tribes, he will rise to his destiny.

The healers will be needed, as they always are in war. Alexa? Her favor of embroidery shall be vital in their strategy.

And so, they all survived the quest, but the true test will come in battle. There, they will not be as lucky. In war, they will find that the shadow boy called Zephyr will make the difference between victory and defeat, at great cost to himself.

I said I did not have a heart, and I do not lie. It is my task to see that humans follow their destiny.

I can, perhaps, be forgiven if, occasionally, I feel pleased with the outcome.

To Be Continued . . .

ACKNOWLEDGMENTS

If it takes a village to raise a child, then it must also take a village to birth a book. I belong to four critique groups. So many writers helped me not only to revise, but to keep the faith during the long times of querying, entering contests, and being rejected.

So here's my shout out to my village—the wonderful writers who undoubtedly made me a better writer—I couldn't have done it without you!

Anny, Ashley, Charmaine, Chris (always grateful for his male perspective), Diane, Donna, Emily, Joan, Karen, Kathy, Laurie, Linda, Marcia, Melinda, Nancy, Rebecca, Robin, Sandra, Sandy, Sarah, and Wendi. Thank you for your suggestions, your encouragement, and your belief in Zander and Alexa.

A special thanks to Tina Brockett. We met in an online critique group and then actually met at the 2013 SCBWI Summer Conference. She's become a friend who's supported and encouraged me many times! Thank you for loving Zander as much I do.

Much gratitude to the Society of Children's Book Writers and Illustrators for their wonderful conferences and for creating a safe haven for hopeful writers.

Love and thanks to my husband, Mike, who doesn't always understand me, but always believes in me. And even more importantly, he makes me laugh.

I will forever be grateful to my editor, Reece Hanzon, and Jolly Fish Press, for making my dream come true.

And finally, to Kate DiCamillo, who doesn't know me and whom I've never met. I've admired her writing since I first read *Because of Winn-Dixe*. Her books inspired me, and her Facebook posts kept me from giving up.

Before becoming an author, Jeri Baird worked as a handmade paper artist, an entrepreneurship teacher for at-risk high school students, a reflexologist, a rock painter, and a zombie (in a film, not a real one).

As an Illinois farm child, she shared her life with an assortment of pets including mice, hamsters, rabbits, cats, dogs, ferrets, a rescued sparrow named Chicken, and a pony named Red Baron who thought he was a dog. Jeri now lives on the Western Slope of Colorado with her husband and one cat, who both make her laugh. When she's not writing, she enjoys kayaking, the scenery from the back of her husband's motorcycle, and visiting her sons in Wyoming and California.

Visit Jeri online at www.JeriBaird.blogspot.com